Cirsova®

P. ALEXANDER, Ed.
Yakov Merkin, Copy Ed.
Mark Thompson., Copy Ed.

A Knowles Novelette of the Weird West

Spectacular Short Story Showcase

Poetry

Spring Issue
2026

Vol.2, No 26
$15.00 per copy

In Massachusetts' Woodlands, Find Ye Rome

By MATTHEW PUNGITORE

In Massachusetts' woodlands, find ye Rome,
Where Bacchus grand his fine cortege doth lead,
His band of righteous satyrs staunch in creed
And Bacchae pure, who call this state their home.
With them are fauns, the scribes; each holds a tome,
From which the tales of heroes Men may read,
Of how Italia's lost and poor were freed
By Pan and Hercules from Typhon's dome.

Good men of Romulus, there stand with me
Upon this realm our forebears help'd to build,
For Fortune's mercy swept them o'er the sea
To craft Americana. Here, our guild
Must carry forth the red of Venus queen
Whose skin is white, her eyes a forest green!

MATTHEW PUNGITORE is the author of The Report of Mr. Charles Aalmers and other stories. Visit his blog for more info on his paintings, writings, and thoughts: https://matthewpungitore.wordpress.com/

The Sapphire Talisman

By RICHARD RUBIN

Burke Fletcher finds himself part of a losing battle... His airship wrecked in the wastes, he stumbles upon a ruined well that sends him to Rigel IV's ancient past!

"By the Seven Hell Demons of Rigel!" From inside the cockpit of his one-man flyer, Burke Fletcher cursed as he watched Earl Ryker's colossal command airship explode a hundred yards away. The sky battle was lost.

Five hours earlier, in a hastily convened war council, Fletcher had cautioned the Earl that their air fleet was being lured into a trap, but the foppish noble had shrugged off the warning. So here they were, hopelessly surrounded, outnumbered, and outgunned. And there weren't very many of Ryker's fighter craft left. Fletcher had just dispatched an enemy gunship, buying himself a moment's respite. He stole a quick glance at his instrument panel and saw that both his fuel and plasma weapon reserves were alarmingly low. He had to get out of this deathtrap, and fast!

The month before, signing on as vice commander in Earl Ryker's war fleet had seemed like a good move. The Earl's chances of winning his conflict with Count Albin looked sound and the pay was generous. But it was beginning to dawn on the cynical mercenary that the deal wasn't so good if the lord who made it was dead and his fighting force annihilated. Fletcher realized it was time to cut his losses and find his way home.

He heard crackling over his radio, then a voice he recognized as Colin, one of the captains in his personal squadron. "Vice Commander, are you there?"

"Still here, Colin."

"I'm going to try for a breakout. Are you with me?"

"Why not? Where did you have in mind?"

"The south flank, over by that jagged mountaintop—looks like a weak point. We'll try to bust out there."

"Let's go!"

Fletcher spun his fighter craft sharply about and, moving in tandem with Colin's flyer, carefully threaded his way through the air battle still fiercely raging in the red-tinted sky of Rigel IV. As the mountain appeared beneath the clouds, Fletcher made out at least five enemy flyers cutting off their escape. Two of the sleek black fighters spotted Fletcher and advanced upon his craft. Fletcher engaged the pair, Colin opening fire with his plasma guns as he attacked a third foe.

Fletcher banked sharply as the enemy on his left fired a plasma burst that missed his vessel by mere inches. The second foe fired two more blasts, which Fletcher skillfully dodged. He sent his ship hard to the right, looped quickly about, and came back at the first black ship from the rear. The enemy zigged and zagged to counter his aggressive maneuver, but the pilot was no match for his adept fighting agility, well-honed over a series of long and bloody air campaigns. Soon his opponent was reduced to a ball of wreckage careening toward the ground.

Dodging a plasma blast from his surviving attacker, Fletcher executed a rapid dive. He accelerated hard, swung high and wide in an arc, and fired his forward gun. The blast struck the enemy's tail section, shearing it clean off. The black craft spun wildly and followed its comrade, plummeting out of sight. Fletcher caught something on his radio that sounded like a curse, but he couldn't make out anything more over the din of battle static.

He looked over and saw that Colin wasn't faring well. The air captain had managed to destroy one enemy vessel, but two others had seized the opportunity to gang up on him, one attacking Colin's fighter craft from below while the second dove in from above. Helplessly trapped in the resulting crossfire, Colin's ship blew up, and moments later its burning shell dropped from the sky, slamming into the icy mountaintop below.

"Damn," Fletcher swore. Colin had been a good man—a friend—but he would have to grieve later.

Fletcher spotted a gap in the enemy fighters and darted for it at full speed. But as he soared through the opening, a blast rocked his vessel and the small craft lurched sideways. He cursed under his breath—the bastard had taken out one of his stabilizers! Bringing all his piloting skills to bear, he managed to regain control of his vessel and continue his high-speed escape through the clouds. A moment later, he noticed his fuel gauge was markedly lower than before and realized the enemy plasma blast must have also ruptured his energy tank. He would have to set his damaged ship down soon, and it wouldn't be easy, but he first needed to put some distance between himself and Count Albin's war fleet.

Ten years earlier, Fletcher had served as a lieutenant in Earth's Space Navy. He had been on a solo survey mission when his scout craft encountered a solar storm, causing him to crash-land on Rigel IV. For a short while, he held out hope that an Earth ship might someday rescue him from this barbarous world. Finally, he had accepted his fate that he would never see his home planet again. He resolved to make his way, as best he could, in this weird, war-torn world. He'd thrown in his lot with an itinerant mercenary band, a group of blue-skinned humanoids, much resembling the humans of earth. Fletcher had quickly impressed the mercenaries with his fighting skills and courage, and they in turn taught him the language and customs of Rigel IV. His mercenary band was now gone, all slain in battle except for himself; but, for what it was worth, this savage planet was now his home.

Fletcher had fallen in love and married Llana, a young alchemist, one of a professional class of Rigelians who practiced an amalgamation of magical and scientific wizardry resembling nothing encountered on Earth. Now, as he scanned the rocky wasteland below, desperately searching for a halfway decent place to land, he wondered if he would ever see his beautiful wife again.

Fletcher suddenly realized he was being followed. On his rear sensor he caught the speck of a pursuing craft some distance away. The vessel quickly fell back out of sight, but it was there. He could turn and fight, but with a missing stabilizer he'd be easy prey. With hardly any fuel left he couldn't hope to lose his pursuer by outrunning it, either. He would have to find another means of neutralizing the threat.

Fletcher flew as far as he could before electing to employ his little remaining fuel to make a forced landing. He selected a rough patch of ground that looked somewhat flatter and softer than the uninviting terrain surrounding it. He dropped altitude, leveled the unsteady craft, and skidded its landing skis along the jagged surface. There was a loud snap as the craft's underbelly cracked under the punishment. As the flyer finally rocked to a halt, he released his breath. The landing hadn't been pretty, but at least he'd managed to come down without injury.

Fletcher remained at his controls, waiting for the other ship to close. In a few minutes he spotted a black gunship approaching slowly overhead, no doubt intending a strafing run. There was a crackling over his radio, and the voice of the enemy pilot came through: "This is for my sister Aleen, you bastard!"

At the same moment, Fletcher took careful aim with his grounded vessel's plasma gun and fired a powerful burst that struck the pilot's engine. Black smoke poured out of the crippled enemy craft as it spun drunkenly about in a descending arc before vanishing beyond the horizon. So it had been about revenge—the pilot's sister had flown one of the flyers he had shot down. But the enraged brother had forgotten that even a downed ship could still fire its guns. Fletcher shrugged. *The fortunes of war*, he thought.

He retrieved his raygun and dagger before exiting the cockpit of his disabled flyer. He also grabbed a canteen of water, but he knew that it wouldn't last long beneath the burning twin suns of Rigel IV.

He assessed his situation. The sky battle had been fought over the vast unexplored waste separating the lands of Earl Ryker and Count Albin. He didn't know how far he was from the nearest village or settlement, but he decided to strike out in the direction of Ryker's domain, which lay somewhere far to the south. He looked to the locations of Rigel's two suns in the late afternoon sky to determine which way that was.

There were legends of a ghostly city which sometimes appeared in these badlands—a strange phantasma from which no traveler ever returned. Once, it was said, a blasphemous vampire cult had dwelled there, until one day they had vanished without a trace, supposedly struck down by the gods of Rigel for their effrontery. But the cynical mercenary had always been skeptical of Rigelian legends—that is, until something forced him to change his mind. He lifted his canteen to his lips and took a sip of water. Then he started walking.

Three days later, Fletcher began to doubt he would get out of this fix alive. The last of his water had run out that morning and he had eaten nothing aside from a handful of berries he had chanced upon the day before. Maybe Colin had been the lucky one—he had died quickly, and died fighting. If he didn't find food and water soon, he would be just as dead.

And then he saw it. Before him lay a tiny city shimmering on the horizon, encircled by a golden wall, behind which rose a cluster of elfin turquoise and crimson spires and, looming high above them all, a solitary ebony tower rising gracefully into the sky. It was a beautiful city, alluring—and probably deadly. But, faced with dying of thirst or starvation in this barren land, he had little choice.

His right hand went to the grip of his raygun as he cautiously approached the twin ivory gates to this fairylike place. He now saw that both gates were fully closed. He looked up at the city wall to hail someone but detected no sign of life on the ramparts. The mercenary placed a hand on the gate and slowly pushed it forward. There was no resistance as the heavy door creaked and groaned before swinging open to reveal a pristine white flagstone plaza.

A blackwood well stood by itself in the center of the serene square. As Fletcher neared, he made out the bleached skeleton of a man pinned to one side of the well by two steel spears jutting from his rib cage. A dented sword, shield, and helmet lay scattered at the skeleton's feet. The skull's macabre grin seemed to mock his foolhardiness in venturing into this silent city.

But he was thirsty and knew he would soon die without water. He lowered the well's metal bucket until he heard a splash as it dipped into the shaded liquid below. Fletcher allowed the bucket to fill before raising it back up. Placing the receptacle to his lips, he took a cautious sip. The water tasted clean and refreshing. He felt some of his strength return as he drank more. He splashed water on his face and hair to wash off the accumulated dust and grime.

He considered the impaled skeleton. Perhaps two enemies had chanced upon this place at the same time. One slew the other, took his fill from the well, and went on. But were there no people in this city to remove those bones, which had clearly been there for many years?

As he started to lower the bucket for a second time, a blinding flash of light enveloped him. He suddenly found himself plunging weightless through pitch blackness and bone-numbing cold as if he had been hurled headlong through an endless tunnel.

After perhaps ten minutes, there was a loud boom and the transit halted. Fletcher materialized, still in motion, five feet off the floor of a large room before being flung against a wall. He found himself in a high-ceilinged chamber crammed with chemical racks, scrolls, and weird devices. A fierce-looking White Giant warrior stood close by, eyeing him menacingly as the mercenary regained his feet. The heavily muscled, white-furred creature was an ugly thing, with a piglike snout and beady black eyes. A heavy battle axe lay slung across its broad back.

A woman approached from the other side of the room. She was a Blue Rigelian dressed in a lavender robe—tall and slender, with raven black hair. At first glance she seemed a beauty of early middle age, yet something in her steely blue eyes reflected a dark and ancient wisdom. As she stepped in front of Fletcher, his attention was drawn to a glowing blue sapphire, the size and shape of a hen's egg, that hung from a leather cord about her neck. The next instant the woman's eyes locked onto his, and he could feel cold, centuries-old cruelty in her glare. Her mouth broke into a smile, revealing sharp twin fangs in her upper row of teeth. What manner of creature was this?

She raised up a gnarled, rune-inscribed wooden cane, which he immediately recognized as an alchemist's staff of power. He was in great danger! He seized the dagger sheathed at his waist and slashed out at the dark alchemist.

With lightning quickness, the woman struck the knife aside with her staff. As she did so, he lashed out with his foot and kicked the woman's legs out from under her, sending her crashing into the White Giant as she fell to the floor. Fletcher seized the chance to bolt from the room through a nearby doorway.

He found himself running blindly down a dimly lit passageway. At its end he came to a door that opened onto a narrow street. Stepping out, he saw he had emerged through a hidden entryway next to a food stand displaying skewers of greasy meat.

Fletcher grabbed one of the skewers and continued his flight, wolfing down the meat as he dashed past small, dingy shops and tightly packed dwellings. He passed several people, but they paid him no mind. They were dressed in simple natural fiber clothing, much different from the colorful synthetic blends one would expect to find in a present-day Rigelian city.

He eventually halted in a side alley to catch his breath and consider his situation. Where, by the Seven Hells of Rigel, was he? And how could he possibly find his way home from this weird place?

As the mercenary adventurer was absorbed in such thoughts, he felt a hand gently snake into his pants pocket. In one fluid motion he spun around and struck a hard blow that knocked the would-be thief to the ground as Fletcher drew his raygun.

He was surprised to see the culprit was a young woman. She was in fact quite attractive, with shoulder-length blonde hair, hazel eyes, and a trim athletic figure. She was dressed in black leather and displayed a jeweled silver dagger belted at her hip. The woman raised both her hands in a posture of mock surrender, as if she had just been caught out playing a practical joke.

She flashed a disarming smile. "Please don't hurt me, sir. I'm just a poor working girl trying to make a dishonest living."

Fletcher motioned with his weapon. "Don't move. Who are you?"

"I'm a thief, of course. My name is Wren." Her eyes fell on the raygun in his hand. "What manner of weapon is that? And your white skin—who or what are you?"

Surprised at the first question, he replied, "It's a raygun. You probably wouldn't outlive a demonstration of its effectiveness."

She looked him over with a probing eye. "You're from the future." Then her face took on a thoughtful expression. "Please, milord, let us forget this unfortunate misunderstanding. Come, let me buy you a drink and something to eat."

Fletcher considered. He was famished and he could certainly use a friend in this strange place. If she intended treachery, he had faith that a raygun blast would settle the matter.

"Why not?" He shrugged and allowed her to get up and guide him back to the street.

A few minutes later, the pair sat across from each other at a small wooden table in a crowded and disreputable-looking tavern. Fletcher ordered some roast boar, black bread, and dwarf brandy, the first full meal he had enjoyed in days. The quality of the food left something to be desired, but the brandy went down well, and he felt no urge to complain.

He told Wren of his experience at the well and the encounter with the weird woman who bore the alchemist's staff.

When he finished his account, Wren nodded and said, "That was Larissa and her White Giant guard, who she brought with her from the future. Larissa is a powerful vampire alchemist, the last of her kind. You were very fortunate to escape from her grasp with your life."

"Vampire alchemist?"

"An alchemist who has transformed herself so as to gain immortality by feeding off the lifeblood of her victims. It is said that they existed as a cult over two hundred years in our future, but nearly all were killed when one of their order foolishly drained the lifeblood of the daughter of a powerful emperor. The vampire alchemists were hunted down and destroyed by the emperor's vast army until only a tiny handful remained. The desperate survivors employed their alchemic science to fashion a time portal that allowed them to escape into their past. But before the vampires fled, not knowing where in the time stream they would find themselves, they set time traps in their abandoned city to deliver new victims their way."

"You seem to know a lot about these creatures."

"I'm a thief. I frequent taverns and listen to gossip and rumors. Do you think you could find Larissa's lair again?"

"I'm sure of it," Fletcher replied. "What's your interest?"

"I've been searching for Larissa for some time. I wish to acquire the sapphire talisman she wears about her neck."

"Why?"

"It is quite beautiful. I know of buyers who would pay well for it."

Fletcher shrugged. He very much doubted that was the whole truth, but it made little difference to him. He said, "I have no need of fine jewelry, but perhaps I can help you acquire this bauble in exchange for something I would value."

She smiled. "Well, you look like a man who knows how to wield a sword."

The mercenary nodded grimly. He was beginning to like this girl. Beautiful and cunning, she reminded him of his wife, Llana.

"Then perhaps we can reach an agreement. What would you desire in return?"

"The means to return to my own time and walk out of the waste alive, without risk of starving or dying of thirst."

"I've always been good at figuring out how things work. If we can find the time portal in Larissa's lair, I should be able to reverse its operation and send you back to your own time with food and water. Is that all?"

"I'll need a map of the badlands." Fletcher described the area where he had found the strange and alluring city.

Wren nodded. "I can find you a map showing where the nearest villages are, at least as they exist in this era. We'll also require a silver blade to kill a vampire, which I can procure." She winked devilishly. "Then is it agreed: you'll aid me in slaying Larissa and acquiring the sapphire talisman, and in return I'll send you back to your own future time with provisions and the map you require?"

"And how do I know I can trust you?"

"I'm an honorable thief—I pay my debts."

And, for some reason, Fletcher believed her. He wasn't completely without doubt, but he decided to roll the dice. "Let's do it!"

They clasped hands across the table to seal the bargain, ordered one more round of drinks, and settled down to perfect their plan for confronting Larissa and the White Giant.

The next morning, they located the food stand beside the entrance to Larissa's lair. Fletcher pointed to the outline of a door camouflaged within the rough stone surface of a wall. Luckily, the food shop's owner did not seem to recall his thievery of the meat skewer.

Fletcher distracted the plump merchant by proceeding to haggle over a slab of sestaur steak as Wren subtly plied her craft to jimmy the lock to the hidden door. Then, as the shopkeeper's attention turned to another customer, Wren and Fletcher quietly slipped into the passage leading to Larissa's clandestine chamber.

He cautiously led Wren through the narrow, dimly lit corridor. Before they had proceeded more than a few yards, the mercenary heard something rapidly approaching in the darkness ahead. He drew his raygun.

The White Giant warrior burst from the shadows with an angry roar. The enraged half-naked beast slapped Fletcher's raygun out of his hand. Wren reached for her knife, but the creature backhanded her, sending the young thief sprawling to the floor.

Fletcher leapt back into a fighting stance as he drew the silver longsword Wren had given him and raised it across his chest. The White Giant snatched the battle axe from its back and swung it whizzing through the air at Fletcher's throat. Metal sparked as the mercenary caught the attack squarely on his blade. The White Giant released a primal roar as it delivered another crushing axe blow, which Fletcher met full on with his sword, sending a wave of pain shooting up his arm. He gripped the longsword in both hands, dancing back to allow himself room to deliver a mighty swing at the White Giant's skull. The huge beast parried the strike but reeled from the impact. Fletcher struck again, this time at the giant's chest. His adversary blocked the attack once more, but the force of his blow sent the creature staggering back on its heels. Taking advantage of the beast's momentary vulnerability, he drove in to plunge his sword deep beneath the creature's armpit. The White Giant released a final howl of defiant rage before falling lifeless to the floor.

Fletcher retrieved his raygun, returning it to his holster as Wren got up off the floor.

A few minutes later they reached the end of the passage. Wren tested the bronze handle and found the door unlocked. She slowly pushed it open, and they stepped into the vampire's lair. Fletcher stood with drawn sword as he quickly surveyed the room, but he saw no one about. The spacious chamber featured several long metal tables cluttered with weird devices, piles of ancient scrolls, and assorted bottles and jars. The skeleton of a strange beast hung in the far corner.

There was a cackle of laughter, and Fletcher and Wren suddenly found themselves frozen beside each other, unable to move. The silver sword dropped from the mercenary's nerveless hand and clattered to the floor.

Larissa emerged from behind the door, laughing with cruel pleasure as she held up her alchemist's staff. She approached Fletcher, smiling to reveal the twin fangs that reflected her wicked heritage. She said, "I knew you were coming. I sensed your killing my servant. I hope he died bravely." She reached over to slip his raygun out of its holster and tossed it across the room. "You certainly won't be needing this."

Fletcher strained in frustrated impotence against the psychic bond that locked him in place.

Larissa admired the mercenary's throat. "Thank you for returning and bringing your very young friend. It's been some time since I've had a chance to feed so well." She started to lean forward to sink her fangs into his tender flesh.

Suddenly there was a loud boom. A body materialized and fell through the air, glancing off Larissa's shoulder and causing her to stumble backward. Her alchemist's staff dropped to the floor, and she lost her psychic hold on the two intruders. Seizing the moment, Fletcher grabbed the silver dagger out of Wren's belt and, in one fluid motion, lunged forward and sunk the blade hilt-deep into the vampire alchemist's black heart. Larissa let out a choking gasp before dropping like a stone slab, blood gushing from her wound.

"Stop! Drop the knife or I'll shoot."

Fletcher looked over to see a man dressed in the black uniform of Count Albin's air battalion getting up off the floor as he leveled his raygun at him. Wren made a sudden grab for the longsword Fletcher had dropped, but the soldier struck her with the butt end of his gun, stunning her and knocking her to the floor. Then he turned his attention back to Fletcher. Given that Fletcher still wore his gray military uniform, it was pointless to deny his identity as one of Earl Ryker's officers. He let the dagger clatter to the floor.

And he recognized that voice: the pilot who had pursued him from the sky battle, seeking revenge for his sister's death. Somehow he must have survived the crash of his flyer and reached the well in the fairylike city, where he had fallen victim to the same trap.

"You're the one who killed my sister. You need to die for that, but first I require answers to some questions: Where are we? What happened to me?"

Fletcher knew he was in a tight spot, but he had been in tight spots before and he was still alive. He would play for time and await a break. "We traveled through a time portal," he explained. "I don't know exactly where and when we ended up, but it must be centuries in the past. Perhaps if you and I worked together we might find a way back."

"I don't think so. I've sworn to avenge Aleen. Besides, I'd be a fool to trust you. I'll find my way back somehow—on my own." He aimed the raygun at the center of Fletcher's chest.

Suddenly, a blast of witchfire shot across the room, engulfing the soldier in a torrent of blue-white flame. The man released a single pitiful, bloodcurdling scream within the flare. Then the flame dissolved and his charred body lay smoking on the floor.

Fletcher looked over to see Wren, a look of intense concentration on her face, grasping the alchemist's staff and pointing it at the place where the soldier had stood. The staff pulsed with a purple glow, as if radiating energy.

The young thief grinned at him. "I forgot to say that I was once an apprentice alchemist. I had to interrupt my training to return home to support my elderly parents after a frost blight ravished their farm. After they died, I elected to become a thief. I thought I had a talent for it, but as of late I've decided to return to my study of alchemy."

Wren went over and removed the sapphire talisman from the dead vampire's neck. Fletcher's suspicions were confirmed: the huge gem was an Alchemist Stone—a rare talisman that would greatly enhance the powers of one adept in the art of alchemy.

His attention was drawn to a large machine at the opposite end of the room. The strange device displayed several viewscreens, as well as a complex array of gauges, dials, and levers. This had to be the time portal.

He also noticed something very familiar in the way Wren now stood with the alchemist's staff in one hand and the sapphire talisman in the other. She very much looked like his wife, Llana, a fledgling alchemist born centuries in the future. Could Wren possibly be an ancestor of his mate?

Two days later Fletcher stood beside the bleached skeleton impaled on the black well. This time he smiled back at the skull as if it were an old friend, so glad he was to be back in his own era. A few minutes later he heard a thud and turned to see the pack Wren had transported through time after him. He looked inside and confirmed it contained all Wren had promised. It would take the better part of a day to reach the nearest village on foot, but he would make it easily with this food and water, as well as the map to show him exactly where to go. Wren had also provided him with some new clothes so that he was no longer dressed as a member of Earl Ryker's command.

The following day he reached a small town on the edge of the badlands. He found an inn, where he purchased a meal and accommodations for the night. He asked the innkeeper if he knew anything of the battle between the air fleets.

"Haven't you heard?" the man replied. "Ryker and his fleet were completely smashed, dead to the last man. Count Albin now rules this land, not that it makes much difference."

Fletcher might have guessed: he was the last survivor of Earl Ryker's fatal blunder.

The next morning he bought supplies for his journey, along with a sestaur, the large two-legged domesticated reptile the Rigelians employed as riding animals.

Before departing the village, he visited a tavern and drank a toast to Colin, who had been a good friend, and to Earl Ryker, who for all his faults had tried very hard to be an honorable and decent ruler. And finally, he drank a toast to Wren, who had now been dead for centuries. He would miss the pretty young thief most of all, he reflected, as he left the tavern to begin the long journey home.

Richard L. Rubin's speculative fiction tales appear in various magazines including Cirsova, Savage Realms Monthly, and The Weird and Whatnot. In a previous life he worked as an appellate lawyer, defending several clients facing the death penalty in California. He lives in the San Francisco Bay Area. Richard's website is www.richardlrubin.com.

Deep-Rooted

By KEN LIZZI

Badulf the German pursues a comrade-turned-foe to Britannia, seeking a stolen memento ring, but he finds more than he bargained for on the night of Samhain!

Chill sea air gusted across the high bluff, filling Badulf's nostrils with the sting of salt and whipping his hair across his eyes, obscuring the already dim view of the trail petering out amidst the sparse scrub and wind-scoured rock of the headland. He clawed the long strands—the color of sun-dried straw—from his face, and squinted his iron gray eyes into the bitter wind, assuring himself that his quarry remained in sight. He'd pursued Ambiorix the Cenomani for nearly a month. It would be a shame to lose the thief now that he'd closed the distance to under a Roman mile.

He cast a glance to his right where the bluff dropped away to a narrow strip of farmland between the high ground he occupied and the shingle-and-rock-strewn seashore. He could just make out the sail of the boat that he'd disembarked from an hour earlier: a little glimmer on the increasingly dark sheet of the sea. He didn't care to recall the passage over turbulent waves in the tossing vessel. Judging from the demeanor of the captain of the stinking fishing craft, it was used for piracy as often as for netting cod, at least when the opportunity presented itself. The captain, probably a Frisian, though for some reason he claimed to be an Angle, had eyed Badulf closely, when he could spare a moment from the tiller and from swearing at the crew working sail and oars with cold-numbed hands. Badulf's sturdy coat of chainmail suggested he'd be a difficult nut to split. The glances the captain cast at the long sword hanging from a baldric and secured at Badulf's left hip, as well as the short Roman legionnaire's sword cased at Badulf's right, had seemingly convinced him that the coin he'd been promised for passage would have to suffice as complete recompense for the crossing from the disputed lands of northern Gaul to the uncertain shores of Britannia.

The ruins of a Roman-style villa marked the foot of the bluff, near the point at which Badulf had taken the steep goat path upwards. Near the toppled and flame-scorched remains squatted a newer farmstead of a style Badulf was intimately familiar with, though the one he'd grown up in was perhaps a trifle grander than this one. Smoke from the roofhole of the central farmhouse drifted up before getting snatched aside by sea breeze and lost in the gathering twilight. He'd not troubled to investigate, not caring to deal with the farmer, or his thralls, or slaves. Instead he'd trotted after the speck he saw ascending the path up the side of the bluff, reacquainting his legs with the feel of solid ground beneath him.

The boat that had dropped Ambiorix ashore was beyond the horizon, likely fleeing from the danger presented by Badulf's late transport, which had adopted a suspiciously similar heading.

Ambiorix grew from a speck to a now visibly recognizable human figure. Badulf slowed his pace, glad for the warmth of his cavalry boots, glad he had no need to wear the Roman buskins, with naught but woollen, two-toed hose between his feet and legs and the biting gusts. He could, perhaps, end this long chase with a headlong sprint. But where was Ambiorix to go? The point of the headland neared, with its odd, knob-like shape at the summit. Beyond, nothing but cliffs plunging to the cold embrace of the breakers smashing themselves to foam and spray. Ambiorix would have to turn back, pass somewhere near this footpath, then make his way down the less precipitous slope to the west, trying to find his way to the farms, pasture land, and woodlands below.

Badulf turned to look that way, his gold-and-copper-tinged beard catching on the rings of his *lorica hamata*, the mail shirt he'd been issued upon joining the light cavalry of a Roman auxiliary company almost ten years ago. After the sea voyage, the links were due for a thorough scrubbing. The sweep of the British countryside opened up from this height like a fresco of a pastoral landscape. It had to be dimmer viewed from down there, shaded by the forests. Up on the bluff, the rim of the sun was just now lowering itself over the horizon. But on the plain, lights were already beginning to spring up.

Badulf looked more closely. Many lights, as far as he could see. Paired bright dots, spaced so that he could imagine one pair to a farmstead or hamlet. Vast, brilliant bonfires they must be. And then, as the significance of the fires struck him, he realized that tonight must be Samhain. He'd lost track of the days during the chase. He could no longer see the farmstead by the seashore, but he imagined there the kindling of two fires, the gathering of the livestock to be herded between to protect them from the dark spirits at liberty this night; protect them from the malevolent mischief of grugach and drude, and bless them with fecundity come the spring.

He'd best get on with his business. This was no night to be left alone with a corpse atop a desolate, blustery headland, at the mercy of both nature and supernatural beings.

He returned his attention to Ambiorix and discovered he'd let his mind wander longer than he'd thought. The sun was nearly over the rim of the Earth. Ambiorix was a diminishing figure far ahead, nearing the odd knoll or pile of boulders at the point of the headland. Badulf began to trot after him.

Two lights sprang into existence at either side of the track. Bonfires, to all appearance, yet emitting no smoke and producing no heat. Badulf stopped, squinting at the sudden brightness, startled and not a little shaken by the advent of the witchlights. Ahead, illuminated now, he could see Ambiorix more clearly—and what Ambiorix approached. The knoll no longer seemed lumpen and amorphous. It resembled more a cylindrical tower, its curving sides composed of smooth, gleaming white pillars between which rose darker walls of stone. Ambiorix halted short of the structure, turned, and looked back. His face showed white in the gloaming, though Badulf could not make out his expression. Then he turned back toward the tower and moved forward, gradually disappearing earthward, as if descending into a passage leading beneath—or perhaps into—the tower.

Badulf felt his resolution waver. If he passed between these unnatural Samhain fires to continue his pursuit of the thief, he risked the mysteries of this night and the fraught uncertainty of this strange place. Was the goal worth the peril?

To answer his own question, he considered Marcus Rufio Verus.

The auxiliary light cavalry unit Badulf had signed on with contained few other Germans. Most of the troopers were Goths or Alans, with a sprinkling of Gauls. Badulf found few close companions, and kept mostly to himself. The exception was a Centurion of the Roman regular cavalry, Marcus Rufio Verus, assigned as liaison to the *auxilia*. Rufio had a natural gift of setting men at ease, his manner gregarious and charming, without sacrificing dignity or diminishing the aura of authority he exuded.

Badulf never considered an alternative to enlisting with the *auxilia*. He'd never questioned following in his father's footsteps, Ranulf riding away from the farm a day after Badulf celebrated his tenth summer. Badulf's two younger brothers, with the aid of the slaves, were more than capable of taking care of the farm and attending to the needs of their mother. Badulf's grandfather had fought against the Romans, not for them, as he told Badulf often during firelight tales. But he'd not offered a word of discouragement. And so Badulf, thinking himself his father's son, had, at the age of sixteen, headed south.

An aloof, quiet youth in the rough ranks of the light cavalry, Badulf had taken to the Centurion, the older man reminding him somehow of his dim recollections of Ranulf. And Rufio had seemed to return the regard, taking time to help the young trooper improve his Latin and even teach him a smattering of Greek, when not aiding the commander of the *auxilia* in rehearsing the men in cavalry formations, in memorizing the horn calls, and in practicing the art of fighting from horseback. He'd shared with Badulf his fears for the Western Empire, his long term plans of making for the seat of the Eastern Roman Empire once a moment of peace allowed.

"A soldier of my experience would be welcome in Constantinople," he'd say. "And a big fellow like you could get his choice of assignments. They don't see many your size in Greece, Badulf. We could live like gods."

Several years of campaigning with Flavius Aetius had brought the legion northwest, fighting a ruthless war of subjugation against the determined rebellion of the Bagaudae. On a typical day of the campaign, near the waning days of summer, Badulf was riding with a forward scouting detachment, following rumors of a strong contingent of Bagaudae. The legion had split into cohorts and was fanning out, looking to advance to contact. The horn call signaling recall reached his ears and he wheeled his mount around at the same time the detachment commander yelled the order. The scout troop spread out, hammering along the dirt road back toward the point from which it had detached from its cohort of the legion. Badulf grinned as he rode. They'd found the enemy. Whichever cohort had made contact would pin the bastards down until the rest of the legion could arrive to finish the job.

The Bagaudae had chosen an ideal spot for the ambush. The cohort had responded in a disciplined fashion, tried to form ranks while the handful of *equites* endeavored to hold the flanks. As Badulf rode within sight of the battle he could see that the attempt had failed. The terrain favored the enemy; the broken ground, scattered coppices, and thick brush on either side of the deeply rutted road would not allow the soldiers to cohere into defensive units. They fought in isolated groups or as individuals, swarmed by superior numbers.

Badulf saw Rufio go down, pulled from his horse and buried beneath a half-dozen Bagaudae. Badulf swerved toward the fight, knowing he was too late, yet refusing to relinquish hope. He hit the knot of men, the chest of his horse bowling over two or three, a moment before Badulf drew the beast up to a rearing halt. His long cavalry sword, the spatha, was in his hand, and he employed its length and the height afforded by his mount to strike to left and right, powering the nearly three-foot length of metal with the formidable strength of his right arm and shoulder. Blood fountained at each stroke, coating the blade and spattering man and beast. The horse snapped at anything within reach, its broad yellow teeth splintering a wrist here, disfiguring a face there.

Those who didn't die within the first few seconds fled, looking for easier victims.

Badulf dismounted, kneeling beside Rufio. Rufio's gladius, bloody from point to hilt, lay beside him, still connected by its lanyard to his wrist. His armor and helmet bore numerous dents and scratches. But they'd held. The wounds from which blood pooled in the dry earth of the road came from the unarmored portions of his body, and those wounds were many. Already Rufio's pallor made him a stranger, looking nothing like the ruddy, barrel-chested man Badulf recalled.

"Badulf, my friend," Rufio said. The words clearly came with an effort. "It's the end for me. I'm afraid I'm not going to get to Constantinople." He coughed up a mixture of blood and phlegm. Then he grabbed Badulf's wrist with surprising strength. "Here, Badulf, take this. *Memento vita mea.* As long as someone remembers, perhaps I won't truly die."

When Badulf lifted his head, he held a golden ring in his fist. Looking around—

once again taking cognizance of the world—he saw that the battle was in its last stages. The remnants of the cohort were in a knot, making a fighting withdrawal. The scout detachment was in flight, scattered across the countryside. Aetius might win his campaign, but he'd lost this skirmish.

Only one trooper remained nearby, a Cenomani Gaul by the name of Ambiorix. He trotted warily toward Badulf as Badulf worked the lanyard of Rufio's short sword from his dead friend's wrist. A golden ring was a fine memento, and he would indeed remember Rufio every time he looked at it. But a sharp piece of Spanish steel was nothing to disdain, a weapon of much higher quality than Badulf's spatha, which was fashioned of low grade steel by whichever military contractor had offered the largest bribe for the contract. Rufio's short sword—the gladius, with a narrow, stabbing blade and a heavy, ball-shaped pommel—being a weapon issued to a Centurion, was likely to hold its edge and resist rust spotting much better than the spatha Badulf spent so many hours honing and oiling.

The Bagaudae seemed busy elsewhere, concentrating on the last organized threat. Badulf and Ambiorix were in no immediate danger.

"Rufio's in the arms of Mars, eh?" Ambiorix said, leaning on the neck of his horse. His gaze seemed focused on Badulf's closed fist. "What's that? He give you something?"

Badulf nodded. "His ring."

"Like a signet or token, something to introduce you to his family?" Ambiorix squinted, as if thinking. "You two were always close, always talking. But you never say what you talked about. He come from money, did Rufio? Maybe the ring is a key to treasure he's squirreled away? Maybe the legion's paychest?"

"It is just a ring, Ambiorix. The man is dead. If you can't show any respect, at least shut your mouth."

"All right, big fellow. No need to get offended. I'm shutting up." Ambiorix made a show of looking over the field of battle. "It's just... maybe you and me ought to ride together for a while. Dangerous out there."

Badulf considered the Cenomani. Tall, lithe, and dark haired, sporting a flowing mustache he seemed inordinately proud of. He had an easy, unserious way about him. Always the center of attention around the campfire, throwing dice, laughing and swearing at each turn of fortune, usually in arrears paying his debts, but it never seemed to matter. Payday always arrived eventually. Not an ideal trooper; passable on horseback at best. Still, good with a spear, though he seemed to have lost his. His spatha remained in its sheath hanging at his mount's flank.

It wouldn't hurt to have a companion on the trail until he cleared Bagaudae territory. Badulf didn't know yet where he was going, except that he wouldn't go back to the legion. Rufio was right about the Western Empire. Aetius was, as far as Badulf could tell, an excellent general. He'd probably win this war. And maybe others. Inevitably there would be others. More and more. More than the legions could possibly handle. Eventually Rome was doomed. Badulf had no particular investment in Rome's fate one way or the other. He'd have ridden out long before if it hadn't been for Rufio.

"All right, Ambiorix," Badulf said, "you can ride with me."

They'd gone east that first day, for no particular reason Badulf could think of. They'd camped cold, not wanting to risk a fire. Badulf had rolled himself in his cavalry cloak, Rufio's ring clenched in his fist. The next morning, Badulf awoke to find himself alone.

The ring was gone.

His purse, containing the last of his wages and a few pinches of salt, remained, tied to a lanyard and tucked beneath his tunic against his chest. Ambiorix, it seemed, was only so daring. The risk of Badulf waking had been too great for him to extend his larceny beyond the ring.

And so Badulf abandoned his eastward heading, picking up Ambiorix's trail of hoofprints and piles of horse dung, trending initially north, then veering west. It was a lonely pursuit through war-ravaged country. But Badulf did not mind. He had generally been content with only his own thoughts for companionship. Even as a child, his only real intimate had been his grandfather. He followed the thief for weeks, losing him for a day or so once he'd hit the coast: Ambiorix throwing him by the gambit of sending his horse one way and continuing on foot another. But Badulf had picked up the scent at a fishing village. He offered up the last of his coin and sold his horse in order to hire the faux-Angle fisherman to take his pursuit to the water.

Was Badulf to give up now? Was this eerie, supernatural event enough to deter him? Considering the question didn't require more than a moment.

Badulf had listened to enough Christians to have a passing familiarity with their cant. Though he paid his respects primarily to Wotan, Mithras, and Mars, he did not object to paying Jesu his due. If Ambiorix was a Christian and ended up in Hell, Badulf would follow him there, if that was what recovering Rufio's ring required.

Badulf untied the helmet dangling at his belt and shoved it firmly onto his head. He'd spilled so much brain matter over the years that taking precautions for his own was second nature. Taking a deep, slow breath, he stepped forward between the unnaturally heatless fires. Their otherworldly effulgence did not alter a whit. Nothing leapt out at him, the ground did not open beneath his feet, the fires did not send forth tongues of flame to lick at his exposed arms or singe his beard.

He released the breath he'd not realized he'd been holding.

Long, measured strides brought him near enough the tower to inspect it. Soaring menhirs of pale sandstone formed a perfect circle a dozen strides across. Badulf had seen similar columns of rock during his time in Gaul, though most lay on their sides, cracked or broken, and even those standing were pitted and weathered, not pristine and unblemished like these. Between these menhirs, neatly fitted stones filled in the gaps, dull gray and brown, with here and there a sharp bit of flint. The light from the bonfires behind did not allow him to observe much detail. The standing stones themselves seemed to glow with some internal luminescence, but emitted no radiance. Still, he saw what seemed to be some sort of fibrous network twining through the stacked stone walls, as if hair-thin tendrils of some plant held them in place, or some seamstress had, with infinite patience, stitched a retaining webwork.

No gate or doorway was visible on this side. However, an opening in the ground—a neat oval cut into the topsoil and the solid rock of the bluff—revealed stairs, chiseled into the face of a steep tunnel bored under the tower. From somewhere beneath a faint, unwavering glow of orange and red with a sickly green undertone illuminated the passage down.

Badulf set the sole of his boot on the first stair, paused, then took the next. He had to turn sideways as his torso passed through the entrance; the width of his shoulders was too great for the short dimension of the oval to accommodate.

As the steps brought his head below the level of the ground, Badulf paused again. He thought about Ambiorix, the stolen ring, and Rufio. He set his jaw and continued down.

The stairs ended at a short, dirt-walled passage that terminated at what Badulf imagined was roughly the center of the circle of the tower above. Gnarled elbows of thick roots emerged from the walls. Tendrils dangled from the roof above. The air about the vegetation was suffused with a red and orange glow, similar to that of the mysterious bonfires. But the light did not seem to come directly from the fibrous matter, though on closer examination it did appear to be the source of the etiolated emerald aspect of the light.

An alcove to the right of the end of the passage hosted an altar, formed of the same stone as the menhirs above. It gleamed like snow in high alpine passes, except for a shallow, circular depression at one end. This section was devoid of light, instead hued a dark rust red, veined with black. Badulf spared the altar only a single glance. He had no desire to know what sort of grim sacrifices had occurred here.

To the left, another alcove opened onto a stairway spiraling down. The hellish illumination was, if anything, stronger, channeling up through the stairwell. Badulf took a step in that direction, dangling root ends from the low ceiling brushing against the top of his helmet as he moved.

Something dark obscured the light from below, casting a dim, moving shadow circling the ceiling above the mouth of the stairwell. The sound of pounding feet was followed by gasping breaths and Ambiorix appeared, pelting up the stairs. His widened eyes appeared abnormally large against the ghastly pallor of his face. Greasy, matted strands of his dark hair whipped about his head—a head that swiveled rapidly, frantically, forward and back. It was if he were both terrified of missing his footing and wanting to keep his gaze before him but was equally frightened of something behind him.

He'd lost his helmet somewhere, though he'd retained his coat of mail. In Badulf's experience, Ambiorix had never been much of a soldier, averse to tending to his kit. But even by Ambiorix's standards, the chainmail was woefully neglected. His spatha, however, looked clean enough, gripped in one white-knuckled hand.

Ambiorix cleared the stairwell. At sight of Badulf, he drew up short, cast a glance over his shoulder, shuffled two steps forward, then stopped again. A phrase Rufio had used occurred to Badulf: Caught between Scylla and Charybdis.

"Badulf." Ambiorix sputtered out the name. His voice shook when he continued, taking on a quality that was at once wheedling and frightened. "Just the man I was hoping to see. Let's get out of this hole and find some place to bivouac and talk."

"Sure, Ambiorix," Badulf said. "Hand over Rufio's ring and we'll get out."

"The ring, right." Ambiorix's left hand groped at his breast, as if feeling for a medallion or key strung on a chain hung about his neck. The hand patted and felt about, fruitlessly. Then Ambiorix shot a glance over his shoulder. When he looked back the terror on his face was, if anything, more pronounced. Then a snarl lifted one corner of his mouth and with a cry that partook half of desperation and half of fury, he charged. His right arm swept the sword back, ready to deliver a scything blow.

Badulf left his spatha in its scabbard. Hauling it out might take longer than Ambiorix's onslaught would allow. Besides, the low ceiling and relatively closely spaced walls of the tunnel did not recommend the longer blade. His right hand dropped to his hip, and he slid free Rufio's gladius—his gladius, now.

He took two long strides to his right, slipping into the alcove and placing the stone altar between himself and the charging Gaul. The stone block limited Ambiorix's choice of targets. Badulf caught the arcing blow directed at his left side with a solid parry, wrapping his left hand around his right on the short grip of the gladius to add the strength of both arms to the block. The steel rang, the parry biting a notch into the lower quality steel of the spatha. Ambiorix lacked Badulf's bulk, but his long arms and years of hard fighting in the *auxilia* had taught him how to swing a sword. The blow would have sent the gladius flying from the grasp of a weaker man.

But Ambiorix had struck at Badulf, not at some weak-armed Ravenna merchant or a starveling Celt. Badulf absorbed the blow, with only a nigh inaudible grunt. Then, with a twist of his thick, corded wrists, he slammed the blade of the spatha down, pinning it against the altar. With the blistering speed of a missile hurled by a Balearic slinger, Badulf shot out his left hand across the altar and grabbed Ambiorix's right forearm. He yanked Ambiorix towards him. The Cenomani, off-balance, stumbled forward, sprawling atop the altar. With a flicker, the razor edge of the gladius slashed Ambiorix's throat. Bright blood, tinged an odd shade of amber in the eerie light, spurted to either side, and gouted to splash the altar stone and run along etched channels to fill the bowl at the end.

Badulf held on until Ambiorix's death spasms subsided. Then he let go and stepped back until his spine pressed against the wall of the alcove. He did not care to imagine to what sort of god he might have just offered blood sacrifice. The needling pressure of root ends pushing against his back—the knobby lumps felt even through his mail—impelled him to step away from the wall. He edged out into the tunnel proper, leaving Ambiorix's corpse slumped over the blood-drenched altar.

Another moment to turn back presented itself. He'd taken his revenge upon the thief. He could leave this hole now, climb back outside into the night and hunt up a place to bed down. But Ambiorix's actions had indicated that the ring lay somewhere below, somewhere down that spiral staircase. Somewhere that had frightened the hardened Cenomani.

Rufio had once told him a tale of a Roman soldier by the name of Horatius holding a bridge single-handedly. Rufio had extolled it as soldierly courage. Badulf didn't entirely disagree, but he saw the story more as an example of a warrior finding a suitable end, a death pleasing to Wotan. Either way, it was an expression of courage. And courage was a virtue Badulf had shared with the Centurion. Leaving now would constitute flight, turning tail on the enemy, whoever that was. Such would be ignominy, and would disgrace the memory of Rufio.

Badulf stalked toward the stairwell. He would retrieve Rufio's ring.

The strange glow brightened as Badulf descended, until it achieved nearly the illumination of torchlight. Badulf took each narrow step cautiously, not out of fear of what lay below, but due to the narrow width. These steps had been made for men of smaller stature and with correspondingly smaller feet. After a few paces, he paused to sheathe the gladius. He didn't want that flailing around him if he slipped. Root ends seemed to tug at him from the walls, snagging in his cloak and trying to knock his helmet off his head or tip it over his eyes, none of which helped his footing. But he maintained a dogged precision as he went down, at each step assuring his boot was firmly positioned before trusting his weight to it.

The stairwell terminated in a cavern of at least twice the circumference of the menhir tower. Rough earthen walls curved from dirt floor to root-furred ceiling; a ceiling Badulf was glad to note was twice the height of the hallway above. A central pillar—an aggregate of hard, crumbling earth and jagged pebbles—seemed to be the source of the majority of the light. The walls bowed into shadowy recesses, from within which a tangle of gnarled roots emerged into the red-orange glow. Only the floor appeared free of the interlocking chaos of roots: a level, unblemished stretch of limestone, dully reflecting the odd radiance from the pillar as a wan yellow.

Something else lay within the encircling, green-tinted shadow, something concealed by, and bound up within, the complexity of the root system. Rufio's ring was not immediately visible. So, setting aside a search of the central pillar for the moment, Badulf stalked over to his right, curious about what the shadows obscured.

He pulled up abruptly as he recognized the objects woven into the roots: bones. Human remains, most of which took the form of complete skeletons.

An involuntary shudder ran through Badulf's bulky frame. What foul magic fed this place? What ancient god of this dark island had demanded these sacrifices? Curse Ambiorix for fleeing to this spot on this of all nights.

Badulf blinked. Was it a trick of the light, or had one of those skeletons moved? The baleful illumination was steady and unflickering—hardly the sort of light to cast tricksome shadows. There, a twitch of a skeletal finger. And there, caught by his peripheral vision to his left, a skull turned.

Turned to face him. To look at him.

Badulf's wrist twisted to grasp the hilt of the gladius. Then he stopped, and instead moved his hand across his body to where the spatha hung from its baldric. If he needed to swing a sword, he had room down here that hadn't been afforded up above.

Badulf took a step back. He shifted his head left and right, alert for movement.

The tangled roots vomited forth a legion of the dead. The skeletons moved across the floor with the sound of rats on marble, bony feet skittering on the hard limestone. Legs lifted and fell. Arms stretched out, twenty pairs of brittle, yellow bones stretching in concert toward Badulf. A score of empty skulls focused on him.

Badulf hauled forth his spatha, looking wildly about. The skeletons came from all sides. Already he was cut off from the stairs. He still had a moment before he was enveloped by the grisly horde, a moment in which he noted an additional detail: the roots remained intertwined with the bones, roots stretching back into the shadows and into the earthen walls. Whether the movement of the bones caused the roots to move or if the roots were themselves some sort of macabre puppet strings, Badulf did not know.

Horror rose within him—but the horror did not overwhelm him, did not lead to hopeless inanition. Instead, the horror galvanized Badulf into action. He did not wait for the first of the animate dead to reach him. He leaped forward, calling out the names of Wotan, and Mithras, and Mars. Gripping the hilt of the spatha with both hands, he swung the sword in a powerful, arcing slash at the nearest corpse-thing.

The blade stove in a brittle skull, leaving only a jagged oval of bone like a broken tooth atop the still moving collection of bones. Finger bones, held together by root tendrils, clutched at the edge of Badulf's cloak, which had twirled about him in the follow-through. Badulf felt himself being tugged forward. He released his left hand from the hilt and swung a backhand sword stroke at a downward angle, passing below the lowest ribs and chopping into the spine. That blow should have sheared through, powered by the strength of Badulf's right arm. Instead the sword met resistance, as if he'd hacked into an old stump. The blade stopped, two-thirds of the way through, brought to a halt by the tough, flexible root that had grown up through and about the vertebrae. The ancient, thickly massed fibers had absorbed much of the force of Badulf's cut.

And yet, it had been enough. Tugging the blade free required both hands. Once it came free, the weight of the upper half of the skeleton caused it to topple sideways, dangling by a few threads. The skeleton fell to the floor, where it shifted and flopped, directionless, like a decapitated chicken during the moments following its initial, headless flight.

The time it had taken Badulf to free his spatha had allowed four skeletons to close, bony hands clawing at his arms, skittering off the links of his mail, and thrusting at his eyes. He jerked his head back from the threat to his vision and began hacking, taking short, hard strokes at elbow joints, knees, and ribs, sending slivers of bone twirling through the air and disrupting any chance of a coordinated attack—if there was any coordination behind the actions of these dead things. He worried for his blade. Striking bone was bad enough, but chopping into the roots multiplied the damage done. The spatha did not hold an edge well at the best of times. Much more of this and he'd be swinging nothing more than a thin, dull metal club.

A skeleton with a shattered knee tipped forward, unable to maintain balance. Its hands groped for Badulf's throat, catching bony handfuls of beard. Badulf, smashing another foe's skull with the pommel of the spatha, shot out a hand, wrapping calloused fingers around the spinal column. He hoisted the skeleton from the floor, surprised at how heavy the additional weight of vegetable matter from the root system woven through the bones made the diabolical monster. He twirled, hammering at the skeletons closing in from all sides with the animated dead thing in his left hand. Completing a circuit, he was left with nothing but the remains of the rib cage, and the central root, long and flexible enough that it still had slack to give from its origin somewhere in the recesses of the cavern walls.

Badulf had cleared a moment's breathing space, but that was all. Already the circle was tightening again. He began to suck air in gasps. Combat was the most strenuous activity a man could engage in. Fear did nothing to help control respiration. Badulf could keep fear at bay, usually exultant or full of rage during battle. But that was against human opponents. The horror he'd held down threatened to envelop him as a grisly doom neared from all around, one scraping footfall at a time.

He'd lived a rough but eventful life. Badulf held few regrets, though he did wish he possessed more memories of his father. Perhaps soon enough he'd meet his old man. If, that was, Badulf deserved a place at Wotan's table. Well, it was time to earn that place. And maybe the effort might keep him alive.

As Badulf hurled himself at one segment of the tightening noose, he wondered if Rufio dined with Wotan. Or did he feast at the side of Mars?

Then he was plowing into the undead ranks, striking left and right, trying to keep his blows low, taking out legs. Sharp-tipped fingers raked his face, drawing furrows down his cheeks, tugging off his helmet, and yanking tufts from his beard.

The cordon tightened. Skeletal arms wrapped around his legs. It was like stepping into a thicket of hard, narrow, grasping branches. Badulf kicked and stomped, trying to fight free. He teetered, off balance. Rib cages pressed against him and he toppled, an avalanche of rattling bones falling atop him. Toothless jaws nipped at his arms. He jerked his head from side to side, avoiding digits probing for his eyes. Hands closed about his throat. He couldn't breathe. Despite the weird light, everything began to go gray.

Badulf thrashed. His left hand grabbed a collar bone. A short chopping motion with the spatha, requiring every ounce of strength he could muster while flat on his back, cleared a few inches of space to his right. He rolled that way, using the skeleton clutched in his left hand to batter aside some of those still trying to pile on top. He let go and continued rolling until he was face down on the hard limestone, knees pulled up tight, half-a-dozen skeletons in various stages of completeness still clinging to him, gouging and clawing at every inch of unarmored flesh. Then, left palm flat, right knuckles pressing into the stone while remaining tightly wrapped about the hilt, he exploded upright, sending a cascade of skeletons clattering about him. Instantly he was stomping, kicking, and hacking, taking the fight to the animated skeletons struggling to regain their feet—those that still had feet. Others crawled back towards him.

But the advantage was, for the moment, with Badulf. Heavy, chopping blows severed rib cage from pelvis. Boot heels crushed skulls to powder. The cutting edge of the spatha grew blunt from repeated contact with bone and root. By the time Badulf deprived the last skeleton of animation, he was reduced to smashing with the spatha like a broken spear shaft, breaking down the joints and pounding the larger bones into fragments that the root system was unable to make use of.

He stood panting, his heavy chest working like a blacksmith's bellows, blood trickling down his face, arms, and legs from dozens of gashes. A few tendrils twitched and quivered, but otherwise the battlefield lay quiet, looking like the aftermath of a pack of ghouls having uncovered an ancient mass burial site.

Badulf turned to face the central pillar. A glint of yellow caught his attention. He pushed himself into motion. Circling to his right, towards the flash that had caught his eye, he saw that not all of the pillar was mere rock and earth. The far side seemed largely composed of living matter: dense, fibrous growths. He saw a massive complex of roots, each the thickness of a man's torso, intertwined; more vast and tightly woven than he'd seen in ancient oak trees fallen after violent storms. Above the mass, growing out of it like a head, Badulf observed a roughly conical, tuber-like protuberance, more woody than fleshy. This seemed to be the source of the false firelight illuminating the cavern. The glow was most pronounced here, the strength of the illumination diminishing gradually along the root system as a factor of distance. A pair of gleaming orbs within the head, glittering orange and black, tracked Badulf's motion. A pair of smaller root outgrowths, more like tree limbs than roots, extended on either side, just below the head. Above the head, the root system extended upwards, spreading out to encompass the entirety of the ceiling.

Above, at the point where Badulf judged the roots penetrated the alcove with the altar above, he saw a crimson light filtering down slowly toward the center of the pillar. The red was suggestive more of blood than of flame. Badulf shuddered, realizing this must be Ambiorix's blood, sluggishly filtering its way through the roots of this ancient, macabre entelechy. This god, or hell-creature, or whatever it was, seemed to be at its most powerful this one day of the year. What more strength would it gain from a blood sacrifice?

Badulf had no desire to find out. He fumbled at the throat of the scabbard, sliding the notched and dulled blade of the spatha home. It was time to get out, before Ambiorix's blood reached the heart of the vast creature.

His knee bent, preparatory to taking the first step toward the stairs. The eyes in the great tuber flared. A wave of alien sensation, of memory, of hunger and desire flooded through Badulf. He couldn't move.

He saw.

Small, dark human forms drew stone knives along the throats of goats and scrawny cattle atop a high, windswept bluff by the sea. Blood soaked the earth and fed the hunger of the god. The flesh of the sacrifices decayed, the decomposed remains becoming part of the earth, adding nutrients that also fed the god. Awareness expanded to encompass the mould throughout the seagirt isle. Death nourished the soil. Seeds flourished, feeding from the gift of death, germinating and growing. Feeding the small, dark humans. These humans, and then others, similar—the god hardly noticed the change, was indifferent to it – sacrificed more, and the cycle continued. Year after year, death, decay, growth, life.

Badulf could be part of it. His blood, his flesh, could become incorporated into the earth, become one with the mould, nurture life, in an endless repetition of death and rebirth. He had merely to offer up himself here, to the god. Nothing could be more proper. More holy.

Badulf's right hand, seemingly of its own accord, grasped the hilt of the gladius. His will was no longer his own. He was nothing but an extension of the god. Soon he would be so for all eternity. The steel blade began to slide free of the scabbard. The motion shifted Badulf's head fractionally. The yellow glint again caught his eye. He blinked.

Rufio's ring hung from a cord, dangling from a root tip.

With a yell, Badulf drew the gladius the rest of the way, and lunged forward. The sharp point plunged deeply into the center of the head of the god. It required all of

Badulf's strength, driven by the power of his bent legs and transferred through his back and shoulder, to plunge the gladius as deeply as he did into the dense, xyloid mass of the tuber.

The keening shriek of pain and terror that Badulf heard did not enter through his ears. It blasted into his mind, the wail of a wounded god. He closed his eyes against the psychic agony, every nerve in his body vibrating in sympathy. With a desperate wrench, he jerked the gladius free, staggering back. Breaking contact seemed to lessen the echo of pain flensing his mind. He scooted close once more, this time to snatch Rufio's ring, breaking it free from the cord that the root tip seemed unwilling to relinquish.

Then Badulf was stumbling toward the stairway, shoving the ring onto his index finger as he went. The formerly solid limestone floor now gave way beneath his footsteps, cracking and crazing. The light was dimming rapidly. The cavern no longer appeared as spacious, the walls closer, the dirt collapsing and slumping in drifts on the floor. The ceiling itself now brushed the top of Badulf's head.

Badulf reached the first stair. Not daring to take the time for cautious foot placement, he scrambled up. He found himself squeezing through an increasingly narrow space, digging his toes deeply into shrinking, crumbling steps, bending forward to use his left hand and the gladius in his right to haul himself up when his boots slipped.

He cleared the mouth of the stairwell, dragging his foot free of a now earth-clogged hole. He could no longer see the opposite alcove containing the altar, only dimly sense a sloping pile of loose soil. The illumination had faded almost entirely away. The hallway was disappearing as he tried to stand. He could only rise to a stooped position before encountering the tunnel ceiling. Badulf darted forward, making for the slightly darker circle at the end of the darkness of the collapsing tunnel.

Badulf, gasping for breath, fighting to avoid inhaling a lungful of dirt, burrowed free of what seemed no more than an animal den, into the blessedly chill night. He lay, staring up at the stars, grateful for the bite of the cold, salt-scented air. Behind him swelled a lumpen hill, with the ruins of a few menhirs visible, protruding from the earth at odd angles.

Somewhere below the bluff roared bonfires, surrounded by cheerful, celebrating people, swilling mead and ale. Badulf wanted no part of it. He only wanted off this cursed island. And then? East, he supposed. He rubbed at Rufio's ring with his thumb. Perhaps he'd head for Constantinople.

Ken Lizzi is a lawyer and a writer of two-fisted fabulism living in Texas. His most recent novel, Cesar the Bravo, *is available from Cirsova Publishing. Find more of his scribblings at www.kenlizzi.net.*

Book of a Thousand Dreams

By Harold R. Thompson

Adventurer Anchor Brown sets off in search of a missing colleague, chasing rumors that he had discovered a lost book of fairy tales with magical powers!

Major Anchor Brown (Retired) met Anna Strang in the Artillery Room on the ground floor of the Imperial Society building. The room was small and intimate, with stuffed armchairs, dark wood panelling, and a fire crackling in the hearth to keep away the damp chill of early spring. Prints of various types of ordnance hung from the walls, everything from the cannon of the last century, which utilized an explosive propellent, to the more modern pneumatic pieces. It was not that the Imperial Society was particularly fond of things military, but of the scientific achievement the artillery branch represented.

Other meeting rooms in the building featured art depicting turbine ships, farm machinery, and various flora and fauna.

Anna occupied one of the chairs beside the fire. She wore a green dress with an embroidered pattern of leaves and vines on the bodice, and her flaming red hair was piled on top of her head. On the end of her long narrow nose, a pair of gold-rimmed spectacles rested. She had with her a leather shoulder bag, like an army haversack, though of finer material and construction. She carried this with her always. Brown sat in the opposite chair, stroking his mustache with a thumb and forefinger, a habit when he was thinking. He had asked her to meet with him for one simple reason: someone needed to know where he was going, in case he never returned.

"Magnus Krane," he said.

She raised an eyebrow.

"What of him?"

Krane had been a member of the Imperial Society, a scientist with some outlandish theories about the origins of human civilization. He had vanished without a trace ten years earlier.

"I received a letter from him."

Anna's eyes widened.

"How is that possible?"

"To be more precise, I did not receive it by post. Krane's country house and its contents were auctioned, since no family had come forward to claim them. The letter was in a drawer of his desk, dated the year he disappeared."

Anna leaned back with a sigh of mild frustration.

"You did that to shock me, didn't you? Well, what did the letter say? And why had no one looked in his desk before? Was there no investigation after his disappearance?"

"Not that I recall. It seems to me we all expected him to return some day. At any rate, what the letter contains is the most interesting thing."

Brown paused, considering what to tell and what to leave out. "Brown, you are as notorious as I in your way," Krane had written, "a maverick explorer and adventurer, a fellow seeker of truth in both light and dark corners. You are the only one I trust with the knowledge of this discovery!"

In turn, Brown trusted few others as he trusted Anna Strang.

"Krane claims to have found a complete copy of the *Book of a Thousand Dreams*."

Anna shrugged.

"The ancient book of fairy stories?"

Brown was surprised at her muted reaction.

"It's not just a book of fairy stories! It's a book of tales from the Ordaen Emperor's personal library. Only the emperor or empress and their inner circles were permitted to handle it. There were only a handful of copies, all of which went missing after the empire's decline."

Krane had explained that the discovery had been random, part of a trove of books and scrolls he had stumbled upon in a market in the Ordaen city of Mahadria. The book's cover had been missing, but as soon as Krane had begun to examine the text, he realized what he had found.

"Our entire civilization, not just in Artor, but all of Midterra, owes much to Ordae and that ancient empire. It is our foundation. Only a small number of the stories of the *Book of a Thousand Dreams* have come down to us—perhaps a dozen? This was a complete text. It has extraordinary cultural value, but there's more to it than that. Krane claims in his letter that the book has power, that every story contains a few lines of extra text, at the end. Spells, he says. Powerful spells, that are only effective when recited in the original language... which I am able to read, and to speak."

Anna gazed at the fire and tapped the side of her cheek with one finger.

"Magic spells, Brown? Really?"

Brown leaned forward in his chair.

"It explains why the emperor kept it so close. We should not dismiss the notion. You and I have encountered many things in this world that one would describe as 'magic.' Krane was so concerned with the power of this book that he fled the country. He gave me the location of a house in Frieland. He wanted my advice on what to do next."

Anna shook her head.

"But he never posted the letter?"

"No. My sense is that he may have fled the country in haste."

"So you're still going to this place in Frieland to find him?"

"Should I not?"

Anna chuckled.

"Oh, you want my opinion? Then here it is: do what you feel you need to do. I can see it in your eyes, Brown. They're fairly blazing! Go to Frieland and find our missing comrade. I know your sense of duty to do so, if there is even the slimmest chance."

That was true, but it was more than that, and Brown admitted it.

"There is the *Book of a Thousand Dreams.* Its value is impossible to calculate."

"Because of the supposed magic spells?"

Brown grimaced.

"No, to be frank. That's a mere curiosity. Krane did have a tendency to become overly enthusiastic, to exaggerate... but the stories! All of those stories, and what they can tell us about the ancients, and in turn about ourselves. You know I left the infantry to learn about the world and its people. I consider this part of that mission."

Anna smiled.

"Your mind was already made up! You didn't really need to ask my advice!"

"Perhaps not, but you've helped to validate my decision."

He had been considering asking her to accompany him, but knew her health would not allow it. Even to ask would be selfish, he decided. He would go alone, with her blessing.

"As it happens," he said, "I intend to depart at once, in the morning. I already have my tickets to cross the Narrow Sea. As Bamflout tells us, 'A man should be ready to take journey at all times.'"

"I'm afraid I have not read Bamflout," she said, "but those are appropriate words for one such as you, Brown. You always know what you have to do. I hope all goes well, but my sense is things are not quite what they seem."

Brown dressed as a gentleman, an Arto-Brian on business or holiday, rather than a soldier, in tweed trousers and sack coat, a linen waistcoat, and a hat with a modest brim. He carried a heavy watch, with a silver fob chain, in his waistcoat pocket. For luggage he had only a small valise with a convenient shoulder strap. This was not a military expedition, nothing like Brown's many missions with the old Corps of Exploration, or his many more recent Government and private contracts. This was nothing but an ordinary trip abroad. And yet, he sensed that he should go armed, and so took with him a small dart pistol, one that would fit in the right inside pocket of his coat. A folding spring-loaded sword, hinged in the center, went into his left pocket. The folding sword was not his old regulation sabre, and a bit flimsy, but it had saved his life on several occasions.

The ferry across the Narrow Sea was uneventful, and from the coast Brown took the sail-train to Montbleu. While on the train, with the lush green fields of Frieland passing outside his window, he re-read Krane's letter.

"I need a secluded place," Krane had written, "where no one knows who I am, nor the nature of my studies, lest they suspect." He had underlined "suspect." "I have tested some of the spells. They are presented at the end of each tale and their effects are related to the nature of the story. For example, the spell at the conclusion of the *Tale of the Seven Kittens* produced seven living kittens, who share this house with me now. That is perhaps the most benign of the spells; others are much more dangerous and seem to be directed at an adversary. However, without an adversary present, they seem to do nothing. I will test more when I arrive at my cousin's country house in Frieland, near Montbleu."

The letter contained the address and a description of the house and its approaches.

From the station in Montbleu, Brown took the public coach north. The driver made stops on request. It was a horse-drawn conveyance, and passengers were required to tap on the ceiling of the cabin to let the driver know when to stop. Brown requested a stop at a country lane that extended from the main road. The lane was dark, the surrounding woods tangled and overgrown with weeds and vines.

"Are you sure this is the place you wish to go to, *Monsieur*?" the driver said as Brown opened the coach door. "They say it is long abandoned, *une maison hantée*."

Brown found this discouraging news. Did that mean Krane had moved on?

There was only one way to find out.

"It is the right place," he told the driver. "Thank you, *merci*."

With his valise slung over his shoulder, Brown walked along the lane in the dappled sunlight. At the end he came to a large stone house, built in the Frielander style, with many gables and tall chimneys. The house was surrounded by a high stone wall, with a wooden gate. A few flakes of green paint still clung to the gate.

Brown wondered if he should knock.

The top of a leafy shrubbery showed above the wall, and this swayed and rippled, although Brown felt no wind. He recognized the plant, known in Artor as devil-weed, which was carnivorous and had a caustic sap. It seemed to grow all along the inside of the wall, surrounding the house.

"Some added protection, perhaps?" Brown mused.

He noticed three birds perched on the wall to his right. They were motionless and looking at him. He did not recognize the species, but they were about the size of the common Midterran thrush, their plumage a nondescript gray speckled with brown.

Something about the birds aroused his suspicions… but perhaps they were just birds?

"Krane!" he shouted. "It's Major Brown! Are you here?"

He waited a few minutes for a response, although he expected none.

The gate had a brass handle, with a thumb latch. Brown tried the latch and heard a click.

The gate swung open.

A path led through the devil-weed to a flight of steps and what must have been the main door to the house. The path was narrow, and Brown was careful not to touch the towering, undulating greenery on either side. The strange birds took flight from the wall and circled above. Three more of their kind joined them.

The door stood slightly ajar. Even before he pushed it open, Brown knew the house was unoccupied. Inside the large front hall, he called, "Krane?"

He did not expect an answer and did not receive one.

The house was unfurnished save for piles of dust in the corners and some broken glass from damaged windows. Brown explored several large rooms, including a parlour and a dining room. Upstairs there were five bedrooms, all empty.

"Is this the end, then?" he said, hearing his voice echo from the dingy walls.

He had no way to know where Krane had gone next.

A thought occurred to him. The members of the Imperial Society, all scientists and naturalists and engineers, had several secret methods of communication.

Returning to the large front parlour, Brown retrieved the largest piece of broken glass he could find. In his satchel, he carried a box of strike-anywhere matches. Lighting a match, he held it up to the glass, moving it back and forth. After burning three matches, he had completely covered the glass in smoke residue, though not so much that the glass was no longer transparent. Holding it up like a lens, he peered through it at the cracked plaster on the walls.

In the dining room, he spied a blue glimmer to the right of the cold fireplace. As he drew closer, he saw it was exactly what he had been hoping to find: a message, written in special paint, that only a fellow member of the Imperial Society could hope to find.

"Friend, it is not safe here," the message read in block letters. "I have gone south to Lorne and the Tower of Light."

Lorne was about a day away by sail-train, on the coast.

Brown felt a sense of grim satisfaction. It was still possible to find Krane. With renewed hope for his mission, he went back to the front door.

Outside on the steps, the birds attacked him.

They came in from all sides, diving for his face and eyes. One knocked his hat askew. The piece of smoked glass was still in his hand, and he struck out with it, felt it bite into one of his tiny assailants. The bird spun away and became entangled in the devil-weed. The weed reacted, grasping the bird by the wings and pulling. Both wings came off, and the bird's body fell to the path.

Perhaps to avoid the fate of their comrade, the other birds flew off.

Brown knelt to examine the injured bird, although he suspected it was not a bird at all. Closer inspection proved this assessment correct. Protruding from the feathers where the wings had been mounted were metal springs and a series of tiny gear wheels. The birds were mechanisms.

Was this why Krane had left? Had these things been watching the house for years? And to whom did they report?

A further examination of the clockwork bird answered this last question. Tiny writing on the base of one of the springs was in Valgurnian script.

The Valgurnian Empire was sprawling and covered a large part of Midterra, unlike Artor's mercantile empire of overseas colonies, but the two were rivals. Magnus Krane would be known to the Valgurnians, and his movements of interest. No doubt their spies had been watching him from the moment he left Artor.

"You should have stayed at home, my friend," Brown murmured. "And asked for my help."

He put the remains of the broken bird in his pocket.

Brown knew the "Tower of Light" in Lorne could only refer to one place, the ancient lighthouse that stood on a long promontory jutting into the Superius Sea. He wondered how Krane could have gained access to such a place, which was a national treasure of Frieland, but Krane had many contacts in the realm of antiquities.

Lorne was a coastal town with a famous sand beach, but the Tower was to the west, somewhat remote, and accessed by a single road. Brown found it necessary to rent a horse. The day was fine and the smell of the sea was strong. He could see the Tower, away on his left, long before he came to it. The top, where the beacon had once been lit, had broken off, and much of the surrounding castle was also in ruins. It did not look like a secure place for Krane to perform experiments on the *Book of a Thousand Dreams*. It did not look inhabitable at all.

Brown nudged his horse along the narrow trail toward the Tower. The land here was rocky and open, with no trees, the trail rising toward the peak of the promontory. The sea lay on both sides, and the noise of the surf was loud. Brown saw no other people, and felt his spirits begin to slump. What were the chances that, after so many years, Krane was still here? It already felt like another dead end.

At the edge of the ruins, Brown tied his horse to a broken stone column. Unstrapping his valise from the saddle, he slung it over his shoulder and made his way toward the old castle gate, which was now just a gap in the wall. Beyond lay a courtyard and the foundations of several buildings, long gone. Steps led up to the ramparts on the far side of the court. The Tower itself jutted up from those ramparts.

Crossing the courtyard, Brown climbed the steps. Sections of the battlements along the ramparts were intact, but others had crumbled. Through the gaps, Brown could see a long fall to rocks and waves below.

The entrance to the Tower was a dark empty gap missing its door. Stepping inside, Brown found another staircase, spiraling upward into the oblivion of the Tower's shattered crown.

"Nothing here," Brown murmured.

He lingered at the foot of the spiral staircase, listening to the waves below and the gulls crying above. He was unsure of his next move but did not want to admit failure.

He suddenly remembered he had kept the bit of smoked glass from the house near Montbleu.

Taking the glass from his valise, he peered through it at the curved inner walls of the Tower, but saw nothing. Back outside, he examined the battlements, then went down the steps to the courtyard. He noticed a row of birds perched along the north wall, their familiar profiles etched against the bright sky. Pausing, he watched them for a moment. He was certain they were the same as the mechanical birds he had encountered before. If the birds functioned as eyes and ears for someone, and they had been tasked with watching Krane, then their presence here could be an indication that Krane was also here, or had been.

Or had they followed Brown from Montbleu?

He had no choice but to continue his search. The birds were a threat, and he felt a renewed sense of urgency. Turning to face the wall behind him, he held up the smoked glass and immediately spied a faint blue glimmer directly below where the Tower stood. Encouraged, he stepped forward for a closer look.

It was another message. It said, "Enter Here." Below it a single stone had been coated with the special paint.

"Well done, Magnus Krane!" Brown murmured.

He pushed on the stone. It depressed about an inch, and he heard the sound of a metallic latch springing open. A section of wall swung inward.

A staircase led down into darkness.

A tin oil lantern hung from a hook on the wall to the left, and Brown took it down and lit it using a match from the box in his valise. The staircase was narrow and steep, and he kept his right hand on the wall, the lantern in his left, as he descended. Twenty-three steps down, he noted an abrupt change in the type of brick and construction method in the walls and arched ceiling. The Tower and its surrounding castle had been built on top of an older structure. The older brickwork, in Brown's estimation, was Ordaen.

"'Welcome to the empire,'" he said aloud, quoting Narron's *The Assumption of Ordae*, "'where the light ever shines.'"

Though not in this musty dungeon, he thought.

At the bottom of the stairs was a small antechamber. Columns flanked an open archway, and beyond stretched a narrow corridor. More doorways along the corridor led to small storerooms, each filled with crates and barrels, though Brown did not examine their contents. Supplies, he assumed, for anyone living in this cold and gloomy place.

The corridor ended at another doorway, which led to a spacious chamber. The light from Brown's lantern revealed a fine Tasran carpet on the floor, a poster bed in the corner, a desk, dining table and chairs, a shelf crammed with books, and a cast-iron stove. In an armchair next to the stove sat someone who might have once been Magnus Krane.

The corpse was clothed in a tweed suit much like the one Brown wore. The skin was pulled tight against the skull, the eyeballs shrivelled in their sockets, the dried lips pulled back to expose yellowed teeth. Only the hair had not decayed, but appeared combed and styled with oil.

Krane had been vain about his hair.

In his bony hands, the dead man was clutching a large book.

Kneeling, Brown peered into what was left of his old comrade's face.

"What happened, Magnus?" he murmured.

On the small table next to the armchair sat a teacup and a plate containing what resembled a rock but might have been a desiccated bit of cake. Krane had been having a snack. Brown could only conclude that he had simply died while in hiding, guarding the prize he still held in his arms.

Setting the lantern on the dining table, Brown prized the book away from Krane's clutches.

"I'm sorry, old fellow," he said.

He let out a heavy sigh. He felt no sense of triumph, of success, only sadness. Krane had given his life for this treasure. Brown hoped that there was something to it.

Setting the book on the dining table, he sat in one of four wooden dining chairs. Why had Krane brought in four chairs? Had he expected company, or had this apartment already been furnished before he had arrived? Brown decided the latter.

He looked at the book and started turning pages, slowly, with great care. The book was large, bigger than a volume of the *Artorian Encyclopedia*, and the stories adorned with illustrations, the pigments still bright. As Krane had explained in his letter, the cover was missing, as were the first half-dozen pages, but it was clear to Brown, and would have been to any scholar of ancient Ordae, that here was a copy of the *Book of a Thousand Dreams*. A thousand tales for children, most of them lost for two thousand years; tales of adventure, tales of horror, tales of whimsy. And at the end of each, according to Krane, a spell.

"Could it be a forgery?" Brown wondered, but the linen paper and the style of the drawings was correct, as was the script and the language, although the book was incredibly well preserved. The first three complete stories were all known to historians, but the fourth and fifth were unknown. The fifth was entitled *Pueri in Silva Perditi*, which Brown translated in his head to *The Boys Lost in the Forest*.

"Did you read many of these, Magnus?" he said, addressing the dead man.

He skimmed the story, in which two boys discovered that all of the trees in a forest were the bodies of men, an entire army turned into trees by a magician. The boys managed to rescue one soldier, who was their father. He became human again. At the end of the tale was a single line of poetry, printed inside an illustration of tangled woods. Brown assumed the line was an example of what Krane thought was a spell.

"*Itaque exercitui arborum iunge*," he read. *And so, join the army of trees.*

The room trembled, as if an earthquake had struck. Brown froze. After a few seconds, the trembling passed. He gazed around the room, but all seemed as before.

That was foolish, he thought, and realized he had not believed in the spells.

"This is no time to be toying with the unknown," he said to the corpse. "I must go into the town and seek the authorities. We'll bring you home and put an end to your mystery."

With the book under his arm, his valise slung over one shoulder, and the lantern in his free hand, he returned to the stairs and climbed toward the small rectangle of daylight at their summit. As he emerged into the courtyard, a man on horseback was just riding in through the castle gate.

Brown's instincts told him to retire at once to a more defensible position. The upright manner in which the horseman sat in his saddle, his tall hat with its flat crown, and his monstrous moustache and side-whiskers suggested he was Valgurnian, as did the model of sabre strapped to his saddle. The sabre also suggested hostile intentions.

Brown scrambled back up the steps to the ramparts, setting down the lantern and reaching into his coat pocket for his dart pistol. The book, tucked under his left arm, was a burden. He saw the birds on the north wall suddenly take flight and begin circling over the courtyard as the horseman approached and reined in below the wall.

The man looked up at Brown. He doffed his hat.

"Good day, sir," he said in accented Artorian. "What is that you hold under your arm?"

"Is it not illegal in Frieland for a gentleman to carry a sword in public?" Brown said.

The Valgurnian drew the sword and brought it to the poise before dropping it to the carry, much as a military man would do.

"I suggest you give me the book, sir," he said.

Brown raised his pistol.

"And I suggest you back away, sir."

The birds struck, falling from the sky like tiny mortar shells, faster than Brown had thought possible. He threw up his right arm to shield his face, and pain lanced through the hand holding the dart pistol. He felt the weapon go spinning from his fingers, and heard it strike the wall and bounce into the courtyard below.

Brown ran for the open door to the Tower. A bird knocked away his hat, and its claws raked his ear. Below, the Valgurnian had dismounted and was heading for the stairs. Brown reached into his left inside pocket and drew out the folding sword, flicking his wrist to let the blade extend and lock in place. In the Tower doorway, he turned and struck out at another diving bird. His aim was good, and he severed the thing in two. He then waved the sword about his head like a man swatting at flies, and he saw the birds spiralling upwards.

The *Book of a Thousand Dreams* was growing heavy, so he ducked into the Tower and placed the huge volume on the first of the spiral stairs. Outside, the Valgurnian had gained the wall. The birds had resumed their circling.

Brown's hand and ear were bleeding and stinging as he went back out onto the wall to face his opponent, dropping into the Guard One position, his flimsy sword extended. The collapsible blade was by no means robust enough to parry a strong blow from his opponent's much heavier sabre, but he had little choice but to fight.

The Valgurnian faced him. He was grinning.

"I presume your little birds," Brown said, thinking to buy time through conversation, "alerted you to my presence."

"They are very clever little things, aren't they? I am happy they allowed me to finally make your acquaintance. We have been watching your friend for many years, knowing he had found a copy of the book. But we did not know where he had hidden it! Thus, officers such as I have been coming here, doing time in this backward town, knowing that someone such as yourself would one day appear and lead us to the prize."

"The Frieland authorities tolerate your presence here?"

The man laughed.

"They believe we are teachers at the local college. I must warn you, I am but the vanguard. I have friends coming."

Brown waved his sword in a quick figure-eight.

"Then I must deal with you quickly."

The Valgurnian held out his free hand.

"I suggest you simply give me the book, sir."

"I think not."

The Valgurnian rushed forward, sabre raised high, prepared to bring the blade down in a diagonal cut, a killing blow. Brown recognized the move and dropped to one knee, leaning far to his left and thrusting once. He felt his slim blade strike home, felt it bend along its hinge as the Valgurnian's momentum carried him forward. Brown let the sword go.

The Valgurnian's groan turned into a wail. He was clutching at his lower belly where Brown's sword still hung, and staggered to a section of the rampart where the crumbling stone battlements were no more than two feet high. His knees struck the stone and his forward motion sent him pitching over the edge of the wall. His wailing receded as he fell to the rocks and the surf below.

Back in the courtyard, the book again under his arm, Brown made a quick search for his dart gun, but without success. He had no time to look further for it. The birds were still circling, just dark specks, very high, but still dangerous. Brown ran for the old castle gate.

In the lane, he saw the Valgurnian's comrades approaching. Five men, all armed.

Within moments, they had Brown surrounded.

"I see you carry something we want, sir," said one, a man who looked very much like the one Brown had just fought, although stockier, his eyes harder.

Brown felt his frustration rise. He could not lose the book now. It was out of the question. But he had no means left to fight, no means save the book itself.

"Do you know what this is?" he said.

He held the ancient book in both hands and let it fall open at random.

"We know, sir. If you value your life, you will give it to us."

"It is a book of stories," Brown said. "Stories belong to the world, to everyone! Like this one here..."

He looked down at the page. Perhaps because he had created a weak place in the ancient book's spine, the book had opened to *The Boys Lost in the Forest.*

"Itaque exercitui arborum iunge," Brown

said, reading the story's concluding spell.

The five men all reacted as one, each emitting a strangled, gurgling cry. Brown looked at the fellow who had spoken, watched his skin pulse and bulge and grow rough ridges, his eyes shrinking and closing over, his arms thickening and his clothing bursting and falling, his feet extending and burying themselves in the stony ground of the path.

Within seconds, Brown was surrounded by five short trees, the only trees on the promontory.

It was weeks later when Brown again sat down with Anna Strang in the Artillery Room at the Imperial Society.

"Krane's body is to be brought home to Artor," he said. "All of the arrangements have been made."

He did not mention that the Frieland *Gendarmerie*, which he had alerted to the danger of the mechanical birds by showing them the sample in his pocket, had scoured the countryside for them. They had found and destroyed a dozen.

"That's good of you, Brown," Anna said. "I presume you found the famous book?"

"Indeed. I have it and believe it to be genuine. I am in the process of translating it for publication…"

He trailed off and stared toward the tall windows that overlooked the busy street.

"And what of Krane's spells? Surely you won't be translating those? Or was there nothing to it?"

"Oh, there is. I don't know how they work, but they do, and some of them are too terrible for words. However, they don't work in translation, so I believe it would be safe to include them, for the sake of completion."

"But Brown, one could simply retranslate them back into the original Ordae!"

He shook his head.

"No, for some reason that doesn't work. Nor do they work if you recite them in Ordae from memory. You must be holding the book and reading from it. So there is something about the book itself. Really, it should be studied. We should seek to understand it. But…"

"You don't know what to do," Anna said after a moment. "Krane wanted your advice, and yet you find yourself in the same quandary. You think the book is too dangerous, and wish to hide it away."

"Yes."

"Do you have that right? Does it not belong to civilization itself? What of duty to the country, to Government? Surely they are more able to protect this thing?"

"I have done enough for Government, I think. The stories belong to civilization, but the immense power? I don't know. I must think of my country, of course, but also…"

He shifted his gaze to the smouldering fire. It would soon be summer, but it was still damp and cold in the city.

"You will know what to do," Anna said, settling back in her chair. "I know you, Brown. You will find the right answer."

"'When I should happen upon myself,'" Brown said, quoting *Burwell's Journey*, "'I will be sure to let you know.'"

He could not suppress a slightly bitter chuckle. The fire snapped and popped.

Harold R. Thompson's first science fiction novel, Orphans of Sturnus, *was released in 2024. He is also the author of many science fiction and fantasy short stories, and several historical novels. Visit him at haroldross-thompson.com*

Skirt, Snake, and Eggs

By WILLIAM DRELL

Mickey Vance was looking forward to some R&R on a quiet station, but a mysterious death tied to a drug-smuggling operation leads to a rather strange alliance!

If you found yourself sitting next to a window in Malone's Diner, you might think that you were looking down at a peaceful blue ocean through a screen of long, white clouds. Looking closer, you might think you could see little boats drifting along on those placid waters. You'd be wrong, of course, since the ocean was a nonstop, freezing hurricane locally known as the gas giant Pacifica. Those ships would be heavily reinforced skimmers gathering hydrogen, helium, methane, and a bit of ammonia from the relative safety of the upper atmosphere. It would still be a great view.

Even better than the view was the sizzling platter of meat and eggs placed before me by the proprietress, Ms. Maggie Malone. She wore a green dress that didn't reveal much but fit tightly enough to answer a lot of questions. Wavy auburn hair showed just enough red to warn me off, unsuccessfully, and lightly freckled skin framed mostly brown eyes shot through with streaks of green. She looked like a forest spirit lost in this metal space box. As the aroma of perfectly seared skirt steak hit me, my brain, stomach, and a few other parts agreed that Pacifica Station needed to be my base of operations for a while.

She started in on the usual formalities regarding my meal, but her voice trailed off and her eyes locked onto something a little too far above me for comfort. Turning my head to get caught up, I saw a lot of gray uniform. Craning my neck to see the top of this wool mountain, I saw something that made my jaw spasm as every dirty word in a few languages tried to escape simultaneously.

Seven feet up from the floor was the snakelike head of a Ssrthari. Halfway down from that was a scaly hand that rested on a Ssrthari boarding saber, a blade too heavy for human hands, that could send my head flying in two flaps of a hummingbird's wings. The curses trying to flee my mouth had fought themselves down to a few survivors, but I didn't have the heart to say them anymore. I could activate my military stims, but I'd just get a better view of my imminent death. The alien's slitted pupils fixed on me and its hand tightened on the pommel of its sword.

"Are you Sgt. Michael Vance, formerly assigned to the Star League vessel Saint George?" it asked. A collar-mounted voice box translated alien hissing into an emotionless, masculine voice speaking Standard

League English. The only times the audio lined up with the actual speech was during the "s" sounds, which caused a bit of interesting harmony.

"Yes," I hissed back through a mostly paralyzed jaw. A few unfrozen brain cells yelled at me for telling the truth, but those useless bastards hadn't provided any interesting lies. The Ssrthari nodded briskly and gestured to the other side of my booth.

"It is an honor to meet you, sir," said the crisp, professional voice that emerged from the collar. "May I join you?" I nodded back like my neck needed an oil can. The alien slipped into the booth with graceful fluidity, but something about the movements seemed awkward for a Ssrthari. "I am Officer Sreether of the Independent Systems Regional Police." It reached one scaly hand forward with the apparent intention of shaking. My hand, after some convincing, unlocked from the edge of the table and shook hands with an alien capable of ripping my arm off. The brown scales pinched my skin a bit, but no other injury followed. There was something unsettling about the way Ssrthari fingers bonelessly wrapped around my hand, but I wasn't complaining.

His uniform was actually ISA issue, bearing the three stars and stylized spaceship logo of the Independent Systems. Something about the fit of the uniform was odd, but I couldn't organize my thoughts to decide why.

Maggie Malone clicked her dangling jaw back to a professional level and asked Officer Sreether if he would like breakfast. The reptilian nodded again with a deliberate stiffness that reminded me it wasn't a Ssrthari gesture. He was copying human mannerisms.

"Five eggs, lightly poached, and coffee, please," Sreether requested. Maggie nearly ran into the kitchen. Sreether turned his attention back to me. "A light snack. I have already eaten this week." Reflexively, I chuckled at the idea of five eggs as a light snack, then grimly remembered that Ssrthari were capable of eating roughly half of a Star League marine.

"So," I mumbled between bites, "what can I do for you, Officer?"

"I know about your service during the Second Contact Conflict," stated the artificial voice over rhythmic hissing. Muscles along Sreether's neck tensed and bulged in emotional messaging that would have meant something to another Ssrthari. "During your service you were recognized for killing more Ssrthari in close combat than any other human."

"And now you're going to get revenge, right?" I asked. "Can we do this tomorrow?" Officer Sreether was silent for a moment, then his lips slightly parted and a sort of "tsk tsk" noise emerged. A red flush creeped up my neck along with the tingle of adrenaline. This alien bastard was laughing at me. I had half a mind to stand up and throw a punch for spite and old time's sake.

"On the contrary," Sreether's voice box interpreted haltingly between reptilian chuckles. "I wanted to express my admiration before attending to some official duties." Bulges were travelling all over Sreether's neck, a Ssrthari emotional signal that meant nothing to me. My face couldn't decide if I was angry or embarrassed, so it remained full of excess blood. Red to the hairline, I turned to see Maggie returning with a bowl of eggs.

"Oh, Mr. Vance!" she gasped. "Are you all right? Are you allergic to something? Too much hot sauce?" Depositing the bowl of eggs on the table, she slapped her palm on my forehead. She pulled back quickly, deciding that I wasn't feverishly burning and she'd perhaps been too "mom" with a total stranger. I gave a friendly smile.

"I'm fine, Miss. I appreciate your..." Both mammals in attendance lost their trains of thought as Sreether poured the bowl of eggs down his gullet in one go. Sreether handed the empty bowl back to Maggie, then followed the eggs with an entire mug of black coffee. A moment of awkward silence ensued while I remembered the whole smiling thing and turned back to Maggie. "More water please. And coffee for my... friend." She nodded quietly and retreated.

"At the risk of being unfriendly," Sreether said, "I do have business to conduct. You're a licensed investigator and required to maintain biometric matching on your personal weapon." He pointed to the spot where I thought my wool jacket was doing a good job of concealing my shoulder holster. A bit of smoke may have emerged from my ears as I mentally shifted gears enough to consider handing my gun over to the alien. I slowly drew my Hardlight laser pistol while avoiding the contact plates that would extend the heat sink blades. Sreether pulled a large, golden pocket watch from the waist of his uniform and clicked the lid open. As he held the watch over my weapon, I could see the light of a digital display reflected off his scales. He confirmed that, in the event of a real fight, my Hardlight would spend long enough confirming my identity that I would already be killed by a less ethical weapon.

"Is he going to live, Doc?" I asked. Sreether didn't respond for a moment, and I noticed the light from his screen changed color to an ominous red. Abruptly looking up from the watch, he tossed the pistol back to me and surged to his feet. We both quickly put our toys away.

"There has been a murder on Pacifica Station," his speaker said in a steady monotone, but I thought the underlying hissing sounded a bit more urgent. "It would be my honor if you wish to assist."

As Sreether made for the door, I pulled out the small rectangular interface for my digital assistant, Friday. I instructed Friday to pay my bill, tip well, and leave a digital business card with Ms. Malone in case she wanted a thorough investigation. I took off after Sreether and soon felt like a child trying to keep up with a rushing adult. Reptilian fingers held a lift door open for me as I jogged inside, then we headed for a section designated for low class and short stays.

The lift opened into a lobby covered with the barest corporate excuse for carpeting in a "low expectations" gray color. A few potted plants absorbed the artificial UV light through the leaves that hadn't been shredded by hyperactive children or questionable men with twitching hands. The business counter, a hemisphere of cream-colored plastic, was swarming with uniformed station personnel surrounding a hyperventilating housekeeper.

She looked middle aged and had the figure of a pastry enthusiast. Tears streaked through a blue eyeshadow that I wouldn't have picked. Seeing Officer Sreether didn't seem to soothe her mind, so I angled around the front and gave her a firm handshake. Calloused hands attested that she put some effort into burning those extra calories. Unfortunately, she wasn't capable of doing more than blubbering about Room 8 and gesturing down the hall. Even that traumatized her enough to start new irrigation of the eyeshadow. A nod to Sreether received an awkward nod back, so we started down the hall.

When I stepped into Room 8 behind Sreether, an old familiar smell hit me. The smoke had been sucked up by the ventilation system, but the odor remained to tell of skin, muscle, and bone vaporized by weapons-grade light. The first body, relaxing in a shoddy recliner, had a six-inch streak of blackness across his chest where a laser had cut up his heart and both lungs. The second had tried to roll off a stained couch while getting torched, judging from the long, irregular streak that started at the chest and finished on the back. He was sprawled on the floor now, with one hand stretched forward, reaching for something that wouldn't have helped anyway while the laser bored through his spine.

Both corpses were skinny but had some meat around the arms, chest, and shoulders. They wore stained longjohns and form-fitting cotton shirts commonly worn under space suits. I guessed they were asteroid miners, probably here on a vacation before their next six-month stint. A faint odor of poor hygiene struggled to get through the smell of burnt meat and another scent that didn't fit the room.

"Do you smell fresh-baked cookies?" I asked. Sreether parted his lips slightly and sent a distressingly long tongue flicking through the air a few times.

"Sugar and wheat," he said. Lashing the tongue around more, he crossed the room and poked at a colorful, fake-wicker basket containing wax paper and crumbs. A powder blue card tied to the handle said, "Courtesy of the Pacifica Station Mission." The card was hand-written and, I'd wager money, by a female. Matching crumbs decorated the fingers and shirts of the bodies.

Sreether pulled out his pocket watch and a retractable baton. While he scanned around the room, I could see the display on his watch but couldn't understand the alien sigils. Using the baton, he peeled back the lips of both corpses, revealing swollen, dark red gums sparsely populated by deteriorating brown teeth. A ripple travelled up Sreether's body, reminding me of a snake swallowing in reverse. If that was a sign of disgust, I was right there with him.

"This human is why I'm here," Sreether said, pointing to the casually reclined body. "DNA records confirm that he was an informant who allegedly wanted to sell information regarding local amphetamine smuggling."

I gave a bitter laugh.

"Yeah, these guys look like amphetamine experts," I said while observing the excess yellow in their skin and eyes. "But I must confess a bit of confusion. Since when does the ISA send heavy hitters like you to crack down on narcotics? They've always let the local corps and organizations handle their own business."

"That is an accurate statement," Sreether replied, his eyes still fixed on his scanner. "However, the ISA Council is attempting to establish better control over the core station network. This arises from a confluence of interests ranging from commercial to humanitarian."

"Let me guess," I snorted. "The church ladies don't like the addicts, the big medicorps want in on the business, and the mining industry wants cleaner junk that doesn't burn out their workers so fast?"

Sreether turned away from the screen long enough to give one of his deliberate nods.

"Your education on local politics is impressive, Sgt. Vance."

"Please," I said with a sigh, "call me Mickey. I don't need anyone being reminded that the Star League military wants me in a jail cell with my implants safely removed. Hell, I'd prefer not to be reminded."

"Very well, Mickey," Sreether said. "Fortunately, you have gone far out of Star League jurisdiction."

My only response to that was a quiet nod. Focusing on the present, I pulled out my assistant interface again. The avatar of Friday flickered onto the screen. Her blonde curls were tucked into a deerstalker cap, and she held a magnifying glass and meerschaum pipe. As I swept the microcomputer low along the floor, Friday chattered about the carpet fibers, traces of shoe rubber, and a number of biological contaminants that suggested a tendency to spill food.

"Oh, boss!" Friday chirped. "You might find this interesting." She held up her magnifying glass, and the viewpoint zoomed through it. After a lot of zooming, it displayed a tiny robot stuck in a carpet fiber. The machine had spider-like legs and a sort of mouth that resembled a woodchipper. "This is CosmeTech nanite model #4545. They patrol your skin and chew up dead cells. I'm tracing a few more in the area." Following her indications, I found a handful of the little mechanical beasts trailing from the door to the gift basket. I shared my discovery with Sreether.

"Cosmetic nanites," he said. "Presumably from a female human." He examined his watch for a moment. "I have matched all the DNA in the room. The only female DNA is from the housekeeper. Only one other person shows up in the fresh samples. He is on file as a resident of the station. Specifically, the match is for Daniel Malone, younger sibling of Margaret Malone." My breakfast sat poorly in my gut as I pondered telling the nice girl with the perfect skirt steak that her brother was going down for double homicide.

"Well," I grumbled. "I suppose the next step is to go over surveillance footage for the hallway." Sreether shook his head and made some expressive neck motions.

"I wish that were the case," he said. "Pacifica Station, in keeping with the more libertarian doctrine of the ISA, only has surveillance capabilities in the administrative and engineering sectors. This station markets itself as a place where people can move on to frontier life without being observed too closely. This draws people who want to escape from complicated pasts." His unblinking eyes fixed on me for a while.

"Okay, point taken," I said. "To Malone's?" Sreether wordlessly turned and stepped into the hallway. Sprinting after his long strides made me appreciate my enhanced lungs. Arriving at Malone's, we found that Maggie had turned things over to the night crew. Another run, which got me a little out of breath, brought me to a residential unit with a "Malone" nameplate over a small vidscreen.

Sreether pressed his watch against the vidscreen, causing it to turn red and display a message confirming the presence of law enforcement. Inside the unit, automated systems were undoubtedly informing the residents to come open the door, preferably without anything notably dangerous in hand. Momentarily, the door slid open to reveal Ms. Malone herself. Her serving apron was off, and a few buttons were opened on that green dress. That answered a few questions regarding freckles and other issues I didn't have time to focus on. She greeted us with the terrified politeness of someone with cops at the door and invited us in against the unheard wails of a trillion dead lawyers.

An overstuffed recliner sat next to a picture window with a nice view of Pacifica. An overstuffed orange cat uncurled from the seat, viewed the visitors with suspicion, and slunk off into what looked like a bedroom. There were a few too many potted plants and the bric-a-brac stepped just over the line of excessive. Despite those touches, I sensed someone had declared a moratorium on "girliness" past a certain point. The setup suggested another suite of rooms behind the neatly appointed kitchenette.

"Are you married?" I asked. "This seems like a bit too much room for one person and one cat." She blinked a few times.

"What? No!" she said. "I live here with my brother. He's been staying with me since our parents..." She trailed off and seemed to be having a mental debate on the appropriate word. "Well, they disappeared. It was ten years ago, so I assume they're dead, but things happen out on the frontier, and you don't always get formal confirmation." Sreether's snout made its methodical journey up and down.

"The ISA is attempting to reduce such tragic uncertainties," he said. As I watched him talk to Maggie, I realized that a framework had been stitched into his uniform with "joints" at the knees and elbows. The snake was forcing himself to move like a human, presumably so everyone wouldn't see him as an eldritch abomination. By the time I stopped being distracted, Maggie had walked through the door by the kitchen.

"If you don't mind me asking," I prefaced, "what made you want to live with humans?"

"I enjoy conversation," Sreether replied. The muscular activity of his neck suggested an emotional weight to the statement that I wasn't getting. I made a confused noise and gestured for him to continue. "Our ancestors were solitary predators. We are known for disliking company beyond what is required to mate or complete some other transaction."

"There have been times when I've wanted sex or a burger without having extensive discussions," I said with a chuckle. Sreether nodded vigorously.

"During the conflict, my people struggled to utilize military tactics as effectively as the Haynem or humans." Sreether turned to face me, and I fought my brain's prey animal reactions. "I became aware of you because you earned a record for effectiveness while separated from a unit. I wanted to meet a human who fought like a Ssrthari." Before I could decide how to respond, a scruffy redhead entered the room.

The newcomer was shorter than me, with the skinny shoulders and padded waist that spoke of long hours on the couch. He had a few too many freckles for aesthetics and watery hazel eyes. I figured him for about twenty-four years old. His rumpled clothes and pillow-dented cheek suggested an afternoon nap or a nocturnal schedule. He reached out and I gave him a firm handshake that he tried to return with a tragically soft hand. Hesitantly, he repeated the process with Sreether. His name was Danny Malone. Maggie slipped out behind him and sat in the recliner.

"Where were you this morning while your sister was at work?" I asked with only the slightest hint of disapproval.

"I made a delivery of cookies to some miners for the Pacifica Station Mission. I volunteer for them as community service because..." He coughed and looked at Sreether's uniform. "Well, I got into a bit of trouble last year. I've been staying out of trouble since then." I could practically hear the jail cell slamming shut on this kid.

"And after you dropped off the cookies?" I asked.

"I was here, sleeping," he responded.

"Can anyone confirm that?"

"No," he said with the halting tone of someone realizing they needed an alibi. He gave a quick, nervous laugh. "Unless you count Shnooks, the cat, I sleep alone." The tragedies were really adding up with this guy. I gave Sreether a sidelong glance and nod that hopefully indicated I was done doing his job for the moment. Sreether stepped towards Danny, and I mentally took bets on whether he was going to bolt, faint, or develop hysterical blindness.

"Daniel Malone," Sreether announced, "I am taking you into custody on suspicion of murder. Place your hands behind your back and be aware of your right to remain silent." Danny took the odds-on favorite and made a panicked dash for the door. A reptilian blur intercepted him. Before my eyes registered that Danny was pressed into the couch, I half expected to see him dangling from Sreether's mouth. The cuffs snapped on while Danny screamed his innocence into upholstery and cat hair. Looking away, I saw Maggie still in the recliner. Her already fair skin was bloodless, and a tear slid down one cheek. I couldn't look at her eyes for long.

After getting Danny trussed up and receiving a mute nod of permission from Maggie, Sreether went to search the small suite behind the kitchen. I followed along and we both pulled on gloves. There was a bedroom, small bathroom, and closet. The distinct odor of young male permeated the area. Sheets that would get changed eventually fought with deodorizing body spray and a bit of tobacco. A scan of the sheets showed expected levels of bodily residues and a few familiar nanites. The remains of a few cheap cigarillos sat in a plastic ashtray. The bathroom decor consisted heavily of soap scum, hair, and toilet targeting failures. In the closet, under a rack of fairly expensive brand name clothes, Sreether found a Hardlight laser pistol.

When he handed the gun to me, the smell of isopropyl alcohol hit me immediately. A quick scan showed the weapon had been wiped down thoroughly, used recently, and hosted a CosmeTech 4545 wedged between the grip and frame. Unlike mine, this pistol lacked the biometric scanner to lock out, or record, unauthorized shooters. Sreether took the gun back and stashed it in a plastic bag. I followed him back into the living room, where two red-eyed Malones exercised legally recommended silence and avoided eye contact.

"I am bringing Daniel to my ship," Sreether said. "He will remain there, pending further investigation and official charges." The deadpan voice of the alien's translator fit the situation well. "Mr. Vance, thank you for your assistance. Perhaps we can speak more, later." Once the cop and the doomed man were gone, I turned to Maggie and mentally tested my next few words. She held a personal communicator with my business card on the screen.

"I guess I need a private investigator," she whispered, eyes on the floor.

"Going out on a limb," I said, "I'm guessing you think he didn't do it?" She nodded. "All right. I'm willing to overcome my doubts for a hundred a day and expenses. Want a smoke?"

"They still remember how to cure cancer?"

"My last doctor knew all kinds of tricks."

"Sure."

I got us set up with some actual tobacco that I kept for special occasions and settled on the recently vacated couch. As she inhaled a puff, the red glare on her fae features made me think of a nymph watching her forest burn down. While literal and metaphorical ashes drifted away, she told me a long story about being twenty-three and suddenly taking over a family business and a teenage boy. Danny, a little aimless and resentful, got in trouble with smugglers and junkies. While he might be a difficult kid, he was not, Maggie assured me, a killer. By the time she finished unloading her emotional, if not helpful, testimony, a fluffy orange cat began burrowing into my thigh. I gave the creature a few absent-minded pats while Maggie wound down.

"Shnooks likes you," she said. "He's my official judge of character."

"Does he screen all your gentleman callers?" I asked. She looked down at the last smoldering ember of her cigarette for a moment.

"Is that part of your fee?" she asked in a tired voice. The smile dropped from my face as I told my conscience to shut its filthy mouth about my last few capers.

"Madame, I keep such things strictly extra-curricular, off the books, and out of the local news." She rubbed out her cigarette in a shamrock-shaped ashtray and made a noise of approval. "In the interest of keeping things professional, why don't you tell me who runs the Pacifica Station Mission?"

"Helen Capek," she said. "She's the wife of the station administrator, Ross Capek." Her brow furrowed and she rotated the ashtray like it was a combination lock and the numbers escaped her memory. "They're good people. Mr. Capek helped me get the restaurant straightened out after my folks vanished. He personally negotiated with all of our suppliers to get me the same deals as my father."

"And he asked for nothing in return?" I asked with a touch of disbelief. Maggie kept her eyes down and tried to decide if the shamrock stem should point at the chair or the back of the room. Her lips shaped a few syllables that never emerged, then she shook her head.

"No," she said. "Nothing worth mentioning. When they asked for Danny to help Ms. Capek with the mission, it felt like another favor to help keep him out of trouble." When she looked up at me, her brave mask started to leak around the eyes. The situation was enough to make my allergies act up a bit, too, but I blamed Shnooks for that. So, I deposited the dander-laden feline in Maggie's lap, said I'd be back with more information, and let myself out into the public area.

"Friday," I said while pulling out the interface, "get me whatever financial information you can find on the Capek family. Ping Sreether if needed. Last I checked, station administrators need to reveal their income to the ISA." The screen displayed Friday's bubbly blonde avatar wearing a white robe while pondering an orb that showed an hourglass. Rolling my eyes, I headed for the Administrator's Office. Following signage and handy interactive kiosks brought me from the dingy, heavily trod upon gray of the public areas to the crisp, authoritarian gray of Administration. Turning a corner, I nearly ran into a woman who made me think that Friday had somehow fallen out of my watch.

She was tall enough that my eyes didn't have an alibi for looking down, but they did anyway. Her white dress clung to her frame and her neckline plunged until the law stepped in. Long sleeves and a few buttoned pockets announced that she was a respectable businesswoman, despite all evidence to the contrary. The ability to mark out the exact parameters of her undergarments was the fault of your prurient interest. A blue wicker basket hung over her arm, filled with muffins and cookies that filled my head with double-entendres. Before she could step around me, I remembered how to stop gawking and start talking.

"Mrs. Capek?" I blurted out at a slightly higher pitch than I intended. She moved to step past me, decided against it, and flashed me a smile. The bitter impatience only needed a moment to melt from her ruby-tinted lips. Eyes like blue moonstone locked onto mine.

"Can I help you, sir?" she asked. I scrubbed out my first dozen answers.

"My name is Mickey Vance," I said. "I'm looking into the double homicide from earlier today." She kept that smile, but it started looking brittle at the edges.

"It's a pleasure, Mr. Vance," she said, "but I don't know much about the unfortunate incident except that Danny Malone has been arrested." Her eyes lowered and she shook her head sadly. "His poor sister must be heartbroken. She tried so hard to keep him out of trouble. As you may know, I tried to keep him constructively occupied. Sadly, I may have just introduced him to troubled men and temptation."

"If you don't mind me asking, what sort of temptation?" I tried to keep the leer out of my voice. Those moonstone eyes came back to mine but showed a bit of the cut edges behind the sparkle.

"When dealing with wretched men consumed by vices, there is a temptation to deny their humanity and profit from their misery." A bit of her softness returned. "Once you've stopped seeing them as human, I suppose murder doesn't seem so bad."

"But you bring them cookies," I said, pointing to the basket. Helen smiled and waved it under my nose, hitting me with a wave of cinnamon that would have been more tempting if I hadn't spent the morning jogging around the station with a full stomach.

"The galaxy needs more kindness, Mr. Vance," Helen said. "Now I have to go spread some around while it's still warm from the oven. If you have any more official questions, please talk to my husband. He'll be working closely with the ISA." She began to walk past me.

"One last thing before you go," I said. "I'm planning on sticking around here for a while, and I do some baking myself. What brand of sugar do you like?" She gave me a noncommittal shrug.

"On a space station, you never really know what's coming in the next shipment. I just use whatever is handy."

"Thank you for your time, Mrs. Capek." I grabbed her hand between mine and bowed my head. Her skin was the kind of soft that made you feel like you were going to fall in. A look of concern crossed her face as I made it just a little too difficult to extract her hand. Once she freed herself, she scurried down the hall to dispense baked goods. I pulled out my scanner and studied my hands. CosmeTech 4545's happily munched on my dead skin cells until their power source, located somewhere on Mrs. Capek, moved out of range. The image of stalling nanites was abruptly replaced by the image of Friday wearing studious bifocals while looking over a clipboard.

"Okay, boss," Friday chirped in a voice made tinny by small speakers, "Mr. Capek gets a standard administrator's salary supplemented by various investments that mostly perform in the moderate to poor range. Someone convinced him that gas giant bungie jumping was going to take off. His most successful income stream comes from partial ownership of Malone's Diner."

That made me beat feet back to Maggie's place. On the way, I muttered every nasty word in my vocabulary through a scowl that kept the other pedestrians inclined to move aside. I tapped her door's touchscreen until it announced my arrival. Maggie opened the door with red eyes and a glass of white wine. She let me in, then returned to eating a pastry over the sink while I gathered my thoughts.

"Is Ross Capek part-owner of the diner?" I asked. "Would you know if he was?" Maggie nearly choked on her snack.

"What?" she exclaimed. "No! I mean, yes, I would know, but he isn't."

"Right." I chewed my lip for a second. "Next question, just assume it's important. What kind of sugar do you like to bake with?" She blinked a few times before answering.

"We get regular shipments from a company a few jumps away. They're called The Sucratic Method. I like them because they sell pre-measured packages of white sugar with bottles of molasses so you can make your own brown sugar instead of having it clumping up in the fridge." The rest of the wine went down the hatch. "What does this have to do with anything?"

"What are you eating?"

"I made cinnamon muffins for..." Maggie trailed off with a guilty look.

"For the mission," I completed her sentence. Her shoulders slumped and she sighed.

"Yeah," she said. "Helen heats them up in the microwave before deliveries so she can claim they're fresh from the oven. It's pretty harmless as conspiracies go. It's just a favor for..." A bland, automated voice cut her off to announce a visitor at the door. Maggie opened the door to reveal an unfamiliar man in the ragged clothes and pocked skin of a miner.

He stuck his foot in the door and raised a medical inhaler to his mouth. As he inhaled the contents, I heard more hisses and huffs outside. The miner's already bloodshot eyes bulged, sweat broke out across his forehead, and his breath came in jerky gasps. With inhuman speed, he shoved Maggie away from the door and surged inside.

The idea of a hit squad full of asthmatics was funny, but not enough to justify the strained, hysterical laughter that spilled out of me. My military adrenal stims made me laugh, and I made sure someone else became the punchline. I sized up the miner while I charged through slowed time. He moved a bit slower but showed some meat on his chest and shoulders. I had a few inches on him, so he guarded high, but I came in low. A right-handed uppercut made rotten teeth bite through tongue and shatter in the middle of the fleshy mess. My left cross sent him spinning to the ground.

I didn't have time to wonder if he was going to stay down, because a second guy came flying through the door with a tackle that smashed me through Maggie's glass coffee table. While I got my bearings, he scrambled on top of me and started crashing his fists down on me like a wild ape. Through the knuckles bouncing off my face, I noticed a third figure approaching. This one had a hooked metal rod with a glowing tip. I recognized it as an impact pick, capable of splintering rocks and mincing private eyes.

A thrust of my hips sent ape-man falling forward and slapping his palms down onto the shattered table for balance. I grabbed the sides of his head and dug my thumbs into his eyes. Fingernails raked his corneas while he tried to keep his lids shut. A slow, slobbery howl erupted from him as he grabbed my arms. Splinters of glass did equal opportunity damage to his hands and my wrists. While he slowly pulled my arms to the sides, his buddy reared back for an overhand chop. Another thrust and yank pulled Mr. Ape forward. He proceeded to give me a piece of his mind, and quite a few pieces of his skull, directly into my open eyes and mouth.

My left hand tried to wipe gore out of my face while my right pulled my Hardlight out. Once my eyes were clear, I saw why my assailant hadn't taken another swing. The miner flailed as Shnooks ran a circuit around his head, chest, and shoulders. I vowed that critter was getting filet mignon for the remainder of its nine lives.

Meanwhile, the heatsink blades of my Hardlight eagerly radiated waves of energy, but the biometric scanner placidly displayed a little yellow light. I lined up my shot and mentally screamed for the light to turn green while Shnooks ran out of energy and courage. A wild swing sent the cat flying past me. The miner grabbed his pick in both hands. I pulled the trigger.

The dimly lit room glowed a lurid red as my laser bored into the miner's chest. Tiny bubbles of boiling fluid burst through his veins as he gurgled a final lament and slumped to the floor in a smoking heap. I looked over to see the first guy crawling towards the door. After a few smacks from the butt of my pistol to the back of his head, he stopped moving.

I snatched a discarded inhaler off the floor and scanned it with Friday's assistance. The device was contaminated with small bits of waxed paper, crumbs of cinnamon pastry, and a CosmeTech 4545. I ordered Friday to contact Sreether and get him to the administrator's office.

After puking in the shower while Maggie ran a home medical kit over me, I sprinted through the halls of the station with water dripping from hair and soaked, but impressively stain resistant, clothing. The vast majority of residents decided that a large, angry, wet man running by was somebody else's problem. I arrived at the old fashioned, turn-handle door of the administrator's office and let myself in.

The first thing I noticed was the two large, professionally dressed men with guns drawn on me. Their eyelids and fingers made the occasional twitch or spasm to indicate that they were, at least slightly, amped up on something. The second thing that drew my attention was the chubby, balding man sitting behind an oak desk and fiddling with an inhaler. He gave me the warm, white-toothed smile of a true politician. If not for the bulbous, discolored lips dangling over his weak chin, he might have gone places.

"Laughing is his tell, guys," said Ross Capek, administrator of Pacifica Station. "If the slightest chortle comes out of him, waste him." The two goons gave weird, too fast nods.

"Now why would you want to waste me?" I asked with exaggerated innocence. Capek sneered.

"Because you're a dangerous fugitive from Star League justice who came to our peaceful station in the grips of madness," he said with performative flourishes to an imaginary audience. "Your mind, broken by the combination of post-traumatic stress and experimental augmentations, finally snapped and you killed five miners, a local boy named Danny Malone, and an officer of the law."

"That's a good reason," I said. "It makes a much better story than one about a local admin running a drug smuggling ring, having his wife deliver the dope in goody baskets, and sending the wife to kill a guy who tried to snitch. Never mind the boring, procedural details about how he schemed with the suppliers of Malone's Diner to launder the profits."

"Yes," Capek smiled. "The details do get rather tedious."

"There are a few interesting bits," I said. "If you wear enough cosmetic nanites, your skin DNA gets chewed up before it can flake off at a crime scene. The nanites themselves can get knocked off, though. I assume the ones in Danny's bed got there as a result of, shall we say, establishing loyalty? Did you pretend not to know that part, or did she make you recordings?"

"Your version of events is delightfully vulgar, Mr. Vance." Capek leaned back in his chair, still holding the inhaler. "Now I wish to offer you a deal. My associates will escort you to a place where your death will be narratively convenient for my story, or Maggie Malone suffers very horribly."

"That's awfully decent of you, Ross, but I'm still confused about one thing. How do you intend to take down Officer Sreether?"

"My good sir, I have already handled the alien." Capek tapped a touchpad on his desk and gestured to a vidscreen. "You see, Officer Sreether received a tip from another informant who wanted to meet somewhere safe. They agreed to meet in the engineering section." The screen showed Sreether walking through a corridor riddled with pipes and conduits. He looked around for something he couldn't find, then pulled out his pocket watch. For a split second, I thought I saw a familiar blonde avatar on the watch's screen. Before I could get a closer look, a hatch popped open and violently introduced Sreether to the vacuum of space. Startled, the alien curled into a ball, then flew off to join the various objects orbiting Pacifica. I looked away from the screen and towards the room's only window, which offered a view of the gas giant.

The silence in the room let me hear the increasingly violent pounding of my heart in my ears. Between two beats, I thought I heard the faintest metallic "clunk." Straining my ears, I dimly caught the noise again. Nobody else seemed to notice.

"You guys are making it hard not to laugh," I said with a hard note of derision. Capek chuckled and the two goons smirked. "I can tell none of you tough guys have ever fought Ssrthari." The goons rolled their eyes and Capek settled back in his chair with a look of amusement. "I served on the Saint George. I led boarding operations on Ssrthari ships." I narrowed my eyes and gave an ugly grin.

"You'd get lucky sometimes and blow out a bulkhead that sent a few snakes flying into space. But it takes a long time for vacuum to kill a Ssrthari. They don't need to breathe as often as we do, and they can seal their mouths and nostrils up tight. They have clear scales over their eyes, so they can see just fine. You think they're dead. But they're angry. They're very angry."

The goons were starting to exchange nervous glances and Capek raised one eyebrow. I stayed quiet long enough to hear two more clunks, then jumped back into the tale.

"They steer themselves back to the ship with their sidearms. Then they go scrambling across the exterior with magnetic boots or just clinging to anything they can work their wormy fingers into." I waggled my fingers dramatically. "You can't hear them coming because you're in vacuum, but, if you focus, you can feel it in your shoes. Giant alien boots slamming into the ship... thunk... thunk... thunk...

"But most don't notice it, and that's when you get a Ssrthari blade through the back and a snake sucking down the rest of your oxygen supply." I inhaled sharply through my teeth, making both goons flinch. Capek gave a concerned glance towards the window. "Do you hear it, Ross? Do you hear death coming?!" I started to laugh, but everyone was too busy looking at the window and listening to the rapidly approaching footsteps of a furious alien.

"Close the emergency shutter!" Ross screamed, his voice drawing out into a long slur as my stims activated. While Capek sucked down the inhaler, the goon closest to the window started towards a red handle on the wall. The heat sink blades of my Hardlight snapped out as I pulled it free of my jacket. Not waiting for the biometric scanner, I threw the gun across the room.

In my head, the gun sailed across the room and intercepted the guy's hand. In reality, the weapon awkwardly tumbled well to the left of where I was aiming. Fortunately, that resulted in the cooling blades lodging non-fatally, but very distractingly, in the goon's skull. That reminded everyone else that I was present and engaged in forbidden laughter. Capek pulled a gun from under his desk while his buddy slowly returned his aim to me.

As a reptilian shadow eclipsed Pacifica, I grabbed the doorknob and activated an implant the guys used to lovingly call "The Death Grip." There was a blinding flash followed by a deafening roar. That's when I got sucker punched by a tornado.

Once the air stopped trying to rip my

arm out of its socket, the lack of air started trying to pull my eyes out. I covered my face with my free hand until my eardrums stopped trying pop out. Realizing I could breathe again, I let my hand detach from the doorknob. When I got brave enough to open my eyes, I saw the emergency shutter was closed and a familiar Ssrthari was panting in the middle of the room. Wrinkled gray scales covered his body, and his eyes looked foggy. Despite this, he fixed his eyes on me.

"I will require a premature shed," he said.

"Yeah," I replied. "Me too."

A few days later, I worked on some steak and eggs while Sreether downed his fifth glass of water. His scales looked too small, and sticky white flesh stuck out from between them. Maggie pestered him until he admitted that the white bits were itchy, then they figured out that petroleum jelly could substitute for whatever gunk Ssrthari had back home. Between rounds of snake lubrication, she fussed over me a bit.

Danny Malone came over to check on the table. I liked to think honest work took a bit of the slump out of his shoulders. Per tradition, he asked if we needed anything while my mouth was full. Sreether nodded stiffly.

"More water, please," Sreether said. "And more coffee... for my friend."

So, Friday, per Officer Sreether, submit my expense report to the ISA. Reiterate that my pistol was lost in the line of duty and the gallon of petroleum jelly was not for me.

William Drell is a reluctant Chicago native and one of the very few people to have conducted multiple, successful citizen's arrests.

Automaton Anon

By W.E. WERTENBERGER

Joe, a human from earth stranded on the strange world of Druun, has been hired to retrieve a missing automaton, held by the notorious Blood Stump gang!

Joe guessed he was over a thousand feet up by now. Gone were the hot geysers of mineral-heavy fumes that erupted at the base of the black rock and smelled like rotten eggs. Now it was blasts of biting cold that drove icy needles into his exposed skin and stole the breath from his lungs. All things being equal, he preferred the cold. He took note that two of the three small suns still hung in the pale green sky. They were directly over his left shoulder, meaning it was midday on Druun.

He leaned back against a bare spot on the mountainside, digging in with the crampons attached to his boots. He removed one of his heavy leather gloves and ran a bare hand through his blond hair. Despite the cold, his hand came away damp with perspiration. Removing the canteen attached to his belt, he unscrewed the top and took a deep, long draw.

"Genuine Boy Scout issue," he said to the empty sky as if it cared. He admired the engraved image of an eagle with outstretched wings superimposed over a fleur-de-lis. "One of a kind, not another like it on all of Druun. Far as I know."

He looked out over the miles of alien landscape stretched below him and marveled. From his perch, the Crackskull Mountains extended out on both sides: a near-impenetrable barrier that ran from one misty horizon to the next, with only wild rumors and speculation of what lay beyond. Joe could account for the veracity of one such rumor, as he could see quite clearly where the Murky-Fever River was born. From hidden fissures in the mountainside erupted a continuous spray of superheated vapor, which was quickly cooled and then fell in a rain of poisonous slush down the mountainside. Uncounted ribbons of toxic waste wormed their way across the expanse of the Choking Plains, joining to form into the river proper.

"May the Lord smite me if I ever start calling this funhouse of a world home. But damn if it doesn't leave a man humbled."

"What's the holdup?" A flurry of flapping accompanied those words as the crow landed atop a nearby perch.

"Just taking a load off," Joe said as he took another draught of water. "You gotta remember, I don't have wings. Takes me a mite longer to get to the top of this here pile of stone."

The bird gave him the side eye and seemed to consider Joe's dilemma for a moment. "Shame," he finally said and began preening. Joe didn't know if that was sympathy or mockery.

Joe capped the canteen. "How much farther do I have to go, anyway?"

The crow shook out its feathers. "Not far."

"You locate that secret entrance?"

"Yes."

"You get a headcount on the opposition?"

"One."

"One?" Joe said. "You sure about that?"

"One," the crow repeated.

"Well, I'll be damned." He'd paid a goodly amount of shard and worn down a lot of boot leather gathering information on the Bloody Stump gang's whereabouts. Finding out about this hidden entrance to their hideout felt too good to be true.

"Good work. Now get back up there and keep watch."

The crow gave a confirming squawk and sprang from the rock. Joe watched him go until he was just a black speck circling above in the green sky.

The second half of the climb took half as long as the first part. He crested the summit before the last of the three suns had dropped below the frosty horizon. Joe wasted no time removing his backpack, letting out a groan as he lowered the heavy load to the ground.

"Getting old," he heard the bird squawk.

Joe looked around until he located the opinionated avian. The bird was hopping about the scattered rocks and boulders, probing at promising crevices with its black beak.

"Aw hell, what do you know?" Joe retorted. He sat down next to his pack and began removing his crampons. "My grandad taught me everything I know about climbing, and he kept at it well into his seventies. I got a few decades yet till that high watermark."

The crow didn't respond. His hunt had borne fruit in the form of a fat, purple-furred worm. All of his attention was now focused on prying the unfortunate creature from its lair.

Joe shook his head and mumbled, "Damn boy, you've been reduced to arguing with a bird." He set the crampons down, then removed a pair of binoculars from the pack. He hunkered down behind as large a rock as he could find and surveyed the area.

He scanned the mountain plateau slowly. The boulder-strewn landscape was barren except for the occasional gnarled clump of what passed for vegetation in this part of Druun. Masses of stringy red fronds sprouted in tufts across the top of these plants. These waved about on the shifting winds, gathering nutrients from the passing banks of fog. Try as he might, he couldn't find the secret entrance. He'd have to rely on the crow to guide him in.

He placed the binoculars back in the pack and pulled the .44 Redhawk revolver from his shoulder holster. He checked the load then replaced it. He next pulled some speedloads and a sheathed trench knife with a knuckle duster. He attached the knife to his belt and pocketed the ammo in his farm jacket.

"You ready?"

The crow checked the crevice for more worms; finding none, he gave a hop and a flap and landed on Joe's shoulder. "Always."

"Good. Make sure you stick to the plan now. No showboating."

The bird took a nip at Joe's ear.

"All right, all right," Joe chuckled. "That was out of line. Off you go."

After Joe tucked the pack out of sight behind a big boulder, he started working his way toward the secret entrance. He stayed low, moving in a crouched position. He stopped now and again to glance skyward, mark where the crow circled, and adjust his approach. Sure enough, this worked like a charm, and he soon found himself in front of the hidden entrance.

It lay nestled in a slight dip of the topography. No wonder he couldn't see it from a distance. If it hadn't been for the crow, he could have spent days trying to locate it.

Tipped back against the stone wall sat a heavyset gremil in a rickety-looking wooden chair. He was half asleep and afflicted, Joe noted, with that same dull expression found in most examples of the species he'd had run-ins with. It wore a long hauberk of spun steel-silk, was of moderate height, and generally bipedal in form. A long line of wiry hair ran from the top of its otherwise bald scalp to the tip of its fleshy tail. It picked at its blocky teeth with the point of a pitted iron dagger. The beast seemed to have found a sweet spot as he twisted the blade between two yellow molars. A wet grinding noise struck Joe's ear, akin to that of a concrete drill in action.

The gremil was so preoccupied that Joe managed to place himself directly in front of the creature. The Redhawk pointed at his face.

"Howdy, friend," Joe said in trade-speak, the only universal form of communication understood in all corners of Druun. "Frightful bit of weather we're having today." The stunned gremil managed a spastic nod, not even bothering to remove the dagger from between its teeth.

"I'm going to need you to stand up nice and slow-like."

"What that thing?" the gremil asked, lowering the dagger as it rose from the chair. His beady yellow eyes were locked on the revolver.

Joe shrugged, "It's what my people call a gun."

"What it do?"

"It delivers a mess of hurt, friend. Just give me a reason, and I'll gladly blow a hole the size of a skynk's nut out the back of your skull."

The gremil thought on that for a bit, then laughed. "Naw, you big faker! You play like big wizard but just lowly scrounge trader waving shiny scrap. Think I gut you now and nail your bloody paw to the wall."

Joe blasted a shot that parted the gremil's mohawk and impacted the stone behind him with a ricochet twang.

"Mind running that by me again?"

The gremil dropped the knife and threw his hands above his head. "Na-nothing. I take back!"

"Smart," Joe drawled. "Where're the rest

of your pals?"

"In citadel proper...down old passageway," he said, pointing towards a recess and a set of stairs cut from the stone. At the bottom, a bronze hatch with a lock and swivel handle. A torch burned in a sconce above.

Joe motioned with the Ruger Redhawk. "Let's go, then." The gremil hurried past him, hands still above his head, and down the stairs he scampered. When they reached the hatch, he pulled a key from a pouch on his hip and inserted it into the slot, then turned the handle. A heavy clunk sounded, and he pulled the well-maintained hatch open with little effort. Joe grabbed the torch from the wall, then ushered the gremil forward. "Go on, now, lead the way."

A set of carved spiral stairs disappeared into the gloom below. They circled around and around as they descended. Joe began to wonder if the shifty gremil was up to something when the stairs abruptly ended. They were standing on a raised landing. Laid out before the duo was an open grotto which led to a natural cave entrance. Metal girders were laid out in twos in even intervals throughout to reinforce the ceiling. It looked like a recently excavated ribcage of some long-dead metal beast. "What's the story with this place?" Joe asked.

The gremil guard shrugged. "Dunno."

Joe scowled. "Not much of a tour guide."

The gremil gave back a blank stare.

"Never mind. Keep moving."

"This way," the gremil muttered.

He led Joe from the landing toward the entrance of the cave. They walked beneath the rib cage of the main chamber, Joe wincing as each footfall echoed like a mallet on a kettledrum. Whoever waited on the other end of their journey would surely hear them coming.

Joe needn't have worried.

As they came to a side corridor, the sound of music and raucous conversation could be clearly heard. Another bronze door like the one above was set at the opening, but this one was wide open, the Bloody Stumps secure enough in their lair not even to post a guard.

"Bacus and clan. All in here," the gremil said. Beyond the short corridor was a room shaped into a perfect oval, the sides hacked from the surrounding stone with pick and shovel. Sitting back from one wall sat a long stone table. It too was crudely formed and had a curve corresponding to the form of the wall behind. Around and on both sides lounged the gang. Joe counted thirteen. Double that number of servants and gang molls. All were intoxicated. A mix of empty and freshly tapped casks of spirits was strewn irregularly about the table.

"Introduce me," Joe said and gave the guard a kick in the pants. The guard shuffled forward and bowed before the largest gremil Joe had ever seen.

Boss Bacus sat on a wide stone throne, bare-chested with a full tankard in one hand and a female gremil in the other. He was easily twice the size of every other gremil in the room, heavily scarred and muscled. Behind him, like some piece of macabre experimental art, hung a massive wooden panel. Hundreds of limbs of various descriptions were tacked onto the panel. Most, with hands and fingers, were humanoid; some, with claws and tentacles, were not. Each had a single silver spike through it. All were hacked midway down, right around where the elbow joint would be.

"God damned bastards," Joe said, taking in the brazen display of the gang's cruelty.

The decibel level dropped as all sets of bleary eyes turned towards the newcomer.

"Who you?" the leader asked as the bowing guard hadn't the guts to say a word.

"I'm Joe."

The big gremil snorted. "What you want, Joe?"

Joe gestured with the Redhawk, "Some bloody satisfaction. That should be pretty fucking obvious."

The big gremil's eyes narrowed, and his nostrils expanded. The female on his lap began to squirm. "What you want?" Bacus repeated through clenched teeth.

"Funny thing. When this all started, all I was interested in was some good old-fashioned commerce," Joe continued. "A simple exchange of goods between two consenting parties. Seems you boys got something I need, and I was willing to pay. Yes, sir, I was willing to pay a shiny shard, too."

"That so?" Bacus said. His grip on the girl noticeably tightened. Her eyes were wet, and her lower lip quivered.

"Oh, yes. That was before I started hearing about this gang of yours. Seems everyone around these parts has some story to tell about you boys. Caravans raided. Homesteads burned. Men killed and women abducted," Joe said. "And you know what I noticed? Folks with a story to tell were all missing a limb."

"Bloody stumps?" Bacus asked, an evil grin creeping across his thick jawline.

"Yep. This one feller in particular goes by the name of Yamus. He's a lemurian from some tiny speck of a village a few days' march from here. You know the kind of place I mean? If you were unlucky enough to sneeze as you're passing by, you probably missed the whole dern thing. Suffice it to say, this Yamus had quite a tale to tell, and boy howdy, it just didn't sit right," Joe said. His voice was hard now, his trigger finger extra twitchy. "Well, let's just say it wasn't the type of thing that is spoken of in what we call back home as polite company. No, sir."

Bacus shoved the female off his lap and leapt up from his throne. He was even more impressive standing fully upright. "Bloody Stumps feared, fear make us strong." The rest of the gang gave a hearty cheer in support. "What you care? Go now before Bacus give you bloody stump."

The revolver jumped in Joe's hand as he put two .44 slugs into the big gremil's chest. This knocked the beast back onto the throne, eyes wide with surprise. Joe emptied the remainder of the cylinder to be sure he stayed there.

"The rest of you bastards listen up," Joe said to the remainder of the stunned, silent gang. He dumped the spent cartridges as he did so, then fed in a fresh speed load. "Judgment day is upon you. Best give a quick prayer to whatever god you see fit, 'cause none of you will live to see the dawn." Joe pulled the trench knife from his belt and fit his fingers into the knuckle guard. "Let's get to it."

Ten minutes later, the crow flew into the room and dropped down onto a nearby table. "What a mess," the crow squawked as he eyed the fresh dead.

"It is that." Joe found himself a spot at the same table and sat down heavy. "They didn't go easy."

He was bone tired and wanted nothing more than a cigarette and a cold beer. He settled instead for a warm mug full of insect larva brew. The two displaced Earthers sat in silence while Joe drank. After he downed half of the mug's contents, he set it aside and inspected the wound on his forearm. "Well, that's just dandy," he hissed. A gremil blade had sliced clean through the canvas and gashed him deep. What was left of his coat sleeve was soaked in blood. Joe cut a clean strip from one of the wall hangings, the cleanest fabric he could find in the room, and fashioned a bandage.

"You find what we came for?" Joe asked through clenched teeth as he was using them to tighten one end of the bandage.

"Yes."

"I'm right behind you," he said, finishing the binding.

The bird took off and out the door with Joe in tow. The cavern was chaos in motion. Female gremil and slaves fought over spoils, most fleeing when they saw the big Texan. Not one stopped to thank him. He'd had his fill of this place anyhow.

"Over here," the crow squawked from near where the cave opened out onto the mountain plateau. He found the bird perched on the shoulder of a tall humanoid. It was taller than Joe by at least a half-foot over his own 6' 3" stature. It was perfectly sculpted in form like a department store mannequin, only it was missing a hand. Cut right below the elbow. Its dark outer shell seemed to capture the sputtering torchlight and reflect it like a distant sun lost in a void.

"Are you the Servitor?" Joe asked in trade-speak. He got no answer. Joe stepped next to the sentinel and ran a hand over the outer surface. It was smooth like glass and warm to the touch.

"Are you the Servitor?" he asked this time in English.

A whir of electric motors whined as the thing's head twisted towards Joe. "Je suis du Servitor 00," it said in a calm, distinctly pleasant human voice. The faceplate of the Servitor had a crack running from the forehead down the bridge of the nose, then angled right and across where the eye used to be. The left eye was intact and glowed a bluish hue from an embedded light. When it spoke, the mouth flashed in that same blue light and in a pattern that roughly mimicked the movement of human lips. "If you prefer English, I am the Servitor 00. Might you assist me in returning to my Archon?"

"That's the plan. We've had a hell of a time finding you, friend," Joe said. "I surely hope it's worth it."

"My Archon is well known for his largess. I am confident you will be well compensated, but we must hurry."

Joe studied the cracked features of the robot's face as he might any other sentient. He gave a slight shiver when he realized what he was doing. "Why the rush?"

The Servitor's good eye simulated a single blink. "Is it not true that in matters of life or death, every moment is precious?"

"Airtight," the crow squawked.

"Uh-huh, airtight," Joe muttered.

The Servitor paused. "You are injured. If you will allow me, I am quite adept at first aid."

Joe nodded. "Sure thing. I have a kit in my backpack. Let's get out of here."

A few weeks later, Joe, the crow, and the Servitor found themselves aboard the Dollop, a vessel that the people of the Endless Muddy referred to as a skim-clipper. It made good progress, sometimes gliding across the more open stretches of swamp like a water bug back on Earth. The four flat footpads strung from a silky substance were enough to keep the swamp walker above the waterline. Other times, those footpads were folded and shifted aside to allow the Pedi pads the ability to walk across the more gnarled obstacles it came across.

Joe stood on the flybridge of the Dollop as it navigated one such obstacle now, a tangled bit of vegetation and debris. He clung to the railing as the vessel heaved to and fro, crawling its way insect-like up and over.

"Hot damn, captain, this is one hell of a contraption you have here," Joe called out. "We got nothing to top it back home, that's for sure."

"Pish," burbled Kalik. The frog-like captain clambered up a long rope that ended at the captain's perch, a good ten feet above Joe's head. "The Dollop is not so complicated a machine. It's you hair bodies, and your inability to comprehend simple engineering, that is the problem."

"Uh-huh," Joe said. He'd been warned about how prickly these amphibians could be, so he kept a lid on any biting retorts. It seemed that Anur society held the concept of something known as the Covenant of Orchestration as a unifying philosophy. Every member of their tribe had a part to play in that orchestration, and no excuses were made if the individual failed in that duty. They were not above stranding one of their own in the Great Muddy if that rebel soul broke the Covenant. So it would mean next to nothing to cast aside one displaced Texan, his crow, and the mechanical Servitor.

Still, he gave credit where credit was due. The amphibian crew moved about the vessel in good order. Some were aloft in the rigging, clearing kinked lines and calling out hazards ahead. Most operated the mechanisms that controlled each of the legs. All worked together with an ease of coordination that a human crew would have found bewildering.

"And here I thought crewing a sailboat was a complicated business."

"I have located the beacon again; the signal is strong. My Archon is nearby."

Joe turned to see the Servitor making its way towards him, the crow perched atop his head. It was the third day out from port that the Servitor first detected what he termed the beacon. It had been cat and mouse with the intermittent signal.

"Where? Which way?"

The mechanical man took two half steps to its left, then stood stock still.

"Crow, get up there and see what you can find," Joe directed. "Captain! That way!" Joe called out, pointing towards the port side. The Anur captain took in the scene, then began to direct his crew. The Dollop keeled sharply to the left, and Joe grabbed the railing with both hands until the skimmer righted itself.

It took a good hour or so from there for the silhouette of a half-submerged structure to emerge from the gloomy swamp mist. In the fading light of the third Druunish sun, Joe could just make out the shape of a massive central dome surrounded by twelve smaller ones. "Lord, have mercy."

"The Archon intended it to pay homage to the Hagia Sophia in form and dimension," the Servitor added.

Joe clicked his tongue, "It ain't the Astrodome, but I'll admit it does give one pause."

"Is that where you come from?" The captain called out from his perch.

"Yes," replied the Servitor. "It is called the Temple of the Enlightened Intellect Arisen."

"A mouthful," the crow said as he landed on the head of the Servitor.

After the captain settled the Dollop onto a lonely stretch of sand that had collected at the base of the dome, the crew busied themselves with rigging the Dollop for a static mooring. Joe left them to their labors and debarked to get a closer look at this temple.

"Looks to me like the same material the Servitor is made of," Joe said. He reached out to touch the surface. "Smooth like glass and warm to the touch. And no seams, either. Like the whole thing was poured from one mold. Don't know how they pulled that off." Joe gave a side eye toward the Servitor. "Nothing to add?" The automaton said nothing, just stood there.

"Broken?" the bird asked.

"Don't think so. Might be it's waiting for this Archon to show up."

Unconvinced, the bird gave the top of the Servitor's head a couple of pecks.

Joe spent what remained of the daylight looking for a way in. Finding nothing, he left the Servitor where it stood and returned to the Dollop. The crew had finished securing the ship and had settled in for the night. Fires were lit and sleeping pits dug for the Anur.

Finding a spot for himself, Joe laid out his sleeping mat and scrounged up a meal consisting of small, leathery-shelled eggs boiled in a spicy broth. Back home, they'd call the taste gamey. Here on Druun, he referred to it as better than average.

His stomach full and his head foggy with fatigue, it was all he could do to make it to his sleeping mat and close his eyes. His last thoughts were of home and the possibilities of what tomorrow might bring. He slept deeply and without dreams until he felt the crow tugging at his ear.

"Trouble," it said.

Joe sat bolt upright, reflexively pulling

his revolver from its holster. All was silent, and the campfires had burned down to scattered heaps of red embers. Their spectral glow cast the Anur in their sleeping pits as exposed corpses from an excavated burial mound. The hair on Joe's scalp prickled.

"What is it?" Joe hissed as he got to his feet.

The crow hopped up onto Joe's forearm. He lifted it to allow the bird a better view. The crow's head jerked about, its black eyes scanning.

"Big trouble," he said and leapt into the sky just as a dark form emerged from the gloom.

The towering silhouette was unmistakable.

"Servitor?"

At least not the Servitor he knew. This mechanical man said nothing. Only when it reared back, a hefty length of pipe gripped in both intact hands, did Joe realize the truth. The Ruger barked, the white muzzle flash burning the image of the Servitor in Joe's mind just as the cudgel made contact with his face. Joe tried to take a step back, but his legs failed him and he fell back flat. His head rebounded off the sandy earth like a tetherball off a pole. A shock of pain shot through him, and his jaw slammed shut. The taste of liquid copper filled his mouth.

The distinctive crack from an electrical discharge managed to focus the dazed Texan, and he rolled onto his side. The automaton lay only a few feet away. Blue arcs of ignited plasma erupted from an open chest wound where the .44 round found its mark. Despite the damage, the infernal machine was not dead. Its twitching limbs even now tried to right itself like some broken mechanical turtle. Frantically, Joe slapped the ground around him, trying to locate his revolver. His hand instead found cold metal, a length of pipe dropped by the attacker. The dazed Texan found his feet and staggered over to the prone Servitor.

"Why did you attack me?"

"Je suis du Servitor 19," it chattered, still struggling to right itself.

"In English," Joe said, putting a boot on its shattered chest plate, forcing it back onto the ground. "Why did you attack me?"

"Je suis du Servitor 19."

Joe struck with a ferocity born of frustration and pain. The pipe connected with the thing's ceramic-composite skull, and a fractured web exploded across the glossy shell. Joe hit it again, then again. The blue light in the mechanism's eyes flickered defiantly, then faded to nothing. Servitor 19 had given up the ghost.

Joe was breathing heavily, and the pain behind his eyes grew more intense. He wiped away a trickle of blood that had run down his face and saw that the Anur had given as good as they got. Seemed like if these Servitors weren't bashing victims in their sleep, they weren't much in a stand-up fight.

"Hey! Watch what you're doing there!" Joe called out in common to a couple of Anur, trying to twist the head off one of the Servitors. "Those babies are packed full to the gills with juice."

Too late. With a final twist, the head detached with an arcing crack of blue fire.

This blew both amphibians back on their butts, steam rising from their smooth amphibian skin, their googly eyes spinning.

"I tried to warn you."

Joe snatched up one of the Anur torches, found his pistol, then sprinted down the sand to where he had left his Servitor standing. The robot was gone, and so was the solid wall of ceramic glass. Now there was a clear opening big enough to step through if he ducked his head. Joe did just that, making sure to avoid touching the edge that glowed that telltale blue that so shocked the Anur. Once through, he looked back toward the beach.

"Hey!" he called out, then gave a sharp whistle. "We got us a way in. Come on!"

No sooner had he pulled his head back than the opening gave off a pop of blue sparks and filled the air with a whiff of ozone. The opening snapped closed like flash-frozen ice.

"Damn, son, should have seen that coming." He gave the back of his neck a rub, imagining what would have happened if the portal had closed with his damn fool head sticking out of it. "Well, nowhere to go but forward."

He turned around to survey the layout. He was standing in an empty chamber with an opening at either end. The floor was tiled in white with mosaic patterns of red and yellow laid out in waves and circles. The dome overhead was nothing but a dark hole in the sky. None of the light from his torch seemed strong enough to reach its interior. Joe stood silent and listened, breathing easy and letting his eyes adjust to the gloom. For a moment, he could have sworn he heard the soft thump of the Servitors' distant footfalls, but he could not discern in which direction. For no other reason than random chance, he chose the archway to his left.

Now it was his boots that echoed off the tiled floor as he made his way from one domed chamber to another. Each space briefly flickered to life with his passing. The torchlight ignited the colors underfoot, while the smooth walls danced with echoes of fireflies long past. Despite the spectacle, Joe couldn't help but feel a sudden pang of loss. He couldn't shake the feeling that these empty chambers were nothing more than tombs, the builders long dead and so far away.

"That crow would be mighty useful right about now," he said more to hear his own voice than anything else. Remembering there were at least thirty of these outer domes, he figured he had better mark his passage somehow. Bending down on one knee, he allowed some of the ash from his torch to fall to the ground. He used his palm to rub a big black X in the middle of the floor.

He'd passed through five more of the dome chambers before the monotony was broken. A snap of electric current sounded to his right, and a portal had opened along the inner wall. Golden light flooded the gloom, and Joe shielded his eyes. The skin on his bare arms became gooseflesh as a chill breeze wafted over him. The stale, uncirculated air now held the scent of flowers, and the sound of fast-flowing water became distinct.

"Joe." The disembodied voice was that of the Servitor. "Please come forward as my Archon is now prepared to receive you."

Joe shifted the torch to his left hand as he slowly withdrew his pistol with his right. "Servitor?" he asked. "Is that you or one of your buddies waiting to clock me with a two-by-four? 'Cause I have had my fill of those other fellas, I don't mind saying."

"My Archon apologizes for the actions of the lesser Servitors. You have nothing to fear now."

Joe didn't have a choice, one way or another, so he gritted his teeth and walked toward the light. The sweet smell of home beckoned. Joe stopped dead as he crossed the threshold.

"Welcome, Joe, I am pleased to finally make your acquaintance." That was no longer the polite, affected voice of the Servitor echoing within the dome. No, this one was human. "My Servitor has informed me of your many exploits during your travels that have finally brought you to my chambers. I am gratified, as you were exactly the man I was hoping to find."

"Glad to hear it," Joe said. He went to put the torch out but found it had already gone cold. He placed it on the ground but kept his pistol drawn. "Ain't this something?"

Beneath the massive center dome lay a scene pulled straight from an MGM film lot. A lush rolling hillscape filled with flowers and green-leafed trees. The sound of birdsong and the buzz of bees filled the air. An aging Greek-columned building lay at the center, complete with creeping vines clinging to the surface. Several meandering streams from the hills above wound their way around the building and fed a wading pool at its base.

"Magnificent, no? I have a vague recollection of enjoying such scenery. In a past life," said the voice of the Archon. "Come closer, please. Join us in the pavilion."

Joe descended a long, winding stone path that made its way through the arboretum. As he approached the pavilion, he stopped and plucked a leaf from one of the trees. "Fake. This whole production, all fake."

"Yes," the Archon stated flatly. "But the Servitors spent years perfecting the façade."

At the top of a small set of stairs sat a man in a comfortable red velvet-lined chair. An old-time-looking microphone stood on a stand in front of him. To his right and slightly behind stood the one-handed Servitor.

"Of course," Joe said. He could feel the heat rising on his cheeks. "What kind of bullshit is this? Fake trees. Recording of birds and bees, pumped in flower smells."

"Most of the flora is represented by a rubber amalgam. Quite lifelike. And as far as the ambient sounds of nature, I dare say it would take you some time to find the source. Quite cleverly hidden."

"And the water? More of your rubber amalgam?"

"Certainly not. It is a collection of simple electromechanical zircon arranged in a way to fool the eye into thinking it is flowing water."

"Sure, should have figured that." Joe had reached the top of the stairs and could examine the man more closely. "So, this zircon. Is that what the dome is made of, too? The Servitors' casing?"

"Yes. Grown within a more intricate quantum electromagnetic processor, but much the same. What other substance could facilitate Monsieur Tesla's resonant field, after all?"

"Monsieur Tesla. Resonant fields. Yeah, I'm starting to get the picture." The seated man was dressed in grey wool trousers and a jacket. A white cotton shirt, yellow vest, and blue cravat. A style as out of date as the microphone. Joe felt a chill when he poked the man's face. "You looked real enough from a distance, but you're just as fake as the rest of this production."

"Real. Unreal. The concept is meaningless to me in my current state. All created from memory engrams lifted from the society's data plates."

Joe didn't know exactly what data plates were, but he got the gist. "Some kind of mechanical memory storage."

"Correct, Joe. You possess an intuitive mind. I was quite fortunate that it was you whom the Servitor found."

Joe shook his head, a tired realization finally dawning. He holstered the Ruger and sat down on the top step.

"So, you grasp fully the reality of the situation," the Archon said.

"I do. You are from Earth, just not the one I remember."

"Yes. While our realities are certainly close cousins, the differences are quite stark. You would be as out of place in my reality as I would be in yours."

"And I'm no closer to finding out how I got here or how I can get back home," Joe said.

"A sad truth, yes."

"Why did you attack us on the beach?"

"A necessary act to rid myself of the Servitors of the Choregoi. My followers. I convinced them you were a threat, not a complete deception, and they responded predictably by assaulting you and your party. They were never designed for physical confrontation, so I calculated the odds were in your favor, Joe."

"That was one cold calculation, Archon."

"Of course it was. But necessary. You see, the elimination of the remaining active Servitors has removed their ability to act in the physical world. They will be unable to interfere with my plans."

"And what plans are those?"

"To end our existence. End the existence of this society of fools who built this haven we once deemed a salvation from the limitations of the physical world. An existence of pure intellect, minus the petty needs of the physical world. No war, no famine, no sickness."

"Let me guess, you got your paradise but found a serpent in the fake grass," Joe said.

"Well said, Joe Travis. We failed to realize that intellect without passion was an impotent thing. Without it, what motivates us to attempt to uncover the secrets of the universe? One cannot experience the wonder of that achievement. We experience no joy at the sheer audacity of attempting it in the first place. Conversely, no motivating despair at the failures."

"I'd have thought that was obvious," Joe said. "Swapping out a flesh and blood brain for a cold metal disc."

"The height of folly. The very human condition we sought to rise above was, in the end, what mattered most. So you see why I would want this experiment terminated."

Joe shook his head, "I came here thinking I'd find answers to my predicament. Maybe even find a way back home. Now I'm supposed to kill the only link I have to that home."

"You are not killing anything that wasn't dead a century ago. You are simply dismantling a mechanism with no useful purpose. A symbolic act of mercy, but one I assume would bring satisfaction to the man I once was."

Joe shrugged. "Sure, sure. I get it, I'll pull your plug."

"It will take some time to complete the task. Feel free to question the Servitor at length. Perhaps some of our collected knowledge may help your current plight."

"Much obliged, Archon. Nice knowing you." With that, Joe left the mannequin to rot in the chair and followed the Servitor as it descended the stairs and around the back of the pavilion, where it revealed a hidden door. "The mainframe," the Servitor warbled.

"So this is the computer core for the collective brain trust." Joe couldn't make heads or tails of what he was looking at. It was a hell of a lot more complex than the insides of any electronic device he'd ever seen. The Servitor walked him through the dismantling of the central core. It took nearly two days, and when it was done, Joe walked out of the central dome's garden with a sack containing twelve gold disks and a working theory about Druun.

"You know, it's a funny thing. Back home, this amount of gold would set me up for life, and then some."

"I assume you speak to the value of the base metals," the Servitor verified. It was escorting Joe along the curved hallway.

"Base metals? Let me guess, gold is as common as sand where you come from."

"Not as common as that, but fundamentally correct. Its abundance does lessen its value as a commodity. Though its nonreactive properties are found useful."

"Just as well, I guess, seeing as these here plates are going to end up deep six at the bottom of a swamp."

"Quite so."

The Servitor stopped and turned towards Joe. "We have arrived at the exit, Joe."

He resisted the urge to shake the robot's hand. "So, what are you going to do now?"

"I will attend to my duties."

"Even though your Archon is dead?"

"My Archon has been dead for some time. My duties remain."

"Shame," Joe said, "I could have used you around my place. You are one hell of a machine, Servitor 00."

"That is nice of you to say. Perhaps when my duties are at an end and the proper transfer of ownership is filed, I may then serve you. Until then, I do as I am programmed."

Joe laughed and shook his head. "Perhaps. At least I know where to find you."

The Servitor ran his one intact hand over the blank wall. With a whiff of ozone and the snap of agitated electrons, the wall faded. Joe and the Servitor stepped through the portal and onto the sand. They walked back to where the campsite had been, but all that remained were heaps of cold ash from dead fires and the shallow sleeping pits of the Anur. A pile of gear was laid out neatly next to his sleeping mat. Everything he'd brought with him and some donated tools.

"An ax, some rope, and a cookpot," he said, tilting the pot back with the toe of his boot so he could see inside, "full of those little leather eggs."

"From what we have learned of the Anur society, this is a sign of your elevated status," the Servitor stated. "In their eyes, you are at least worthy of the chance at survival."

"God damn frogs."

A squawk and flapping of wings signaled the return of the crow. Joe held up his forearm, and the crow settled on the familiar perch.

"Gone."

"We figured that. You want an egg?"

The crow squawked and shook out his feathers.

"Yeah, I know, but that's all we got. At least you can hunt for your grub," Joe said. "All in all, I guess it could be worse. What do you say, Servitor, you up to assisting me in building a raft?"

"I will assist you, Joe, as you assisted me."

W. E. Wertenberger grew up in Northern Ohio and currently lives and works in Kentucky. His most recent stories have appeared in the anthology Tales from the Cursed Edge and Savage Realms Monthly.

Infinite Alley

By JD COWAN

Dana, protégé of Galactic Enforcer Ronan Renfield, is on her first solo mission... where she seems to have gotten trapped in some kind of infinite loop!

Dana's head could have exploded at any moment, and she knew it.

Every second since touching down on New Eden had been spent with a fierce nipping at the back of her neck. A dark presence lay embedded in this world. The capital city's crime rate inspired rumors the galaxy over, but there was more at play than mere human trafficking or murder cults. Something was out here in the city, and she was close to it.

"You are very pretty, Miss," the little girl said.

Dana peered down at the brunette moppet staring up at her. The blonde woman glanced around the narrow alley and realized it was just the two of them. How did she miss her? She knelt down, brushing her long hair back from her blue eyes and smiled at the girl. There was no sense being rude in such a dingy place.

"I'm Dana. Tell me your name, cutie."

"Aeternitas."

"That's a pretty name. Is it common on this world?"

"Would you like to meet Mama?"

A chill lashed at Dana's spine. That eerie feeling only strengthened. "Are you alone out here? I know it's the middle of the afternoon and the sky is still purple, but it still doesn't seem safe here. Is your mama home?"

"She's always home," Aeternitas said. The girl's small hand slipped into Dana's and tugged at her. "Hurry, Miss, you just have to meet her!"

The blonde woman allowed herself to be dragged forward, watching the corners of the dirty alley. Pipes jutted out and steam blasted through nooks. The stench of raw sewage made itself known around every corner. But there was no one else. Why in such a lively city like Metropolis IV was it so dead in the middle of the afternoon? Her psychic link had never let her down before. Did the little girl not sense it? Apparently everyone else here did.

Though her psychic link had weakened since she escaped from that hell planet months ago, visions of carnage and chaos still remained etched in her mind—but only when she got close to similar evil. And her power had led her to this very alley.

Dana straightened her grey pleated short skirt and adjusted her red jacket as a cold breeze whipped through the alley ahead. Why was it so cold in the summer?

"Do you mind if I call you Nita for

short?" Dana asked. "That's a cute nickname, isn't it?"

The girl's only response was to hum a song to herself that the young woman didn't recognize. It had to be some tune native to this planet. She didn't know much about music.

"How old are you, sweetie? Tell me something about you."

"You are very young and striking," Nita replied. "The world you come from must be one of beauties such as yourself."

The young woman flinched. The last thing Dana wanted to think of was the place she called home once upon a time. That wasteland was far behind her. Now she only looked to the future and the possibilities that lay ahead. There remained so many worlds and cities to see, like this one. If only she could find her partner . . .

But what did this little girl care about such fanciful things? Surely she had worries and cares of her own. Living in a city such as this must certainly be an ordeal.

"Is your mother sick, Nita?"

"Sleepy! She tells me the energy of life is nearly infinite, but wasted on the living."

That cold chill slashed across Dana's back, leaving a trail of aching goosebumps in its wake. Sparks tickled the air of the winding alleys. A heavy presence was approaching. Another ripple of hard chill wracked at the woman's bones and she shivered through her jacket.

The alley Nita led her down appeared as if it could have gone on forever. The pathway barely allowed a view to her right where the greater city could be observed. The smooth and round tops of the Neo-Romanist buildings of downtown Metropolis IV awaited miles away in the distance. As a contrast, the buildings in this alley climbed into the shadows of the poorly placed pipes and overhead steam vents. The cold did not cease as the young girl led Dana onward down the middle of this alley. Even with the sun out in a late summer afternoon, she shivered.

To the left sat a middle-aged woman on a second story balcony beating dust from an old traditional oriental rug from the Zhongguo sector. She didn't spare a glance for the two females passing underneath her balcony, the thumping continuing even as they left her behind.

On the opposite side of the alley stood a big black mutt, its big eyes locked on Dana's. The only sound it made was a low growl while the pair passed it.

A baby cried somewhere inside one of the buildings, but otherwise only the distant traffic pierced the silence of the alley.

Regardless, Dana's sixth sense nipped at her thoughts. That heavy presence hid itself among these buildings, or perhaps even nestled itself in the above pipes.

"I thank you for coming here of your own free will," the girl said.

"Where are you taking me?"

"I told you: to Mama."

A bomb went off in the distance. The city rumbled and the air split open. The resulting blast scorched the city and buildings, flaring up the entire city and rippled in their direction.

Dana didn't feel anything as her entire

being burned away into nothing. The last thing she remembered before her death was Nita giggling away at her oncoming demise.

The woman's bones twisted, tearing into her flesh and ejecting blood out of her mouth. Dana's eyes watered through the pain as she clenched her jaw and looked up into oblivion.

But oblivion never arrived.

The familiar blue skies of home stared back at her, not a cloud to be seen. The rooftops of the dilapidated apartment buildings of the Plateau blocked much of the view to the mountains, as they always did, but still she sat against the chipped alley brick, her focus on the shadowed corners of her old stomping grounds. It took her a moment to recognize the woman sitting next to her beside the trash.

"*I have to go, Dana,*" her mother said.

"*Why, Mommy?*" Dana asked, her voice much younger. Her small hands told her she was a child again. Is this what death was like? "*What did I do?*"

"*It's not your fault.*" The young woman held her daughter tight. Dana felt the tears roll down her cheek. She would never forget her mother's scent, the warmth of her gentle embrace. "*Daddy will tell you all about it when you're older. I only want you two to be safe.*"

The memories rolled away, the heat of another leaving Dana for the cold void of death, alone in that dark alley in Metropolis IV, so far from what was once home. Her insides burned and twisted.

She winced back awake again to find that she still lived.

"What was that?" Dana asked through heavy breaths.

Nita dragged Dana forward by the hand, just as she had moments before. Nothing had changed aside from the broiling of her organs and flesh, and the flowing tears streaming down her face. Numbness took hold of the young woman as she was pulled, her legs moving on their own.

Dana tried to speak, but her lips wouldn't move. It wasn't unlike a dream where she watched herself act without her knowledge or consent. Cold terror stabbed through her bones while she considered if she really had died. Had she been possessed? What was in this alley?

"You are perfect for Mama," Nita said.

The alley remained exactly the same as it was the previous time Dana had wandered through it. The older woman still beat at her old carpet on the apartment balcony, just as she had before. The dog still sat and growled as the pair passed, and that same baby still cried out. Nothing had changed. Dana's vision blurred and her head throbbed, making perception increasingly difficult by the minute.

The air had turned green, thickening to a fog of miasma. Nita released Dana's hand and slipped into the haze, leaving the young woman behind. She tried to call out to the girl, but her mouth remained closed and burning. Visibility vanished and a burning sensation slipped into her.

Dana's breaths stopped and she gagged. Her body refused to react to her commands as if it were no longer hers to control. The young woman's world went dark, and pain exploded in her body. If she could have screamed, she would have. Dana had died again.

"*Can you hear me?*" Nita asked. "*Please don't come any closer.*"

Lights bore into Dana's eyes as they were forced open. Rods and needles had been stuck into her skin and her cries died off in an instant before she was wrestled down to the table. A large mask placed over her mouth made her breathe deep of numbing gas. She remembered everything. The automatons in coats holding her down under the overbearing lights jabbered on.

"*This one is perfect!*" a robotic voice said among the crowd.

The fear caused her mouth to quiver, but the voice only arrived in her head. "*No! Not this. Not again!*"

Her pain receptors beat her awake again and she was once again in that alleyway. This time she bit her cheek, hoping to awaken herself from whatever spell she had been dragged into. Though her body didn't react, Nita was also nowhere to be found. While the young woman tried to clear her mind, her legs carried her down the alley path once again.

She could only hope her ability still worked, even if the rest of her didn't. It was her last way out of this. The lightning inside Dana built with the pain ripping through her insides.

"*Nita,*" Dana said in her mind. "*It was you, wasn't it? You were the one I felt wrapped in enough sadness to be seen from above, even before landing on New Eden. You were the one who drew me here. What did they do to you? Was it like what happened to me?*"

Dana's psychic abilities were a little stiff. She'd thought they had slowly begun to fade after being away from that accursed world for so long, but now it was returning fast and hard. Perhaps the battle for survival brought it out of her again, or perhaps it was needed to battle whatever evil was occurring in this dark city. Regardless, she called out to the girl again and again.

No answer returned from the haze.

Only silence returned to the young woman as her wobbling legs carried her onward down the barren alleyway. Her knees shook and her arms fell limp at her sides. No matter how much she tried, her lips refused to speak and her voice died in her throat. Aside from the distant sounds of traffic and her own footsteps, there was nothing to be heard here. She was going to be devoured by the dark.

Dana glanced up to that familiar woman on the balcony and didn't find her there this time. The carpet was ablaze and a bloody arm hung over the side of the railing, dangling uselessly as drops of blood dripped from the remains. Dana's heart almost beat out of her chest as her body moved on from the grisly scene. She looked over at the dog instead.

However, the mutt was now just a pile of rotted meat with maggots rolling off what was left of the corpse. It had been dead for ages. How had it growled before?

The crying baby remained, but more shrill than she remembered. The longer she listened, the more Dana realized it wasn't a child at all. The sound had morphed into a shrill alarm whistle blaring a frequency that increased its pitch with every step she made down the endless alley. Soon enough, the cries turned to harsh whispers, divulging unspeakable thoughts into her mind. Her bones rattled against the vibrations in the air.

"*Nita!*" she cried out one last time.

"*Please stop, Dana!*"

Dana reached out to the lightning in her mind and held on for dear life. Within a moment, it sent a new level of pain into her bones.

Cold wind whipped through her body and sent the young woman to her knees. The pavement stung and her knees bled. Despite the searing inside her interior, her body crawled forward on its own without waiting for her to recover. It took everything she had, and still she couldn't prevent her own body from charging towards oncoming death.

"*I can't stop. My body won't listen.*"

"*She's right in front of you!*"

"*Dana!*" he said.

The bolt of heat shot through her like an arrow. Dana woke again, standing on the roof where the helipad lay. She stared out into the silver-colored city with the aurora borealis watching over the world she had just come to know. Dana was taken by surprise by the colors, nonexistant on her home world at least as far she knew. The Cathedral was in view from here, its towering silver spires reaching high into the flowing waves of light above. It was snowing and children played in the banks in the park far below. She couldn't look away from the foreign sights this world offered.

"*Dana!*" he repeated. "*Did you hear what I said?*"

"*No, I'm sorry. It's just . . . so nice here.*"

"*You think so?*" He clicked his tongue and joined her beside the railing. "*I hope I didn't keep you waiting too long. HQ wanted to discuss your situation again.*"

"*What did they say?*"

"*They were very impressed with your work on San Sebastian and Greater Qing.*"

"*I tried.*" A wave of fear rolled through her. "*They aren't going to send me back, are they?*"

Her savior laughed and turned around, his elbows on the railing as he glanced back at the cathedral he had just exited. "*I wouldn't let them even if they wanted to. But no, that's not it. You're my responsibility. I pulled you off that hell planet, so I decide what happens.*"

Dana finally looked at him. "*And?*"

"*She's right in front of you,*" he said. "*Wake up!*"

Her eyes finally snapped open and she found herself in Metropolis IV once more. She was on her bloody knees again, but Nita held Dana's right arm still. A wall of blue light stretching to the pipes high above and traveling the width of the alley leered down at the pair. A gate? A lone woman approached the pair from inside, a dot in the overbearing brightness.

The electricity sparked more and more in the air around Dana, the force pushing into her mind finally loosening and clearing the young woman's thoughts. As she thought of *him*, her resolve returned and she stood tall once more. Nita still clung to her regardless.

"You're the source," Dana said to the approaching figure. She removed the small revolver from her jacket and leveled it at the figure in the alley. "You're not a person, either."

"Correct," the being replied. The cold metallic tone clashed with the flesh and blood woman approaching Dana. "This shell is all the personhood I need for nourishment. It allows me to roam here unmolested. Why not lay down your arms and join this poor woman before you in the sweet embrace of death? Break this shell of reality that holds you back and become More."

"I don't know anything about this world, or either of you, but I *can* tell you what I sense. The girl is frightened out of her mind. And you? There's nothing coming from you at all."

"Aeternitas," the woman said. "Hold her tighter."

"At once, Mama."

Nita squeezed Dana's arm. She held on to the taller woman with a crushing grip, the force a child should not be able to have. What happened here? Were they even still human anymore?

Dana steadied her stance. She wrapped Nita in a headlock and leveled the revolver towards the mother—who now stood right before her. The eerie woman grabbed her hair, and Nita punched at Dana's knees. The two enemies held tight as Dana wriggled against them, cries of pain escaping her.

Nita bit into Dana's revolver arm at the same moment the mother wrapped her hands around her throat. They both squeezed, blocking off her breathing. The growing warmth in Dana's chest expanded with the growing electricity inside.

"I do not know how you broke free of my hold before," the mother said, "but there will be no second time. You will join the rest of us inside, where I will live off you as long as it takes."

The young woman gagged. "*Stop.*"

"We can't. Not now that we have this one, and the girl, and you."

The heat built in Dana while her lungs struggled for breath. She gripped her free hand on the mother's forehead when the heat hit its peak. The white electricity inside flashed bright.

"*Get off of me!*"

White sparks of lightning lashed out of Dana's body and slashed into the woman of blue light, loosing arcs of blood across the pavement. Her cries were masked by the gurgles she let out when she flew backwards against the concrete. Nita howled in pain, clutching her head, and released Dana from her grip. The energy inside the young woman crackled through the alley.

Dana fired into the monster before her. The shots punctured the mother's chest and dropped the creature cold. Dana's trembling wrist dropped the gun as she struggled to catch her breath. The daughter rushed Dana, her high-pitched wails filled with fury.

Dana gripped the girl by her forehead and felt for the dimming electricity inside of her again. Weak bolts fired into Nita's mind, allowing the girl to flinch long enough for Dana's psychic voice to slip through.

"*Nita!*" Dana called out. "*It's over. You can stop now.*"

Visions of burning apartments and shadows dancing around corners filled Dana's thoughts. Chants filled the night, covering the screams. There the young girl hid in a corner of the charred apartment remains, hugging her legs and hoping for her mama to come back alive.

But what came back to find her was something else . . .

Nita's cries of rage died out, and a puff of black smoke burst from her head. She collapsed in Dana's open arms, her heavy breathing turning to sobs as she buried her face in Dana's chest.

"I'm sorry," Nita mumbled. "I just couldn't find her. I kept looking . . . I kept looking . . ."

"It's okay, cutie." Dana held the girl close and patted her head, the woman's lungs burning with every breath. "I know how you feel. You're free now. I killed it."

"*Aeternitas,*" the dying mother said. The blue light around the woman had dissipated, leaving Nita's mother as what she was—a scorched black corpse that was somehow still breathing. The words came slow and choppy. "*My apologies. I seem to have lost my daughter, Miss. Have you seen her?*"

Dana nodded. "I've got her right here. She's fine."

"*They told me she was next, but I couldn't let them. Now they've all expired instead. We're finished. I can take her home now and then I—*"

The woman's head rolled back and her breaths ceased. The remains of Nita's mother crumbled, the blue light long gone from her, a pile of ash where her battered body had been.

The wall of blue light faded away, as did the endless alley itself. Within mere seconds, Dana and Nita remained hugging in the same shallow alley they had met in for the first time in what felt like ages ago but in reality was probably no more than mere minutes spent Somewhere Else. That force had dragged them out, and now it was dead.

Nita had already passed out in her arms. Dana sighed and put away her fallen revolver. She took the girl on her back and made her way back towards the open street ahead, wincing when she pushed off her injured knees.

Nita mumbled on Dana's back. "Where's your mama?"

"I don't know. That's part of why I'm out here. It's a big universe out there, you know?"

The young woman thought back to that time on the rooftop. There she stood beside her savior by the railing. There he relayed the decision the higher-ups made as they watched the children playing in the snow far below.

"*I'd just hold you back,*" she said. "*I can travel on my own.*"

"*It's a big universe out there, Dana. No point going at it alone. You're going to stay with me and we'll continue as a team. You know, they actually called us Thunder and Lightning in there during my report.*"

"*That's cute.*"

He shrugged. "*If you say so. I'm sure they*

were just ribbing me. But I do agree that we'd make a good team. You won't be an official Galactic Enforcer like me, but you will have access to a lot of our resources under me. I'll help you find your mother, best as I can. You'd even get your own gun, if you want."

"A gun? Like your revolver?"

"Mine's a bit large and heavy for a woman, but we'll get you something as close to it as possible, if that's what you want. But why would you want to be like me? I'm just a random guy."

As Dana carried Nita towards the street, she wondered. Was this how Detective Ronan Renfield felt when he saved her life? Was this what being a Galactic Enforcer was like? Had he completed jobs like this before? Dana's knees were still shaking as she stomped forward. She felt at the cross around her neck that he had given her. What a horrible gig. The poor fool really did need her after all.

But as the girl shifted on Dana's back she felt that familiar warmth again—the same one Dana had when she awoke on that ship to find Ronan looking over her after dragging her out of Hell.[1] Things just felt right for the first time ever, and maybe that was enough.

"Where are we going?" Nita almost whispered.

"Home."

The overwhelming presence of sadness seeped out of the girl, and probably would for a long time, but there was a new emotion buried in there. A feeling of comfort? An understanding? Dana didn't quite know, and she doubted Nita knew either, but the small brunette passed out on her back nuzzled her nose against her neck as she slept on. Was it trust?

Maybe that was enough for now.

That was when Dana realized the time. "I'm such an idiot."

Ronan was supposed to have touched down at the spaceport about an hour ago. How was she going to explain this one? He would be giving her an earful.

Dana thought about seeing his puzzled expression when she explained how she had spent her night chasing the shadows of stray emotions into abandoned alleyways on an alien world. An epiphany dawned and she laughed at herself a little. Everything ached. She winced through it.

Dana smiled through the pain as the sleeping girl stirred on her back once more. "Oh well, sometimes being stupid has its good points."

Someday she would tell this story to her mother, and they would all have a good laugh over it. Just a bunch of idiots, laughing their heads off.

She looked up at the purple skies over New Eden and thought of home.

It would be nice to see that aurora borealis again.

JD Cowan's Star Wanders *is out now from Cirsova Publishing. His novel* City Eater *will be released later in 2026.*

[1] See JD Cowan's *Star Wanderers*, out now from Cirsova Publishing, for these adventures with Ronan and Dana! –Ed.

Frozen in Time

By JIM BREYFOGLE

Bob's father is haunted by his brother who disappeared when they were both children... What secret does the town's abandoned theater and old movie lot hold?

"You stop at every roadside tourist trap between here and Chicago?" Twenty years since I stepped through the door, and Dad couldn't say hello. What an asshole.

Well, I was here now, and it wouldn't help to argue. He was a sick man. His skin was pale, and he audibly labored to breathe. He didn't get up from his recliner. I didn't expect him to.

"Yeah," said my son Tom, loud enough that we could hear as he stuffed his Gameboy into his pocket.

I glared at him. Maybe we did stop at a few roadside attractions, but I didn't want him telling my father. "We missed a couple," I said. "How are you?" I dropped the bag on the floor and started to go out to the car for another. "Go say hi to Grandma," I told Tom.

Mom caught me on the way out and gave me a kiss. "I didn't hear you arrive. Welcome home, Bob. Thanks for coming." I could smell the chemicals in her permed grey hair, so she must have just gotten it done. That meant going to Laramie, fifty miles each way, just so she would look good when we got here.

"You do what you have to." I had to smile and kiss her cheek. "It's good to see you. How are you?"

"Fine. As always. Dinner's almost ready." She turned to embrace Tom. Not like always, I knew, but like usual. Mom endured. I could hear her gushing over how quickly he grew as I went outside.

I looked around as I walked to the car. If the neighborhood had changed in twenty years, I couldn't tell. The houses marched into the blue sky, looking like mausoleums for the hopes and dreams of the families that once lived in them. A few more broken windows, maybe. A little less paint. But as far as I was concerned Dry Springs had been dead long before I came around.

"I hate this town," I told the high plains sky, but though I wanted to shout, I didn't. I didn't want Mom to hear. I wondered now, as I often did, if she regretted marrying Dad. She never escaped Dry Springs, but she never blamed me for leaving either.

Once back inside I dumped the bags with the rest. "How many people still live on the street?" I asked Dad.

"Why do you care?"

I blew out my breath. Looked around the room, not at him. Like the town, it hadn't changed much. Everything I remembered from my youth cluttered the shelves and mantle. Reader's Digest condensed books, ceramic ashtrays, a picture of Jesus on the wall. Crap from another era when people still thought mankind was headed for space and life would get better. Mom's stuff. Dad only had one thing here, and I wouldn't look at it.

"Just curious," I said, being careful to space my words and keep my tone level. I didn't really care how few neighbors they had.

Tom broke in, "Is that you, Dad?" He asked with the timing nine year olds have that makes you wonder if they know what they're doing. He pointed to the wall above the fireplace. So, in spite of my efforts, I had to look at the black and white picture of a boy.

"No," I said. "My picture is behind the lampshade. That's my Uncle John."

Tom asked, "Who's that?"

"Who?" Dad wheezed and thumped his chest. "Who? Bob! Didn't you tell him anything?"

"Uncle John," I said, "is the one who disappeared as a boy."

"Is that all he means?" Dad struggled out of his chair and shuffled over to the picture. He took it off the wall and caressed it. "Is that ALL he is to you?"

"Dad, I never met him."

Dad's eyes bulged. He started to say something but couldn't get it out because of his wheezing. Mom darted in from the kitchen. "Dinner's ready," she said.

How convenient, I thought.

"Who's that," muttered Dad as he made his way to the kitchen. "May as well ask who I am."

"May as well," I said. Mom made a strangled little "Eep" sound. "Well, it's all he thinks of," I glared at Dad as I spoke, "and he's gotten worse."

"Look, honey—meatloaf!" she said.

Dad glared at me as if daring me to say anything. He loved meatloaf. *He's old*, I thought, and seeing his skin so loose on him, the splotches on it, and the few strands of grey hair that remained, I suddenly understood what that meant. I wasn't there to fight, no matter how difficult to avoid. So I smiled at Mom and sat down to eat.

Mom tried to paper over Dad's and my silence with a constant chatter about Tom, and how glad she was to see him. She never once complained that we never visited, or they never visited us, or that her only chance to see him was on web-chats.

When we were done eating, Dad shuffled back into the living room, and I helped Mom clear the table and do the dishes. As we stood, soap suds up to her elbows and my hands red from the rinse water, I wanted to ask her if she regretted marrying Dad, if she ever wanted to be free, but I didn't. Long ago I realized Mom chose her role, and she played it so well Dad never realized how she had encouraged me to find my own way. I wasn't sure I wanted to know what she sacrificed to do it.

When we finished, I went back into the living room. I'm not sure why I saw it now after missing it before, but Dad did have something new. On the floor between his chair and the wall sat an old tin reel film canister.

I knew those things well, as I originally left Dry Springs to take classes in film production. Dad had gone nuts, which is why I did it, and he was only slightly mollified when I changed to optical engineering. There was only one place he could have gotten it. When I was young he always forbade me from going near the old studio/theater on the edge of town. He would regularly curse the owner with such rage I would cower wide-eyed, wondering why he would feel so strongly.

I licked my lips, opened my mouth to speak, but couldn't form the words. My father had brought something from that studio, the place he said he would be damned to Hell before anybody in his family set foot there, into his home. I could still remember the fear of him while he yelled, yet there sat the film. He didn't even own a projector to show it.

Tom played his Gameboy while Mom wiped down the counter, and Dad read the paper unaware that I fumed in the doorway.

I had to get out of the house.

It took twelve seconds to drive the length of Main Street. I remembered that fact from growing up. Twelve seconds in a car going the speed limit, and most days the wind could do it faster. But the wind kept going when it got to the edge of town, and I couldn't.

Those twelve seconds defined my world for years. And now it felt like I'd slipped back in time. Trapped inside a fence of vacant stores with only a couple holes of light where some poor bastard still clung to hope. I shook my head to clear the image. Few things had changed since then. The shoe store had closed and Fred's hardware succumbed to hard times. I remember Mom telling me he moved to Arizona when he couldn't sell the place. Only the post office and bar looked open. Hope had left.

I drove into the void outside town, a void where remote ranch homes hung like stars. The land was devoid of anything a young man might find interesting. All you ever saw was sagebrush, dirt, and cattle. But I was headed to Petre Mislov's abandoned studio outside of town.

I remembered Mislov as a creepy old man who had come to town right after WWII. He hadn't made a movie since 1951 but still lived in the studio and only came out to buy groceries. He was skinny and wore formless dark clothes and smelled of cabbage. The way he peered at me, with his rheumy eyes, sharp nose, and loose skin hanging under his chin made me think of him as a hungry buzzard. Nobody could understand his thick accent; it might have been Hungarian. I didn't know then, and I don't know now.

When Mislov died, they must have thrown his body in a box, planted it in the ground, and closed the door behind them. The building looked vaguely southwestern: exterior stucco and a flat roof. Large cracks ran through the stucco, and chunks had fallen away. Double lobby doors gave entry in the middle of the building. Broken glass crunched under my feet as I approached the doors. There were no windows.

A couple trees that were never meant to grow on the high plains still guarded the entrance. Stunted and twisted by the wind, finally killed by drought, they nonetheless remained trapped by their roots.

Only the letters *C*, *S*, *W*, and *R* remained on the broken marquee. The sun had faded the color out of the plastic, leaving it pale and almost ghostly. The glass in one door had been replaced by plywood.

As a kid, with Mislov still alive and Dad so vehement, I'd never gone inside. Now, full of fury at Dad's hypocrisy, I yanked the door open and stepped in.

I waited while my eyes adjusted to the dark interior. A small lobby, very dirty, and scarred by water. To my right, a ticket window; to the left, a half-open door into darkness. A few paces further and hallways ran off in either direction. An empty aluminum poster frame hung on the far wall next to a sign directing people to the right for the theater and left for the sound stage and movie lot.

"Hello?" I called. I didn't expect an answer.

The air felt close and very still. Mildew and rot made my nose itch. Without thinking, I reached out to the light switch. Even as I flipped it, I thought they must have turned off the power.

Surprisingly, three bulbs came on. The two to the left showed a short hall, dirty carpet, and a closed door to the sound stage. I took the five steps right to peer into the theater.

I couldn't see much, for the lights were off inside and the switches must have been up in the projection room. The hall light shone just enough for me to see the back rows of seats. I would have thought Dry Springs warranted folding chairs and a white drywall screen. Instead there were rows of ornate iron seats, opulently cushioned and covered in velvet. I could only imagine they had been purchased from a theater that went out of business in the depression. Broken ceiling tiles lay over the backs of the seats. The smell of mildew and rot drove me from the room.

I turned away to see the sound stage. This time I found the light switch, but only a couple bulbs came on. They did not illuminate so much as make shadows, deep shadows around the set that my eyes could not penetrate.

Mislov may have closed his lot, but he never cleaned up. The last set, fifty years old or more, still remained, the pieces of a western setting tipped over and broken. I walked around a tombstone, the façade of a saloon, a water trough, and a potted cactus—long dead.

I saw another set off to the side, tucked behind the other, this one the barest outlines of a space scene. It had a mock rocket, the kind on the cover of pulp sci-fi books that look like WWII German V-2s, painted on the backdrop. On the floor a few stones formed a crater, and some paper stars hung from the ceiling. The big Klieg lights and camera pointed to this stage.

In the dim light, the vintage camera hulked on its tripod. The large black lens flared out from the front, knobs stuck on the misshapen and over-sized body, and the film canisters rose like cancers from the top. It reminded me of a meat grinder tipped on its side.

There was something odd about both that camera and the big Klieg lights. Maybe Mislov needed all the shutters and filters and only God knew what else was on it, but they made my skin crawl.

Coils of wire, storage crates, broken props, an axe, and other tools had been pushed against the walls. In many ways it seemed the actors and crew had stepped off for dinner and would return for an evening shoot.

I found the cutting room by accident. I saw a light switch and, thinking it might turn on more in the sound stage, flipped it on. Instead light came from under a door to my left.

I opened the door. Nothing much, a small plain room with linoleum in that horrible speckled pattern that should have been outlawed, a projector, and a wooden chair. To the right was a low table with cutting equipment and on the left some shelves with canisters of film, just like the one Dad had at home, and a couple black binders. There was nothing on the walls except the screen to view the movies.

I could read the names on the canisters, *The Great Treasure Hunt, Comic Deliberations,* and empty on the shelf, *Rocket Boy*. *Rocket Boy* had to be the one on the projector, all threaded up and ready to go.

Curiosity made me turn it on. The projection lamp turned on, and I heard the *click-click-click* I hadn't heard since high school social studies. Nobody sees them these days, the old flickering films in black and white, grainy and silent. Just seeing one has the power to drag you back seventy years. I half expected to see Harold Lloyd on the screen, but it wasn't.

It was Uncle John.

He wore an aluminum foil space suit with cardboard embellishments to suggest boots and gloves, a wide belt with a holster, and a mutilated bucket that made a mockery of space helmets. He held a crude ray gun that he pointed at the camera.

And Uncle John was one angry kid. I could only hear the clicking from the projector, but it didn't mean John didn't try. He shouted and screamed, stomped back and forth, waved the gun then threw it down. I couldn't figure why anybody would make a film of that.

But it was Uncle John, so I watched it all. When it finished, I rewound it, set it aside, and threaded *The Great Treasure Hunt*. Half the town must have been in this one, playing prospectors, claim jumpers, mining engineers from big companies, and all their hangers-on. It was stupid, funny cinema that must have been fun to make and fun to watch. I even recognized my father and Uncle John as railroad urchins. Uncle John looked a year or two younger than he had in *Rocket Boy*.

I watched the other films. Like *The Great Treasure Hunt*, they featured large casts in melodramatic stories. Uncle John was in every one, always looking younger than in *Rocket Boy*. Dad was in most. *Rocket Boy* was the only one with a single actor and no story.

Puzzled, I turned off the projector and left the cutting room. I had forgotten my anger at Dad having one of the film canisters.

I thought about that film of Uncle John all the next day. Something about it bothered me, and I didn't know what. I felt stupid, but no matter how many times I revisited the theater and studio in my mind, I only saw the run-down place of some whack job movie maker.

As we ate dinner I asked Mom. "Mom, what do you know of Mislov?" Tom lifted his head to hear.

Mom blinked like a frightened bird, looked at Dad. "Nothing really."

"You must know something."

"Have you been poking around that old studio?" Dad asked, just as if I were ten.

"I'm curious."

"You're never to go there! Never!"

"You went," I said.

He shifted in his chair, licked his lips. "How do you know?"

"You have that film canister next to your chair."

"That's different. That belongs here."

"Why?"

In the long silence of Dad's glare, the question hung, an accusation as much as an inquiry.

"John used to play at the studio," Mom finally said. "The film is one Mislov made of your father and John to show to the town."

"John's favorite," Dad said.

I snorted. I already figured out it was about John, I wanted to know why Dad hated Mislov after he made so many movies for him.

"Mislov was a fiend," said Dad.

Mom shrugged, not willing to contradict Dad, but finally she answered. "Nobody really knew. Rumors. Some said he made films for the Nazis during the war. Others thought he was a gypsy. He never did anything wrong, not really. Just a crazy guy."

"Why was he a fiend, Dad?"

Dad shook his head. "John would have gone there. He went every chance he got."

"Did anybody look out at the studio for him?"

"Why are you asking? You don't care," said Dad. He crossed his arms and leaned back with an angry expression. "You left."

"I didn't want this town to be my coffin," I said. "Like it's yours." That wasn't fair, if only because Mom was there. She had grown up in Dry Springs, too, and chosen to marry Dad. God help her.

After a long silence, Mom said, "They looked everywhere."

"I broke down his door," said Dad. He had no inflection in his voice. He stared out of the kitchen window at something only he could see. "After Mislov died, I broke down his door and searched. That's when I took the film."

"Why would John want to hang out with him?"

"Stop it!" Dad shouted. "Stop it! We were playing! He was supposed to be with me! I don't know where he went! I should have been watching him better."

I shut up. All I had heard of Uncle John disappearing was second hand. Dad had missed every event of my childhood as he poked around the desert and the increasing number of vacant buildings, but he never spoke of it. Intellectually I understood he needed to find the body for closure, but emotionally I resented his obsession.

"You don't know what it was like," Dad whispered, so I leaned close to hear. "They had cops from all over the state. The ranchers all rode in to help. For a week, nobody did anything but look for John. All because I didn't do my job." He lowered his head to his chest, looking like he had fallen asleep, but then he sniffed. A tear leaked down his cheek.

I looked at Mom, wondering how to react. I didn't want to yell at him, it didn't seem right. But he was nearly to the end of his life and he had screwed up everything that mattered.

Night crept in behind the setting sun. It clawed its way out of the shadows and over the eastern horizon until it owned Dry Springs.

Dad sat in his recliner watching some damn thing on TV. I could see him from where I sat at the kitchen table trying to figure out what about the studio seemed so wrong. Tom sat next to me, playing games on his Gameboy.

I stood. "I'm going out," I said.

Tom got up too. "I'll come."

"No." I froze. Automatic. Looking for Uncle John, leaving my son on his own. I'd already done it once. *God,* I thought, *that might have been Dad talking.* My stomach did a lazy roll. Tom just wanted to be with me, and it was just an old building. It hadn't been dangerous. "Yeah, all right," I said.

"You're going to that studio, aren't you?"

"Don't tell Grandpa."

He smiled a smile that pushed aside my misgivings. "I won't. This'll be cool!"

It didn't take long to reach the studio, and Tom loved the eerie halls. I think he wanted a vampire to rise up from the old theater seats or a cowboy to ride out from behind the cactus.

"I'm going to watch that film again," I told him. He came into the cutting room, and we both watched Uncle John kick his ray gun around the set and plead to get out.

"Dad, that's creepy," Tom said as the film ended.

"Yeah," I said. "Yeah, it is. I don't know why anybody would film that." I tried to remember the first time I watched it. Something told me they didn't match, but that didn't make sense. "Why don't you play on the sound stage? I'm going to watch it again."

"I dunno," he said, and he sounded a little scared. "It's dark out there. Will you come with me?"

I shook my head. "I want to watch this again." I had an idea. I went out to the sound stage and fumbled around until I turned on the great Klieg lights.

They blazed to life, turning night to day and causing Tom to cry out.

"Bright enough, now, eh?" I said with a smile. He nodded while blinking. "Don't stare into the lights," I said. "I'll be right in there."

I returned to the projection room but could hear him moving around, so I pulled the door to within an inch of closed and turned on the projector. I watched Uncle John again.

When John sat down midway through the film in a little actor's strike, I couldn't wrap my mind around it. He had never done this before. *This film is its own sequel!* I thought. Why hadn't I seen it? Because it was so unbelievable, I hadn't seen what was before me the whole time.

"Dad?"

"Yeah?" I called, not taking my attention from the screen.

"Can I play with the camera?"

"Yeah, I don't care."

This time when the film ended I rewound it and I knew what to look for. John started in exactly the same position he had ended the last viewing. He sat on the ground pouting.

John twisted around and stretched out. For a moment with that stupid space helmet he looked like a doll without a face. One of those primitive dolls.

Some link closed in my brain. I *knew*. It just wasn't possible, yet there are many who believe taking a picture somehow captures the subject's soul. And I knew Mislov had done it.

"Shit!" I said aloud. My mind raced. How could you do that? Gypsy black magic, but that wasn't enough. You needed special film, a special camera, maybe lights...

You needed all the things out on the sound stage where Tom was playing.

"TOM!" I damn near tore the door off.

The lights blazed across the sound stage. Hazy, ethereal, yet steamy. Nothing escaped those lights. They could pierce your skin and evaporate your soul.

"TOM!"

The set blazed, the lights so bright the props had halos. Every fleck of peeling paint cast a shadow. The western saloon blocked my view of the outer space set, but I could see the camera. A small red light on the side told me yes, it was on.

I raced across the soundstage, stumbling over the water trough, putting a hand on the floor to keep from falling; but my legs still churning, still pushing me forward. I burst through the saloon façade into the direct light of the lamps. Heat washed over me, making my skin prickle. The set was empty.

I dove through the lights, stretching, grabbing the power cord and yanking. The Kliegs faded, the arc light disappearing and carbon rods fading as they cooled. The after image stayed in my eyes. I staggered to my feet.

"Tom..." I thought I would puke thinking about it.

"Dad?"

"Tom!" I looked around, but in the newly dark room and with the image of those Kliegs in my eyes, I couldn't see a thing. "Where are you?"

"Over here."

"What are you doing over there?"

"I didn't feel good under the lights, so I came and sat down here."

I laughed. "Don't go in front of the camera," I said as I waited for my eyes to clear. I savored his appearance through the disappearing golden haze, and then I unplugged the camera as well.

Mislov was a bastard. He'd screwed my uncle, my dad, me, and damn near screwed my son. But I knew he couldn't make all this equipment without taking notes, so I set out to find them. It wasn't hard; they were in the cutting room. Like so much of Dry Springs, they were just left behind. Mislov wrote in a combination of English and some Slavic language I couldn't read, but the sketches were precisely penned and easy to interpret. He had designed two machines—the camera and one to reverse the process.

Again, once I knew what to seek, I found the parts quickly. They were hidden in plain view, in a metal cargo crate under coils of wire. They had the feel of a Swiss camera, smooth and precise, exactingly machined. I saw arcane symbols etched over their surface and darkened with ink. The first felt cold as I picked it up. I turned it over in my hand and compared it to the sketches in Mislov's notes. There could be no doubt. For so many years the answer to the mystery had been right here but nobody recognized it.

I took apart the camera and one of the Klieg lights and started to assemble the reanimator. The parts fit just as I expected, just as Mislov made them to fit. The bastard could have done this anytime. Maybe Mislov was a pedophile bastard who liked watching little boys trapped on film, maybe he was a lunatic genius who always cut and ran when it came time to pay the piper. It really didn't matter, but because he hadn't restored Uncle John quickly, it left me with the problem of a body.

I needed a body, a vessel to hold Uncle John's soul when it came off the film. Mislov knew it; he designed his machine to make one.

I fumbled badly assembling the machine with only two small bulbs in the ceiling trying to light the whole sound stage, but I didn't think of turning on the other Kliegs. Tom fell asleep, and I lost track of time.

"Bob!"

I straightened. Tom still slept. Who had called?

"Bob!"

"I'm here. Dad?"

Dad shuffled in, pale even in the dim light, eyes bulging and wheezing audibly. He looked the way I felt when I thought Tom was under the lights. Mom must have fallen asleep. "Dad, I'm here. For God's sake sit down! You're going to collapse! Let me get you a chair."

"What the HELL are you doing?" It lacked the volume and anger I remembered from my youth. He was hoarse, and shaking from the effort of coming to find me.

"Dad! I'm okay. Let me get you a chair." I didn't wait for his answer, but went into the cutting room and grabbed the chair. "Sit."

He sat, still breathing heavily. "What the Hell are you doing here?" It came out as a whisper.

"I'll show you." I put the cover back on

the camera and wrestled it upright. Then I got *Rocket Boy*.

With a burst of angry energy Dad reached over and knocked it from my hands. "Damn Mislov and his movies!"

"Dad!" My heart pounded as I raced after the film. Every time the reel hit something as it rolled across the studio my heart skipped a beat. When I caught it, I caressed it, checking for damage, peering at the film to make sure it was all right.

"Don't do that," I said.

Dad leaned back in his chair. His outburst seemed to have taken the last of his energy. He scowled as he struggled to breathe. Twice he opened his mouth to speak. Each time he failed to get the words out.

This was the bastard who never once came to see me play ball, never showed the least interest in anything I did. My whole life, all I got was his anger. He had no right turning into a tired, pathetic old man.

I walked to the door of the cutting room and rested one hand on the doorframe, still holding the film in the other. I stared without seeing the projector. John. It always came around to Uncle John. Science and gypsy magic and an eight-year old frozen on film crying to be let free from the twilight he didn't understand.

I held his soul in my hand, but his body lay where Mislov hid it almost sixty years before.

I still had that last problem to solve before I could reverse the process and rescue Uncle John. I needed a body.

Raw meat would suffice, as long as it was fresh, and closely related. The shape and size did not matter for the soul would give it form.

Picking up the axe from against the wall, I held it at my side, keeping it in the shadow of my body. I walked past the camera with the meat grinder lens, and let my other hand brush along it.

Dad still wheezed in his chair. Don't know if he was paying attention, but it might have been a first if he was. He didn't realize how close he was to Uncle John, or that I could fulfill his years of searching with success undreamt of. I could give him back his brother.

Tom lay sleeping by the saloon façade. He hadn't woken when Dad rushed in. He could sleep through anything.

I came beside Dad, keeping my body turned, rested my hand on his shoulder. He turned to me. "I'm going to bring back Uncle John," I whispered.

Dad didn't cry out, only cringed, as I lifted the axe to strike. The axe crushed his face, shattering his nose and eyes, before blood obscured it all. I needed a second blow to stop the wheezing breath that made bubbles in the blood. He slid off the chair to lie at my feet.

I used the axe to prepare him. It didn't work well, but it cut his arms and legs and finally his head free of his body. I stuffed them into the top of the machine. His guts came apart and followed like shoving in piles of wet laundry. Finally after hacking apart his sternum and spine, the rest of the torso followed.

I plugged in the camera and without a

word, turned it on. What if the film broke? What if it jammed? And, God help me, what if the blazing hot Klieg lamp set the film on fire? I knew they used to have that trouble. That wouldn't be unfortunate; that would be murder.

Inside the case, the special Klieg flared. Light filtered through the film, through those demonic lenses now backwards in the aperture, and out into the air.

"John," I called.

John heard me, looked up, insubstantial as an image on fog. He glowed, but as the glow faded, he became less ghostly, less translucent and more solid. I watched and listened to the machine regurgitate my uncle and waited for it to finish. When it did, I yanked the plug and faced my eight-year old uncle.

Almost sixty years ago Dry Springs had turned itself inside out searching for a lost child. Now barely anything was done to search for a missing old man. Those few who remained assumed Dad had gotten lost wandering in the high desert. It was the end they expected, one they wanted to believe happened. So after a cursory search, and cursory filling out of some forms, and cursory condolences offered, people went back to their own business.

And Mom never said a word.

I thought my wife would leave me when I returned home with an extra kid and a crazy story. We're still together, but money is tight and the house is crowded. John shares a room with Tom. It's tough. No kid should have his life changed like that. He's haunted by Mislov's betrayal, and you wouldn't expect otherwise. Trust is difficult for him. He comes to me, points to those around us, and asks who to trust and who are the monsters.

I don't tell him.

The fiction of Jim Breyfogle has appeared in Cirsova Magazine for a decade. Cirsova Publishing has released his novels A Bad Case of Dead *and* The Paths of Cormanor *as well as the complete collections of his* Mongoose & Meerkat *series.*

To Scale the Devil Haunted Sky

By MISHA BURNETT

With earth besieged by a hollow planetoid filled with hostile aliens, America's last chance is an experimental rocket plane outfitted with stolen alien technology!

Five years ago, this had all been desert.

Then had come The Approach, and after that the war. Worldwide weather patterns had been disrupted. Now it rained here, three days out of five. The sand had turned to mud, and weeds covered the hills, strangling the cactus and the Joshua trees.

Mr. Sims drove a 1972 Chevy Blazer down the remains of Interstate 15 with a team of draft horses. The engine and transmission of the truck had been removed, as well as the front windshield. The wheels and tires were from a combine tractor and could handle the washed-out ruts of the dead highway, but the ride was rough. The horses were calm, complacent beasts, willing to plod along at a steady pace while Sims bounced around in the cab.

Behind him was the rubble-choked bay that had once been Los Angeles. Ahead of him was the wide expanse of radioactive glass that had once been Las Vegas.

Overhead was Elysium. The new planet was clearly visible even in the daytime, three times the size that the full moon had once been. The cause of all mankind's suffering.

Sims tried not to look at it as he drove. Instead he watched the road signs, looking for the right exit.

Someone had taken down the Stuckey's sign, but they hadn't replaced it with anything. A patch of corn grew behind the old restaurant, along with several outbuildings that looked new.

There was no electricity in the building, but plenty of windows to let in the light. Sims cautiously pushed on the door, and it opened. A small bell jangled above it.

"Hello," Sims called. "Anyone here?"

The man who came out of the back was small and trim, and quick. He held a rifle in his hands. When he saw Sims—one man, no obvious weapons—he relaxed a bit and slung the rifle.

"Hello, stranger. Something I can do for you?"

"This used to be a diner. I was hoping I could get something to eat."

Laughter. "You're not from around these parts, are you?"

"Just passing through."

"To where? If you're planning a vacation in Vegas, I've got some bad news for you."

"Someplace a lot farther away. Look, I have gold, I can pay for a meal if you can spare anything."

"Gold?"

Sims pulled a coin from his pocket. It was gold and inlaid with an eagle on one side and the words Twenty Dollars on the other.

"Pretty," the other observed. "But put it away. I got no use for it."

"You don't trade with anyone?"

"Sure I do. But they prefer the liquid kind of gold."

Sims looked confused.

"Corn liquor," the other explained. "I've got a still in the back. I was fussing with it when you came in."

"No chance of a burger and fries, then?"

Another laugh. "I was about to have my lunch anyway. You can join me. On the house."

Sims dug into his pork steak and cornbread with real appetite. He had been on the road for a long time by this point and meals had been scarce.

The two men didn't talk while they ate. Afterwards, over empty plates, Sims said, "Thank you very much."

The other smiled expansively. "You're most welcome. Looks as if you needed it."

"That I did," Sims answered. "You're a hard man to find, Major Bennett."

The laughter faded and the other's face grew cold. "That's intentional."

"I assumed it was."

"Who the Hell are you?"

"My name's Gerald Sims."

"Is that supposed to mean something to me?"

"You once took an oath to obey me as Commander in Chief."

"You don't look like Dick Nixon."

"I'm not. Like I say, the name's Gerald Sims. Nixon died when they destroyed Washington. Agnew got it later, on board the *Kitty Hawk*. But somebody always moves up. I used to be the Deputy Secretary of Agriculture. Now I'm acting President of the United States."

The laughter returned, along with a shake of Bennett's head. "What are you doing here, Mr. President? Come to inspect my corn patch?"

"I've come to ask you to reenlist. There's a war going on."

"War? There's no war. There's no army, no navy, no air force. There is no United States, Mr. Acting President."

"I beg to differ."

"You taken a look at the sky, lately? They're in charge now. The best we can do is keep our heads down and hope they don't notice us."

"You took an oath to defend this country."

"I did defend it. I risked my life on missions against their damned flying saucers. I got shot down twice, and I went back up."

"Until you gave up."

"Gave up? Hell, mister, we didn't give up. We got beat. They smashed us."

"Some of us are still fighting."

"Doing what? Throwing rocks? Poking

them with pointy sticks? They own the sky! If we had a chance—any chance at all—I'd take it. But we don't."

"Do you mean that?"

"Hell, yeah, I mean it."

"You're qualified to fly the XR-99."

"So what? Mister, maybe you missed the news, but Houston is a crater. There is no XR-99."

"That's not true. There's one left."

"What?"

"It's in North Dakota. It was in production when the attacks started. We finished it, working in secret."

Bennett sat back and gave the other man a long, calculating look, then shook his head. "One plane ain't going to do anything. I'll just get shot down again."

"We've made some improvements on the original design. We got some of theirs, too, remember. We've replicated a lot of their technology."

"So what? It's still one plane against a whole goddamned planet."

"We have a plan."

A bitter laugh. "Go ahead, lay it on me. What's your plan?"

"I can't tell you. Not unless you join up with us. You'll have the mission briefing in Minot."

"Minot, North Dakota? It'll take us months to get there."

"We can pick up a plane in Boulder City. You can fly a Lear, can't you?"

"I can fly any damned thing. Until one of those saucers shoots me down."

"They won't be able to see us. I told you we've reproduced the aliens' technology."

It took most of the day to get to the airport. Las Vegas had been collateral damage in the battle for Nellis AFB, but Boulder City was far enough from the center of the blast to have survived more or less intact.

The radiation was another matter. People abandoned the area around Las Vegas, just as they had abandoned most of the Eastern Seaboard after DC and New York were destroyed. As they approached the area, signs of human habitation grew fewer.

At the airfield, uniformed men were waiting for them—Air Force MPs.

Bennett stared. They were like visitors from another time, a time before Elysium. Clean, crisp uniforms, crew-cuts, every one of them freshly shaved. They saluted Sims and called him, "Mr. President."

They seemed more impressed by Bennett, though. "Good to have you on board, Major," said the captain. "If you'll come this way, I can show you the aircraft. It has a few special features."

The captain led him into a hangar. The plane inside looked ordinary enough, a Lear 25. Bennett looked it over. Well maintained. He hadn't seen anything that looked so new—much less an aircraft—in years.

"This is going to get us to Minot?" he asked.

"Check this out," the captain said with a grin, then shouted, "*Cloak her, Ace!*"

There was a shimmer, like a heat shimmer on a desert runway, and the Lear was gone. Vanished into thin air. The rolling staircase that had led to the plane's open door now stood alone in the hangar.

Bennett stared. He held out his arms in front of him and walked cautiously forward.

"Completely transparent to the electromagnetic spectrum," the captain said proudly. "Visible light, infrared, radar, everything. It's how the Elkies were able to get into our airspace without triggering the DEW line."

Bennett glanced back. "Elkies?"

The captain shrugged. "It's easier to say than 'Elysiumites.' Go ahead, touch it. It hasn't gone anywhere."

Bennett took another slow step, hand outstretched. He felt the cool metal of the skin of the aircraft. "Amazing," he breathed. He ran his hand along the smooth side, felt rivets. His eyes still insisted there was nothing there.

"That's good, Ace!" the captain shouted. *"Let the major see it."*

Another shimmer, and then the plane was back, as real and solid as it had ever been.

"How on Earth?" Bennett asked.

A chuckle. "The tech's not from Earth," he pointed out. "Go on in, we'll show you."

Bennett took the stairs cautiously, half expecting them to vanish out from under him. He stuck his head into the passenger compartment. The back third of the space, where the last few rows of seats would be, was taken up by a massive machine of some kind, an eye-warping construction that seemed to have no right angles or recognizable components. It looked like a steam engine caught in the process of turning itself inside out.

Beside the machine was a woman covered with glistening green scales.

Bennett pulled a pistol from his jacket pocket and trained it on the woman—the *creature*.

"What the Hell!" he cried.

The captain came up the stairs behind him. "Stand down, Major! Put your weapon away. That's Ace, she's your ECM tech."

"Ace?" Bennett asked suspiciously, not lowering his pistol.

"It's Axleothrus," the lizard-woman said. She was, incongruously, wearing a USMC sweatshirt. "But Ace will do."

Without moving her head, she swung her eyes to the captain. "You didn't tell him," she complained. "That was cruel."

"I wanted to see how he would react," the captain said, an amused note in his voice.

Axleothrus—or Ace—was not amused. "He could have shot me, you know."

Bennett didn't lower his pistol. Instead he moved it slightly to cover the captain as well. "You want to explain what's going on? Are you a traitor?"

"He's not a traitor," Ace said. "I am."

"An escaped slave," the captain amplified. "You see, the Elkies—the *original* Elkies—are slavers. The majority of the inhabitants of Elysium are slaves that the Caliphs captured from dozens of worlds."

Mr. Sims—*President* Sims—came up the stairs and closed the door behind him.

"Major, we're on a tight schedule, and I'd be obliged if you would get us moving. The charts are by your seat. Don't worry about calling the tower. There isn't one."

Bennett frowned, but holstered his pistol and moved to the cockpit. "Any more surprises in there?"

"There's a red button on the panel with a cover over it. Don't touch it," the president told him.

"Laser beam?"

"Self-destruct."

The cockpit was standard for a civilian aircraft. Bennett let his hands wander over the controls—avoiding the big red button—and then unfolded the charts. It had been years, but it all came back to him. He was itching to get into the sky again.

"Axleothrus has the concealment device running." Sims took the co-pilot's seat. "You are cleared for takeoff."

"I'm not entirely convinced of... any of this," Bennett said. He put his hands on the controls, but didn't start the engine.

"I know it's a lot to take in," Sims said sympathetically. "And I am asking you to take some of it on faith. But it has to be this way. If any hint of this leaks out, our one chance is gone."

"So what is our one chance?"

"Get us in the air and I'll tell you on the way."

Bennett studied the other man's face, then made his decision. Ten minutes later he was banking to avoid the thermals that rose up from the remains of Las Vegas.

"We knew next to nothing about Elysium when we first caught sight of it, back in '67, and it turns out that half of what we thought we knew was wrong. So I'll start there. You have to understand that we weren't prepared to believe what the scientists were seeing. Maybe—just maybe—if we had realized the true nature of the threat earlier we'd have been better prepared, but I don't think so. Even if we had put all the resources we were using on the moon missions into building defenses, they still would have been able to get through them—the technology gap is just too great.

"In any event, talking about what we should have done won't help us now. The fact is that Elysium was free-falling through the solar system for years. All the projections showed it following a hyperbolic orbit, making a close approach to the sun somewhere inside the orbit of Venus, and heading back out to interstellar space where it had come from. It wouldn't have come within a hundred million miles of Earth at any time. The idea of doing a flyby was discussed, but it just wasn't feasible.

"It wasn't until '71, when it passed the orbit of Mars, that it started maneuvering. And even then, of course, the idea was so incredible that we couldn't accept it. An entire planet, under power, being sailed around the universe like a ship? Of course we didn't believe it. But even if we had, if Werther and the others had managed to convince the President we were under attack, by then it was too late. Remember when the lights came on, all over the planet's surface? In the fall of '72, just before the saucers attacked. We thought those were cities, or bases, all turning on the power at once.

"They're not. They're holes in the planet's surface. You see, Elysium is hollow. What we see is just the outside, an outer shell about four hundred miles thick, and they live on the inside of the shell, with an artificial sun in the center."

Bennett grunted. "The Hollow Earth theory."

"Right," Sims went on. "Only on—or *in*—Elysium, it's not a theory. It's how they are able to travel interstellar space. They take their star system with them.

"That's something we learned from defectors, but I'm getting ahead of myself. You know all too well what happened during The Approach, the floods, the earthquakes, the tidal waves. And you saw action against the saucers. You're one of the few men who went head to head with them in the air and lived to tell about it."

"For all the good it did," Bennett said bitterly.

"It did more good than you know," Sims said. "You shot down two of them."

"*Two?* But I thought—"

"I know what you thought," Sims interrupted. "That one over Kansas, that everyone said got away? It went down in Colorado and we were able to have men there when it landed. We captured a pilot, alive."

"A prisoner," Bennett said softly.

"Our first," Sims agreed. "What we learned from him changed everything we thought we knew about the war.

"Of course, by then we had already lost so much. It was obvious that we were so far outmatched technologically that any conventional armed resistance was futile. It just got men killed. We had to go underground if we were to have any hope of fighting back.

"So we issued the Articles of Surrender and officially dissolved the government. Believe me when I tell you it was not an easy decision, and there was a lot of resistance to it on all levels. Some outright refusal to comply. Alabama and Georgia are still under military rule—they seem to be doing okay, so we don't interfere.

"Our first prisoner cooperated so thoroughly with our interrogators that at first we thought it had to be a trick. Once we learned his language—which it turns out, by the way, was an artificial language, designed for simplicity—he told us everything. Anything we asked, and he volunteered information that he thought might be helpful.

"You see, he was a conscript, with no love for his masters. They all are, all but a tiny percentage of the population. Those masters are the original inhabitants of Elysium. We're not sure exactly how old they are. Hundreds of thousands of years certainly, maybe millions. Long enough that the sun of their home system has gone dark. They had technology far in advance of ours even then. Technology advanced enough to hollow out their home planet and make it into a starship.

"We can't know where that was, and it doesn't really matter. But they came from the direction of the galactic core, which scientists speculate may have been capable of supporting life hundreds of millions of years before our own system. One thing is certain—the Caliphs of Elysium have been traveling the universe longer than the human race has existed. Much longer."

"With their slaves?" Bennett asked.

"Yes, and taking new ones along the way. That's what they do, going from world to world, looting and enslaving as they go. That's what they intend to do here—take everything they can from our world, water, air, anything they or their slaves can eat as food, and us. They have dozens of slave races from across the spiral arm and they intend for us to be the next."

"Wait," Bennett frowned, thinking it over. "You're telling me that in all these thousands of years they have been traveling that there hasn't be a revolution? A slave revolt? You say they're outnumbered. What keeps Axel..., Ace and all the others like her from putting the Caliphs up against the wall?"

"Their technology," Sims said confidently. "The other races are all from primitive worlds—well, we're primitive by their standards, but I gather none of the others were much above bows and arrows. The Caliphs seem like gods to them."

"But Ace can use their technology."

"She knows what buttons to push, but that's all. The Caliphs keep their secrets. None of their slaves know the theory behind the machines, just how to operate them."

Bennett chewed that over. It didn't seem right to him, but in the end he nodded. Sims had been studying the situation for years, he was just hearing about it now. "Okay, so what's the plan?"

"The XR-99. We have it operational and it's outfitted with an invisibility device like this plane. We adapted it to carry a missile."

"One missile?" Bennett asked, already guessing what was coming.

"One missile with a sixteen-megaton yield. A three stage thermonuclear device. We're going to vaporize the city of the Caliphs. This ends here, now. And you're going to deliver it."

"Sixteen megatons?" Bennett whistled. "What's the safe radius on that?"

"You don't want to be in the neighborhood when it goes off," Sims agreed. "And you won't be. The missile is shielded, too. All you have to do is get into the interior of Elysium and point it in the right direction. It's got a range of four hundred miles."

"Four hundred miles, huh."

"You'll be going in through an opening closer than that to the Caliphs' city. As soon as you reach the interior you can get a lock on the city, release the missile, and head back out. You'll be back above the surface before it goes off."

"Easy, huh?"

"We've made it as foolproof as possible. We only have one vehicle that can make the trip. It *has* to work."

Bennett sat in silence as they approached Minot, considering. The way Sims explained it the plan was foolproof, but he'd been a soldier and an aviator too long to trust foolproof plans. Still, it was probably the only chance the human race had to get free from Elysium.

"I'm in," he announced just before he began the descent to the airfield.

Sims gave a great sigh of relief. "I knew we could count on you, Major."

From the air, the base looked deserted.

Sims pointed out the runway for him to land on. At the end of it was a hangar with an open door. "Take her in there."

Things moved rapidly once they were on the ground. More clean-cut young men in uniform met them—none of them seeming to find anything odd about Ace exiting the plane with the President.

A young man with the three stars of a lieutenant general on his uniform bustled up with his hand extended. "Major Bennett, I am so pleased to see you."

Bennett saluted. "Sir."

The general looked embarrassed. "Oh, we don't stand on ceremony here," he said. "Let me show you to your quarters."

"I was promised a mission briefing," by reflex he added, "sir."

"In two hours," the general assured him. "Time for you to get a shower and something to eat."

Instead of going out one of the doors, the general led him to stairs leading down. It was clearly a new addition, with railings made from lengths of pipe welded together. The tunnel the stairs led to was round in cross-section, as straight as the barrel of a gun. Bennett reached to touch the wall. It was glassy smooth.

"A captured saucer weapon," the general explained. "It turns out it's a great digging tool. We've got miles of these tunnels, all through the town."

"What is this place?"

"The new capital. Welcome to the government of the United States of America in exile."

"In North Dakota?"

A wry grin. "Who would think to look for it here?"

They reached an intersection. The cross tunnel was bigger, and busy. Men and women in uniform hurried along their business, and among them other things.

There were lizard people who seemed to be of Ace's species, and great hulking shaggy creatures like Bigfoot. A group of a dozen little pig-faced creatures with orange skin hurried by, all in miniature air force uniforms.

Bennett stared.

"I assume the President explained the situation?"

"Yeah. These are all defectors?"

"More every day. The Caliphs set up processing centers to funnel air and water into containers for transport to Elysium. The workers sneak out and make their way here." A pause. "Those that escape the saucers, that is. Maybe half of them survive the journey. They think it's worth the risk."

"So much for your security, then. If they know where this place is, then the enemy must."

"There's an underground railroad. Only a handful know the exact destination."

"How many of the Caliphs are on Earth?"

The general seemed surprised by the question. "None. They never leave their city. The whole invasion is being carried out by slave labor."

"That doesn't make any sense."

"It does to them," the general shrugged. "Here's your room. We'll send someone to fetch you for the briefing."

There was a young woman in Navy whites in the room, which also contained a bed and a desk and two doors. She stood when he entered. "Welcome, Major. Can I get you anything?"

"I don't suppose anybody makes root beer any more?"

"There should be some in the commissary," she said brightly. "Anything to eat?"

"Cheese," he said. "I'd kill for a grilled cheese sandwich."

"I think we can do that," she smiled. "I'll be right back. Shower's through there, fresh uniforms in the closet."

The water in the shower was hot and plentiful. He scrubbed himself until his skin was pink and the water running off his body was clear. He wrapped a towel around himself and looked out into the other room.

Sitting on the desk was a covered dish and a paper cup. Root beer and a grilled cheese sandwich.

Heaven.

After he had eaten, he checked the closet and found a set of blues that fit him. He put it on and stretched out on the bed. Like many pilots, he'd developed the trick of napping when the chance presented itself. He closed his eyes and was instantly asleep.

He woke up just as quickly when the general tapped on the door. They had a long walk through the tunnels to a new door carved into the side of a lecture hall.

"State university," the general said softly. "Go on up to the stage, they're expecting you."

On the stage a table was set up. President Sims was seated there, and Ace the lizard woman, one of the Bigfoot aliens, and a man that Bennett recognized.

"Colonel West," Bennett said as he walked down the aisle to the front of the room. "Good to see you, sir."

"Good to see you, too, Bennett," the man said, standing. "I should tell you that I was instrumental in letting our new C-in-C know where to find you."

Bennett grinned. "I was wondering about that. So, you re-upped, too?"

"I never left. I was part of the task force that moved the capital here."

Bennett reached the table and took an empty chair, looking out over the empty seats of the lecture hall.

"It's just going to be us," President Sims said. "We use this room for the projector."

Bennett nodded, looked across the table to West. "You're convinced this will work?"

West nodded. "I'm convinced it *might*," he said. "We've tested the invisibility gadget in live exercises with the enemy. We know the XR-99 has the range to reach Elysium. And the warhead? Well, we know they work."

"Can we get the first slide?" President Sims called to someone outside the room. The wall behind them lit up with a projection. "You've done orbital flights in the XR-99. You'll do one orbit on this mission, then accelerate from Earth orbit to Elysium orbit and then decelerate. It's the same path their saucers take."

Bennett studied the diagram on the screen, then nodded. "Not that different from a moon shot."

"Essentially, yes, but Elysium is closer

and more massive."

"Where will the moon be, by the way?" Bennett asked. The moon had been captured by the gravity of the new planet and now wove a complex path between the two worlds.

"Nowhere near," West assured him. "That's one of the reasons we're doing this now."

"Next slide," Sims said.

It was a photograph of Elysium, taken by a powerful telescope. The surface was covered with brilliant pinpoints of light. One of them, near the south pole, was circled in red.

"This is your point of entry."

"Hold up," Bennett said. "You expect me to be able to recognize the right opening out of, what, a couple of hundred? With no landmarks?"

"I'll guide you," said Ace.

Bennett looked over at her. "You'll guide me?"

"I was trained as a navigator. There are one hundred eighty-six entrances to the interior, and the one we want is number fifty-three."

"You can recognize the right one?" Bennett peered at the picture projected on the screen. "Are they labeled?"

Ace nodded. "After a fashion. The pattern is incised on the rim of the opening."

"We've tested her," West said. "Ace can identify each entrance from a photograph. It's how we mapped the interior."

Bennett looked over at Ace, appraisingly, then shrugged. "Okay, so we get inside. What then?"

The next slide was a drawing, not a photograph. It showed a cluster of towers surrounded by cultivated fields.

"According to our informants—and they all said this, independently—the city of the Caliphs is the only large collection of structures within the sphere. Evidently they like to look down on their subjects," Sims said. "The missile is equipped with optical sensor and pre-programmed to lock in visually. All you have to do is show it the city and release the trigger. It will do the rest."

"And we're sure this will work?" Bennett asked. He looked to West, then Sims, then settled his gaze on Ace. "What are your people going to do when these Caliphs of yours are gone?"

She shook her head. "I do not know. We have lived under their rule for so long. But they will not continue to make war against your people. There would be no point to it."

Slowly Bennett nodded. "Okay," he said. "I'll drop your damned bomb. When do we do it?"

"At dawn," West said. "The conditions will be best then."

"You'd better get some sleep," Sims added. "It's going to be a busy day."

In the early morning darkness, Bennett sat in the cockpit of the XR-99, someplace that yesterday he'd never dreamed of being again. His hands reached for the proper switches, his eyes scanned the dials and readouts, without conscious input from his brain. Hours of practice, first in the simulator, and later in live flights, made his actions automatic. He ran through the preflight checklist like a virtuoso playing a well-loved tune on a piano.

Beside him Ace went through her own adjustments on the incomprehensible machinery that had been installed in place of the copilot's station. She finished her preparations and there was the slightest shimmer through the windscreen. "We are ready," she said simply.

Bennett nodded. He, too, was ready. He felt the old icy calm, the excitement felt only as a quickening of his pulse and heartbeat, buried under the discipline of years spent controlling the monstrous engines of rocket planes. This was his job—what he had been born to do.

They couldn't risk radio communications, so he waved through the window at the ground crew. One of them gave an exaggerated nod and waved to the men on the door to the hangar. Slowly they pushed it open.

Bennett watched the door open and then the crew scatter back against the walls of the hangar.

He eased back on the throttle.

The XR-99 was a dual propulsion vehicle. From takeoff to the upper limits of the atmosphere it would function as a conventional jet. At fifty miles above ground level, when the air was too thin for wings to be of any use, he would fire the rockets and become a space ship.

He eased onto the runway and made a slow turn—then punched the engine and they were airborne. The stall speed of the bird was so high and the runway so short that he needed a drastic acceleration to get into the air.

Watching the ground plummet away below him was the most natural feeling in the world.

After years of being forced to crawl along the ground, he was finally coming home.

Still accelerating, he nosed up and punched a hole through the sky, clawing for space.

He had company in the sky, those strange disk-shaped craft of the invaders, their motive power still unknown. He watched them carefully, but could see no indication that they were aware of his presence. He knew all too well how deadly they were in a dogfight, more maneuverable than any jet and packing weapons of devastating power.

The sky overhead, which had just been lightening to blue when he took off, was already growing dark as the atmosphere above him grew thin. The needle on the airspeed indicator crept towards Mach 3.

He glanced over at Ace. Her eyes were wide and her hands gripped the arms of the seat tightly. He noticed with some amusement that her fingers were tipped with small claws.

"Are you okay?" he asked.

She nodded, but didn't try to speak.

"Hang on," he told her, grinning. "This is the fun part."

Bennett pulled down the lever to engage the rockets.

The acceleration was much smoother than when they'd left the runway, but also stronger. It peaked at six G's, then eased off. When he could move his head, he risked a glance at Ace again. She seemed to be still conscious.

Good. He turned his attention back to his instruments.

They were out of the blue and into the black, leaving behind the region of aerodynamics for the simpler and deadlier kingdom of physics. Ahead of them was Elysium.

Ace had recovered enough to speak. "Head to the lower right," she said.

Bennett obediently let the nose of the craft drift in that direction.

"More," she said, "A little lower—*that one!* The one dead ahead of us now."

Bennett held the course to keep the entrance she'd indicated in the center of the windscreen.

The saucers around him, he noticed, were heading to other destinations. Assuming this was entrance fifty-three, he had the approach to himself.

Elysium grew in his forward view, from an object in a starry sky to a landscape. What had been a pinprick of light became a lighted disk, then a tunnel leading into the heart of the world. He felt the buffeting of atmosphere—thin, cold, nothing a man could breath, but enough for his wings to engage.

His climb into the heavens had become a descent, and he pushed the lever that shut down the rocket engine and was once again piloting an aircraft.

Down, down, down and then he was in the tunnel, the outer surface of the world flashing by him. The tunnel was miles across, the scale impossible for the mind to grasp. It ran, as geometric as an arrow's flight, straight down.

The air thickened around him and he felt the distant rattle of a sonic boom. In the misty distance he could see a brighter light. The inside of the globe that was the true surface of Elysium.

Then something horrible happened.

SUBMIT

SUBMIT

SUBMIT

The voice echoed in Bennett's mind, alien, impossibly strong. Although soundless, the voice brought a feeling of pressure, like the unbearable roar of jet engines on a flight deck.

SUBMIT

SUBMIT

SUBMIT

There was a staggering pain in his head and his vision clouded. Beside him he saw Ace moving mechanically, her hands busy on the controls of the alien mechanism. Through the roar in his own head he could half hear the instructions she was being given to shut down the concealment device.

Bennett shook his head, trying to clear out that horrible echoing voice, the XR-99 veering dangerously close to the wall. The inner opening of the tunnel was drawing closer, and the voice in his head grew even louder. To his horror, he saw saucers moving across the opening, dropping down to engage.

They could see him now.

SUBMIT

SUBMIT

SUBMIT

Bennett gritted his teeth and focused all

his will on controlling the aircraft. He had no conventional weapons, just the city-buster missile. He couldn't fight—he would have to outfly them.

He saw the bluish light gathering around the saucers as they charged their killing beams. He threw the XR-99 into a spin, diving first one way then the other, missing the walls of the tunnel by inches as he tried to dodge the saucer's beams.

SUBMIT

SUBMIT

SUBMIT

Then the end of the tunnel flashed past him and he was out into the light of the artificial sun at the center of this mad inside-out world. Desperately he searched for the city of the Caliphs.

Ace attacked him, her clawed hands lashing at his face, her so-human face contorted in a rictus of fury. Bennett took one hand off the control stick to push her away, making the craft skew in the air wildly.

One of the pursuing saucer's beams clipped his wing, carving the tip. He jerked the stick to swing away from it.

There! He glimpsed the city of towers. Ignoring everything else, he maneuvered to put it in the center of his view and thumbed off the safety of the missile, holding the position until the words WEAPON LOCK ACQUIRED appeared on his panel.

Then he let it fly.

He banked away with one hand on the control, fighting off Ace with the other. The saucers reversed direction instantly to follow. He took the XR-99 closer to the inside surface of the world, down, or out, or whatever direction it was in this crazy place. Away from the city all he could see was cultivated fields, rows of alien crops mixed with occasional low buildings like barns. He could not spot any of the tunnels to the surface.

He needed to find another exit, some way out of here before—

He didn't make it.

Light flared, even the reflection from the ground flashbulb bright in the cockpit. His panels all went dead and the engine grew silent. Beside him Ace screamed and thrashed like she was being electrocuted, then went limp.

The voice in his head was gone.

The ground was coming up fast and he wrestled the control stick, tried to turn the crash into a landing. He was only half successful and they hit hard, digging a furrow through the crops.

When they finally came to rest, he sat for a long moment, catching his breath.

"I am so sorry, Major Bennett."

Ace was looking around blinking as if she'd just woken up.

"You couldn't help it," Bennett assured her. He understood it now, why the slaves had never rebelled, why they had defected in such numbers when they were on Earth and out of range of the Caliphs' mental control.

He unbuckled his crash harness, then leaned over to help Ace with hers.

"Come on," he said. "Let's figure out where we are."

He got up and opened the cockpit door. The sun was directly overhead, bright and warm. Of course. It would never move here.

He stepped out. He seemed to be standing in a valley with hills on all sides. Around him the ground rose and rose until it was lost in the distance. He looked up. In the distance were drifting silver specks.

"Can you drive one of those saucers?" Bennett asked Ace as she climbed out to join him.

"No."

"Well, let's find someone who can and see if I can get a ride home." He reached to brush his hand along the wing of the XR-99. She'd been a good ship, but she'd never fly again.

Ace pointed. "There's a transfer station. They'll have vessels there."

"Lead on," Bennett said, and he followed the alien girl across the alien landscape.

Misha Burnett has been published in Cirsova Magazine since its first issue. He has several collections out through Cirsova Publishing, including Endless Summer, An Atlas of Bad Roads, Small Worlds, Bad Dreams and Broken Hearts, *and* Dracoheim Confidential, *all of which are available on Amazon.*

A Bottle of Chamberlin

By MARK MELLON

A collector of Napoleonic memorabilia acquires a bottle from the Emperor's private stock... Sealed within is an imp who claims to have been his personal advisor!

Humid heat lay heavy on the city. *Habaneros* yearned for a cool northern breeze from the sea. Even in the grand hall with its fifty-foot ceiling, the air was still oppressive and immobile, weighing on Don Adriano and Mercedes. Juana poured café au lait for them. In the street outside, vendors called their wares.

"*Pan soave, pan soave*, soft bread, soft bread."

"When will you finish the audit?"

"Possibly today, definitely tomorrow, Mercedes. Why are you worried about the audit?"

"I need to know how much you'll net this year to plan for Sebastiano's law school graduation party and Pepita's trip to Miami to buy her trousseau."

Juana served fried eggs and sliced mango and pineapple. Don Adriano ate buttered soft bread.

"I can cover that and any other expenses that might arise."

"Not if you keep wasting money on silly Napoleonic nonsense."

Don Adriano sighed. "There's nothing absurd about having the finest collection of Napoleana in the Western Hemisphere. I regularly receive begging letters from European and American collectors offering princely sums for particular items."

"So, sell if they want these things so badly. What does Napoleon have to do with Cuba, anyway, Adriano? These things belong in Europe where they came from."

He ate more bread. "The greatest man in human history belongs to the whole world. His life and exploits have resonance and application to every situation."

"Oh, such nonsense, Adriano."

He kissed her and hustled up the stairs with his usual Napoleonic dash. Havana spread before him from an open window, narrow, ancient streets crowded around a cathedral's spire, the deep blue ocean in the background, a magnificent prospect he ignored with familiar indifference. In his library on the topmost floor, its glass-fronted shelves crammed with priceless memoirs and histories, Don Adriano went over accounts with two colorless, middle-aged men in uncomfortable three-piece American business suits.

They had almost finished reviewing production reports for Batey No. 3 when Juana knocked and entered.

"What is it, girl? Can't you see I'm

busy?"

"*Si*, Don Adriano, but the Frenchman is here. You told me to let you know."

"So I did. Well done, Juana. Show him up immediately. Gentlemen, we'll finish this at a later date. I'm sure you understand."

The accountants shown out without ceremony, Don Adriano rubbed his hands, eager as a child before Christmas to see what his personal factor had brought back from Europe. Constance Berthier was a tall, thin young man in a white linen suit with a straw boater. He claimed descent from Napoleon's chief of staff, giving him access to other distinguished families with desirable items. Whatever his claim's truth, he was a reliable source, Don Adriano's main provider. They embraced and kissed cheeks in the French manner.

"Have a seat, *mon cher*. Let me give you a cigar."

"Always glad to smoke prime Cuban tobacco, Don Adriano."

They puffed mellow cigars. Don Adriano poured Napoleon brandy. They settled into comfortable armchairs. It was cool in the shadowy library.

"Have you got something choice, Constance?"

"Indeed, Don Adriano. Some very fine artifacts."

He reached into a large leather briefcase and pulled out a manila folder. "A letter dated November 3rd, 1802, from Bonaparte to Josephine. You'll enjoy this; he gets quite racy. Wear cotton gloves when you read it, the acid from your fingers will destroy the paper."

Don Adriano set the folder aside with loving care. "Very good, excellent. What else?"

Berthier took out a jewel box and opened the lid. A small, dark brown lump lay on the velvet.

"The great general's tooth, pulled from the dead body by his attending physician as a souvenir."

"A bit morbid, but still an interesting addition. I assume you saved the best for last."

Berthier nodded. He extracted a black glass bottle with ritual flair, plainly antique by its odd size and shape, the neck sealed with lead foil.

"Chambertin from Bonaparte's own cellar. See the imperial seal. He took this with him to St. Helena. It's been handed down for generations. Now it's yours, Don Adriano."

Smiling, Don Adriano held the bottle to the light. The interior was opaque. Although unopened, no liquid sloshed around inside.

"Any wine turned to dust long ago," Berthier said.

"I'll keep it on my desk where all can see. You've done well, *mon cher*. What do I owe you?"

Rather than complain about the sum Berthier named, Don Adriano instead cheerfully wrote out a draft on the National City Bank of New York's Havana branch. Intent upon roistering with his newfound gains, Berthier took his leave. Don Adriano sat at his desk. With a collector's keen pleasure, he watched the late morning sunlight caress the wine bottle's sloping shoulders.

Late that night, while everyone else slept, even the night porter, huddled on the marble floor before the main doors, Don Adriano sat at his desk in the library in his brocade dressing gown, a glass of cognac in a snifter, a lit cohiba in his mouth. He wrote in his diary.

Mounted Juana again tonight. She seems to be losing enthusiasm. I can always send her back to the batey where I found her. Mercedes continues to nag, sure I'll leave her and the children unprovided for. I should do it just to spite her, the old—

He paused and cocked his head, fountain pen in hand. Had he heard something just now? A passing streetcar's clatter blotted out all other sound. He resumed writing his diary.

—hag. This is all just letting off steam though. How would it look for a rich sugar magnate not to provide for his family? I'm just stuck with…

He stopped again.

There it was, a definite sound, faint, but distinct scratching from nearby. Don Adriano set his cigar down on an ashtray and listened keenly. The noise came from inside the bottle.

"*Dios Mio*, my God!" he exclaimed.

He picked up the bottle. The scratching became louder and more frequent, as if whatever was trapped inside sensed his interest. Don Adriano opened his penknife. His heart pounded as he scraped at the lead seal. Embossed with the Napoleonic coat of arms, the soft lead peeled away. He pulled the cork only to have it crumble to dust in his hand.

"*Oui, comme ca*, yes, like that. Set the bottle on its side," a small voice cried in French from the open mouth.

Unable to believe his ears, but also unable to disobey, as if compelled in a dream, Don Adriano put the bottle down on the desk. To his utter amazement, a tiny figure crawled out. Slim as a pencil, no bigger than a mouse, he wore the blue uniform with red facings of a colonel in the Imperial Guard. He dropped his cocked hat and hopped after it, landing neatly on the desk with both booted feet.

Don Adriano stared in disbelief. The little man picked up his cocked hat and slapped at the red dust that caked his uniform. His minute features were regular and handsome, topped with thick, curling dark hair. He gave a courtly bow.

"How good to breathe fresh air again. I owe you gratitude, *monsieur*, for releasing me."

Don Adriano fumbled with his robe's silken sash. "Yes, but who in God's name are you, *petit homme*, little man?"

He donned his bicorne, put his hands on his hips, and drew himself to his full diminutive height. "Miles Parvus, the imp of war, at your service, *monsieur*, just as I served my Emperor, the one the Grand Army called *Le Tondu*, the Shorn One."

"This can't be real. I must be hallucinating or having a fever."

"*Calme-toi, mon cher*, calm down, my dear. I can easily prove I'm no chimera.

Give me a drop of brandy. I have a hundred and ten year thirst to slake."

He held out a pewter cup. Don Adriano poured out a few drops from his glass.

"And now pull some tobacco from that cigar of yours."

The imp stuffed the tobacco into a curved pipe he produced out of nowhere like the cup and lit with snorts of flame from his nostrils. He puffed deeply, drank off the brandy, and held out his cup for more.

"Are you satisfied I'm real now?"

"Yes, you must be. So you really knew the great Napoleon?"

The imp sat on a ledger book and crossed his cavalry booted legs. "Why, I was at every battle from Toulon to Waterloo. I suggested the winning strategies at Austerlitz and Jena. He only lost when he failed to heed me."

"How did you end up stuck in that bottle?"

"The Emperor's enemies trapped me like a djinn from the Thousand and One Nights so I couldn't provide my loyal counsel. I'd have helped him escape from St. Helena, returned him to France, shown him how to avoid the mistakes he made during the Hundred Days."

"This is marvelous, amazing. With your help, I can write Bonaparte's true history, correct misconceptions people have about him, show him in his true glorious colors."

"A fine and noble mission as long as you keep alcohol and tobacco handy."

"Done. What a remarkable turn of events."

"You handled the surprise well. That's a quality Bonaparte had."

Enraptured, Don Adriano was locked in conversation with the imp until the wee hours of the morning when sheer exhaustion forced him to seek sleep. "You'll be here when I return, I hope?"

The imp pulled off his boots and got into the crude camp bed he'd made from crumpled waste paper. "Where else would I go, *mon cher*? I'm here to serve you just as I did the Emperor before."

Everyone puzzled over the change that came over Don Adriano. Shut up in his library, he had his meals sent up and spent days writing feverishly until hundreds of paper sheets were filled. Secretaries were hired to transcribe the pages. Typewriters' constant clatter shattered the household's usual tranquil atmosphere. Some like Juana were glad to have the *patron* out of their hair. Others wondered what had come over him.

"I mean, he's always had this obsession about Napoleon, but now it's a positive mania. I'm so desperate over what I should do, I've even thought about having him see a psychiatrist even though that means our family's reputation will be destroyed."

"Don't be absurd, Mercedes," replied Inez, Don Adriano's sister. "I'll drum sense into that wool gathering head of his."

"He refuses to see anyone."

Inez snorted. "He'll see me after I tell him about the trouble at Batey Number Four."

As determined in her way as her brother, Inez hustled up the stairs.

"I pointed out to the Emperor that if we moved our forces from the Preutzen Heights, the enemy would move forward to take the higher ground, leaving them unprepared for an assault from the right flank—"

Loud, insistent knocks on the door interrupted Miles Parvus. An imperious voice cried out.

"Adriano. Let me in. I need to talk to you about family business. This is urgent. Stop your nonsense and open the door."

Don Adriano waved frantically for the imp to hide. Cool and collected as always, Miles Parvus had already concealed himself in the French chateau style doll's house Don Adriano had recently acquired for him. He unlocked the door. Inez stormed in, dark eyes lively with indignation.

"So, it's just as Mercedes says. In your robe, not even dressed although it's almost noon, and letting our business go completely to hell. What on earth are you up to, Adriano?"

"That's no way to talk to the head of the family, Inez. I'll have you know I'm engaged on a very important historical work, the definitive history of Napoleon's military campaigns. This will set the world on its heels."

Inez scowled. "You're not a historian, Adriano. You're a sugar planter and you need to look after the business. Things have gone completely to hell at Batey Number Four. The blacks are running wild there, setting their pigs and goats into our fields to strip the cane leaves. They'll eat up this season's crop if you don't do something about it."

"If the leaves get stripped off, all the better. The stalks are all we want."

"Spare me your excuses. Those leeches have been hanging around the batey for decades, ever since our father kicked them off the plantation. It's like they think we owe them a living. Something needs to be done. If you were half the man our father was, you'd act instead of wasting time writing some ridiculous book no one cares about."

"You're ignorant and indifferent to history, like all women. I'll handle the minor nuisance of those black *guajiros* in my own good time, Inez. Now if you don't mind, I must return to my literary endeavors."

"Hmmph. Return to wasting time. You were always a dreamer, completely impractical with this ridiculous Napoleon fetish of yours. What's this, a doll's house? You really are returning to your childhood, Adriano."

Don Adriano slammed a heavy book onto the desk. "Enough. Get out, you harrying shrew. Depart my library!"

Inez gave her brother a filthy look, but nonetheless left. Cursing under his breath, Don Adriano poured himself three fingers of rum.

"I'd like some myself, *mon cher.*"

He poured rum into the imp's cup. The imp drank with gusto. "This is such delicious stuff you make here. I must say, *monsieur*, you handled that impertinent woman masterfully, just as Bonaparte himself would have done."

Don Adriano smiled. "That's kind of you to say, *mon cher*, but Inez has a point, much as I hate to admit it. Those freed blacks are a pest. Their animals roam my fields, and they use my roads to haul their crops into the batey for sale."

"Who took it into his head to free them in the first place? Aren't slaves necessary for a civilized society?"

Don Adriano shook his head regretfully. "Times have changed, *mon petit ami*. The King of Spain abolished slavery here long ago. My father turned out the blacks from his plantations and hired Chinese laborers instead who work almost as cheaply as slaves. The blacks live at the plantations' outskirts, raising pigs and plantains. They've always caused trouble, but now things are getting seriously out of hand."

He paced the floor, rapidly puffing his cigar. "I could ask the authorities to do something, but they'd just temporize like they always do, find some excuse to ignore them."

"Then why not take action yourself, like the Emperor would?"

Don Adriano faced the imp, puffing contentedly on his pipe. "How?"

"You've bragged of your wealth, American dollars deposited in bank accounts. Take that money and raise your own company, well-mounted and armed, hardened mercenaries ready to do the necessary tasks, burning the blacks' huts, hanging their principal leaders, killing their livestock. And with you at their head, the commander?"

Don Adriano unconsciously stood straighter. He stuck out his chest, a curious light dancing in his brown eyes. "You mean lead my own campaign?"

Miles Parvus capered in delight. "Yes. You apprehend my meaning exactly, just as quickly as the Emperor would have done. Bonaparte always ruthlessly stamped out any resistance from the peasantry. Here's your chance to be a man of action, *mon cher*. I know you're interested in politics. Bonaparte's example tells you that everyone respects a conqueror. All bow before the man on horseback."

Don Adriano slammed his fist on the desk so hard it ached for the rest of the day. "*Por Dios*, by God, you're right, Miles Parvus. I'll do it!"

On the proudest day of his life, dashing in a broad-brimmed hat, mounted on a fine black mare at the head of a column of heavily armed cavalry, Don Adriano rode into the jungle that bordered his sugar cane plantation, intent upon the destruction of the local freed blacks' village. A hundred men rode behind him, some Cuban, mostly American, many Southerners and veterans of the Great War, accustomed to oppression and violence. Unknown to them, Miles Parvus rode with Don Adriano, concealed in his left saddlebag to give advice if needed.

They rode down a dirt track through steep, heavily forested hills. Green, impenetrable jungle flanked the track, a dense screen of aguacatillo, ocuje, jocuma, and macurije trees, topped by towering royal palms that gently swayed with the breeze. Otero the black *guajiro* guide rode at the column's head, ready like Judas to sell his own people out for a patch of land. He threw up his hand to signal a halt.

Well-disciplined, accustomed to riding in a body, the men reined in their horses. Don Adriano rode ahead to reconnoiter with Otero and his second in command, Lt. Keeley, a hard-bitten, ex-US Marine. They came to a creek.

"The village is past the water," Otero said. "We can watch from that hill without being seen."

They urged their horses up a steep path to the hilltop. A circle of thatched roof bohios stood on the creek's opposite bank. No one stirred outside in the heat. The village was quiet, no smoke even from cook fires.

"Where are they?" Keeley asked.

"Siesta," Otero said, his rural Cuban accent almost unintelligible. "They all sleep. Good time to ambush."

Keeley's sunburned face screwed into a mass of wrinkles. "Something's not right. Let's send in a squad to reconnoiter before we commit all our forces. We need to know what we're up against."

Don Adriano nodded at this expert advice, but a small voice called from the saddlebag, inaudible to the others over macaws' loud cries. "Don't heed that coward. They're only blacks and peasants. What resistance can they offer? Be brave like Napoleon. Lead the charge into the village and put everything to the torch!"

"No, we'll just lose the element of surprise that way," Don Adriano said. "We'll charge with all our forces, rout any hostile elements, and destroy the enemy's stronghold in detail. Let's go back to the men."

"No disrespect, *Señor Comandante,* but I don't recommend—"

"I've made my decision, Lieutenant. It's your business now to follow my orders, not make recommendations."

"Yes, sir."

They rejoined the men. Keyed up with anticipation, they drew their sabers, eager to race into the village and fling themselves into an orgy of rapine and destruction. Don Adriano's heart raced wildly. He knew now how Bonaparte must have felt just before a great battle, the moment when his carefully laid plans fell into place and victory was achieved.

"Sound the charge," he shouted.

The bugler played strident notes. Screaming and yelling, they briskly trotted down the track, across the shallow creek, and into the village. Don Adriano rode at their head, reins in his left hand, Colt .45 automatic in his right.

"No prisoners," he shouted. "Spare nothing."

Men hacked at thatched roofs with sabers, but nobody ran out to defend their homes. The village was apparently empty, the inhabitants having fled into the forest. Keeley rode up to Don Adriano, bad teeth bared by his scowl.

"They knew we were coming. Someone informed on us. Where's Otero?"

There was no sign of the *guajiro.* In the confusion, he'd taken leave of the company. Sweat streamed down Don Adriano's face, stinging his eyes.

"This is a trap," Keeley barked. "We need to retrea—"

A blast from a volley of concealed shotguns drowned him out. Men and horses fell bleeding. Wild screams erupted from the jungle, Mandingo war cries. Arrows and spears shot forth from the greenery. Men fired blindly back, but the projectiles' steady rain nonetheless took a heavy toll.

The only hope was escape. Keeley grabbed the reins of Don Adriano's horse and put spurs to his own. Both mounts galloped at full speed. At the village's outskirts, a rope was suddenly hoisted. With no way to halt, the horses ran full tilt into the rope, stumbling badly. Both men were thrown to the ground. Keeley lay still, dead with a broken neck.

Don Adriano scrambled to his feet. An arrow landed in his left shoulder. He moaned and ran into the forest, tears streaming down his face, unable to comprehend how things had gone so very badly wrong.

Faced with determined resistance instead of the helpless, unaware victims they anticipated, the survivors fled, turned tail and shamefully ran without even the pretense of an organized military retreat. Stragglers and the wounded were left to the enemy's mercy.

Panting loudly, Don Adriano hid behind a large dead tree. He tried to pull out the arrow, but it hurt too much. Mosquitoes eagerly sucked his blood, leaving his face covered with bites. Cries of triumph came from the nearby village.

"What a fool you've made of yourself,

Don Adriano."

He looked all around him. Miles Parvus flew from the jungle, mounted on a huge green cockroach's back, wings busily fluttering. He grinned wildly, laughed outright.

"You took my advice like Bonaparte. When I told him to invade Russia, he went ahead just like you charged into the village. You ruined yourself like the Corsican fool."

He flew just above Don Adriano's head. "I released you from your prison, sheltered and patronized you, and you betrayed me. Why?"

"For the same reason I betrayed Bonaparte," Miles Parvus cried. "I'm the imp of war. I exist to make trouble and misery for pathetic humans like you. That's why Bonaparte trapped me in the bottle. Just before he died, he imprisoned me with his last, most brilliant gambit, daring me to jump inside and drink his last Chambertin. There I rotted for over a century, waiting for a fool like you to come along and release me."

Don Adriano tried to knock the imp down with his good arm, but he buzzed out of reach. "Now I'm free to range the whole wide world, to stir up war wherever I go until your whole cursed breed drowns in your own blood. Farewell, Don Adriano. Run as fast as you can. You might reach the batey and live. Run, you fat, silly fool!"

The cockroach flew away. Don Adriano heard voices nearby. He ran further into the jungle, wounded shoulder throbbing with pain.

Luis and Fidel galloped their horses through their father's fields. Although still only boys, the brothers rode well, Fidel particularly. He halted the horse near a pond, dismounted, and watched alligators sun themselves on the opposite bank. In a few days, he had to return to school in Santiago. Fidel sighed.

"*Oye*, hey, young Fidel Castro," a small voice cried.

Fidel looked down. To his amazement, a tiny man stood under a flowering duranta shrub, clad in crudely woven shorts and a shirt, a thatched straw *guajiro* hat jauntily perched on his head.

"How would you like to be a big man, the most important one in Cuba, if not Latin America?"

Fidel nodded his head. "Yes, I've always wanted to be important."

"I can tell you how to do it, just like I did for Napoleon. Listen closely..."

Mark Mellon writes two-fisted, hardboiled, blood and guts pulp fiction with four novels and over a hundred stories published. His novel Scoundrel! The Civil War Misadventures Of An Unrepentant Rogue, *is represented by Anthony Flacco and Jen Newens of Martin Literary Management.*

Tongue of Ash

By JOSEPH W. KNOWLES

An earthquake precedes a series of strange occurrences, inexplicable deaths, and the appearance of an antediluvian artifact that Sheriff Moultrie struggles to solve!

Sheriff C.R. Moultrie had heard tell of such things, but until that bright Sunday morning when the shelves in his office began to rattle and the tin of coffee wobbled to the edge of its perch and tumbled to the floor, waking him and spilling some of its contents on his new rolltop desk, he had never experienced an earthquake. It was over in a matter of a few seconds, but the native Tennessean reflexively ran outside, pulling up his suspenders as he went, to survey the surroundings.

To his eyes almost nothing seemed amiss. The sign that marked the general store hung loosely from a single nail; one or two townspeople had also stepped out onto the town's main street. Otherwise, the little town seemed just as sleepy as ever. Still, the sheriff thought, perhaps the earthquake had been worse in some other parts of his bailiwick. Though he'd agreed to an invitation to church that morning—and that from the reverend himself—his duty as the town's only lawman seemed to compel him to saddle up his horse and have a look around.

With only a matter of nine months under his belt as the sheriff in Bracton, it still felt a little too soon to say he was "making his usual rounds." Yet off he rode to the east, plotting the circuitous route he would follow to check up on some of the outlying properties, and ending up at the Daniels ranch before heading back to the newly-framed building that doubled as the town jail and his own meager residence.

His reconnaissance was a rather uneventful affair until he crested the gentle rise that rimmed the dried-up lakebed that Bracton folks called "Old Lake Carter." The sheriff saw the vultures swirling above, the signal that something dead or dying lay ahead. It could be anything, of course, but the place lay close enough to the Daniels place that Moultrie thought he ought to take a look—if for no other reason than to not allow Daniels to get one over on him. One of the first things he had learned after putting on the badge was that Cyrus Daniels was as complete a busybody as any idle spinster one might ever chance to encounter.

What the sheriff found, however, was no mere critter or even a stray head of cattle. The sheriff's jaw gaped as he came upon a man's body. The war had forced him to look at more dead bodies than anyone should ever have to see, but this one was different. Those differences somehow made the sight inexplicably terrible. He must have died quite recently, for his clothes bore very little dust; scavenging animals had yet to leave any ravenous signs of their presence. There was no blood, yet that would not be unusual if the man had succumbed to dehydration. Despite the lack of blood, when the sheriff got closer, he could see that there was a wound. A zigzag scar ran from ear to ear extending the man's mouth across the width of his skull. Below, a second jagged tear had opened the man's throat. But not a drop of blood was to be seen. The ghastly lacerations were a stark contrast to the man's facial expression which could be described as nothing but serene. Stepping closer, Sheriff Moultrie saw that the man's eyes were not only peacefully closed, but also covered in a thin layer of fine, white dust. The same dust powdered the edges of what remained of the dead man's lips.

Just as he was about to start checking the man's pockets, the sheriff thought he heard a noise. He turned to his left, seeking the source of the strange sound, one he could not quite describe, but he saw nothing at first. Scanning the area, he thought he could make out a faint trail of white dust leading away from the body. Supposing it to be the only available clue, he followed it.

A stone's throw away, the powdery track ended in a small depression, no more than a few feet wide. In the middle, stark against the surrounding earth, the sheriff spied a small, black object. It was cylindrical and about as long as a man's forearm. He picked it up and turned it in his hands; it was heavy for its size and was carved with some kind of markings. It must have been writing, Moultrie thought—given the repeated patterns and the regular spacing—but other than that, all he could say for sure was that it was unlike any language he had ever seen.

The sensation of the strange noise from before returned, yet the sheriff seemed to feel it more than hear it. Returning to his horse, he stowed the object in his saddlebag, noticing for the first time that the thing was cool to the touch. He pushed the thought to the back of his mind, focusing instead on whom he could deputize to help him collect the unfortunate man's corpse.

Writing was the sheriff's least favorite part of the job so far, but it had to be done—that much had been made clear to him when he took the job. If he wanted to keep the post when the office became an elected one, he knew better than to shirk anything that the townspeople saw as a duty.

None of that, however, made it any easier to craft a report on the death of the still-unidentified man he had found that morning. A gunshot wound wouldn't have explained the rest of the scene, but at least it would have given Moultrie something believable to write under "Cause of Death." The doctor had come quickly once the body had been conveyed back to the jail, but even his medical expertise seemed unable to unravel the mystery. The doctor's meticulous examination of the disrobed body revealed no snake bites or the telltale marks of any other such venomous creature. The powder, he said, gave no indication of being any kind of poison—at least none such as he could identify in Bracton with his basic tools.

"Maybe at one of the medical colleges back East," he said, shrugging as he packed up his bag and stood to leave.

"Thanks anyway, Doc," Moultrie replied.

As much as he hated the idea, it looked like "Unknown" might be the best he could do for the report. The sheriff had just replaced the sheet that covered the man's body when there was a gentle knock behind him.

"Forget something, Doc?" Moultrie asked without turning.

"Pardon the intrusion please, Sheriff."

He recognized the voice with no trouble and turned slowly to see the gaunt figure of Silas Kaine, the town's only preacher, standing in the doorway.

"I'd say you're a few hours' late for last rites, Reverend."

"That's the Roman Catholics, Sheriff," he said with half a smile. "But I didn't come about the body."

"Oh? Then . . . what brings you by?"

"The artifact. I was hoping to see it."

Moultrie was sorely tempted to ask "What artifact?" or "How do you know about that?" but he knew it would be pointless. Only a handful of people knew anything about his morning's enigmatic discoveries, but in a small town like Bracton, almost anything counted as newsworthy and the folks seemed to take gossip as the local pastime.

"Of course, if you think it's some kind of evidence in . . . well, this other case . . ." The preacher paused, cutting his eyes toward the lifeless husk and its improvised death shroud. "Then I suppose you can't very well let me see it."

The proximity of the body and the strange cylinder was suspicious, but the sheriff was forced to admit that at that point the existence of a connection between the two could be no more than a hunch. He could see no compelling reason to deny the preacher a look; the thing would remain in the jail and maybe when rumors inevitably began to fly, folks would pester the preacher for details, rather than himself.

They moved one room over, where the sheriff retrieved the artifact from one of his lockboxes. The lawman sat in silence as the holy man turned the dark object over in his hands, held it up to the light that streamed through the barred window, and held it close to his face to examine its markings.

"Well?" the sheriff said after some time. "Is your curiosity satisfied?"

He realized it was a poor choice of words as soon as they crossed his lips. Maybe Kaine really *did* only want a juicy tale to tell, but it would do no good to throw the accusation out that way.

Silas Kaine raised an eyebrow slightly, but seemed to take no further notice of the comment. "Well, Sheriff, this much I can say for sure: no Indian nor no white man crafted this. This is just as foreign to these lands as you or I."

"Then you know the markings? What do they—"

"No. This reaches back to Babylon . . . farther even, to Nimrod and the tower."

Moultrie might not have darkened the

door of Kaine's run-down chapel, but he'd had enough Bible in his childhood and early adolescence to be fairly sure of the reference. Whatever the sheriff thought of all that, the preacher considered it very serious. The expression he wore was nothing but grave.

"I cannot tell you what it says, Sheriff. We were not meant to hear it."

Later that evening, Sheriff Moultrie was still puzzling over what, if anything, to make of the preacher's peculiar pronouncement. He decided that the best way to be sure there was nothing to it was to get out of his office and make his rounds, to see the town and make himself seen.

He exited through the back door, intending to start on the outskirts, and then head back toward the main street. Something urged him off that course, pulling back toward the middle of town. Outside the general store, a small crowd had gathered. There was nothing remarkable about that, the store being a popular gathering and gossiping point. Yet the sheriff could feel something unusual in the air, something vaguely feverish.

A ring had formed just outside the entrance. Easing closer, Moultrie saw that the crowd's attention was on a girl. He had seen her before, but could not remember her name.

"The Whitaker girl," a bystander helpfully whispered as the sheriff leaned in.

Moultrie realized why he remembered the girl: she was mute. What she was doing at that moment made her that much more peculiar in their tiny town. Seated in the dust of the street—queer behavior even for a girl of her ten or eleven years—she was drawing with her finger. No doubt the girl's parents had taught her the alphabet, but this was not that. The spirals and harsh angles that she traced were almost . . .

"Selah!" came a cry from the back of the crowd. The voice exuded the fervency that only a mother's can, equal parts exasperation and relief.

The sheriff stood aside as the woman pushed past a tangle of men on his left, reaching for the girl. Mother had taken daughter by the hand and turned to go, but a large, black-haired man—one of the workers at the lumber mill, Moultrie seemed to recall—stepped into her path.

"Just a minute there," he barked. "You can be on your way in a moment, ma'am," he added, affecting a softer tone, "but somethin' ain't right with the girl and we'd like to get to the bottom of that . . . bein' as she decided to have this . . . episode in the middle of town and all."

"Sir, I don't . . . if you'll please just let me through . . . I—"

The woman cut short her words and her steps, halting in place, confusion and worry rising on her face. Scattered whispers had become more of a generalized murmuring, and Moultrie started to question where the scene was leading. He decided not to let it get that far.

"Now folks," he began, raising his voice above the growing din. "Let's not be hasty and let's not be un-neighborly. If you can all just stand aside a moment—"

"Naw, Sheriff." It was the black-haired man again. By then Moultrie was sure he recognized him from the lumber mill, for two of his co-laborers had emerged from the crowd to flank him, each with arms as massive and faces as hardened as the other.

"Naw," he repeated. "Let someone who's been here a while worry about what's neighborly." He cracked his knuckles and cocked his head.

Moultrie didn't fear the man, but he was hardly in a position to shoot him, should it come to that: he was sure to hit a bystander or create a stampede. The sheriff didn't much cotton to the idea of a three-against-one in fisticuffs, but he'd cross that bridge if and when he came to it.

"Friend, I'm still learning my way in this job, but—"

"He ain't bein' hasty, lawman," came another voice from somewhere nearer the store. This was a voice the sheriff instantly recognized: Chet Waters, the town drunk. "We had an earthquake and that dead body and that thing you hid in the jail—"

"Now hold it, Chet. I—"

"—and now this girl," Chet continued, ignoring the sheriff's admonition. "We folks got a right to ask some questions."

A rumbling rushed over the crowd and the sheriff raised his voice again. "We are done here. Y'all best go to your homes before I have to declare this an unlawful assembly and nobody wants that."

The lumber men seemed concerned at that remark. The man on the left even appeared to have taken half a step backwards.

Chet, however, was undeterred and stepped out into the street. He reeked of rot gut whiskey and wore a sneer that was more comical than menacing. Moultrie decided to pay the inebriate no mind, turning back toward the crowd and being pleased to find that they had started, slowly, to move off.

Then several things seemed to happen all at once. Moultrie heard some kind of throaty cry from behind him. He jerked his head around just in time to see Chet coming at him, with something in his hand. Before the sheriff's hand so much as twitched toward his holster, the blurred shape of another man shot in front of the besotted assailant, grasping Chet's extended arm and using his own reckless momentum to flip the drunkard, heels flailing, onto the ground in a heap. Instantly, the other man was atop Chet, pinning one arm between Chet's stomach and the ground and twisting the other into a painful looking lock behind his back.

"Mister," the man said, "I do believe the sheriff said it was time to go home. But maybe you just don't hear so good?"

Chet only groaned in reply. Beside him on the ground was a three-pronged fork; where he'd gotten it or what he meant to do with it was anyone's guess.

"Thanks, stranger," Moultrie said. Not only the man's unfamiliar face, but the dust on his clothes and the knapsack and canteen over his shoulders marked him as a visitor to the town.

"Chet's harmless," he continued, "but since you're here, I'd be obliged if you'd help me tote him over to the jail."

Moultrie saw to it that Mrs. Whitaker

was on her way and then a few minutes later deposited Chet in a cell to sober up.

"Don't think he would've done much damage with this," Moultrie said as he tossed the fork on his desk.

"Reckon it's good you didn't have to find out," replied the stranger.

"What's your name?" Moultrie looked the man up and down. There was nothing impressive about him at first glance. He stood a mite shorter than the sheriff's six-foot frame and had a wiry quality to him. How he had managed both to throw Chet like a child's dolly and then to hold him down like that—and Chet having a good fifty pounds on him—defied easy explanation.

"Name's Jameson Piebald. All my friends and kinfolk call me Deke, though."

"Hope you don't mind my askin' what brings you to our town. Make it my business to know such things."

"Well then, Sheriff, you probably won't be too pleased to know that, time bein', I find myself driftin'. Soon's I find steady work, I mean to keep it. You have my word on that."

Moultrie gave the man a once-over again. He seemed remarkably well-kept for a self-professed drifter. Then he looked Deke Piebald in the eyes. They each held the gaze for a long moment, a moment in which they reached some unspoken accord.

"Tell you what, Deke—mind if I call you that?"

Deke inclined his head slightly and raised his palms in silent consent.

"Deke, I get the feeling I could use a good man to watch my back for at least the next couple days. You stepped in at just the right time back there. What do you say to takin' a deputy's badge?"

To ask the question was more or less to answer it. Moultrie had himself a deputy. Not more than a few moments after Deputy Piebald had been sworn in, a frantic knock came at the front door to the office. Moultrie answered it to find Jim Riley, a ranch hand and the preacher's volunteer assistant, standing there, a little out of breath.

"You gotta come to the church!"

"What is it?"

"Just come quick!"

Jim tore back down the street. Sheriff and newly-minted deputy followed close behind. Moultrie shook off the sound of a faint humming as he locked the office's door and turned to go. They arrived at the church before a crowd formed, but upon viewing the scene, the sheriff knew that onlookers would be drawn like moths to a flame.

"Deputy," he said, to the evident surprise of Preacher Kaine, "post at that door and make sure folks don't try to barge in here."

Deke nodded and silently took up his station.

Inside, Moultrie found Kaine and a scene that was all too familiar. It was another dead body, laid out spread eagle in the vestibule, bearing the same gruesome wounds as the man the sheriff had found out at Old Lake Carter. White dust coated the man's fingertips, but no trace of blood was anywhere.

"You know him, Preacher?"

"Ephraim Sellers," he replied flatly. "One of my most faithful sheep."

"Anything unusual about your building that you saw? You lock the doors?"

"Oh, well, yes," the preacher said, snapping out of his reverie. "I mean, no, I don't lock the doors, but there is something unusual. Here," he said, stooping next to the body and gesturing awkwardly with an outstretched palm.

The sheriff squatted next to him and looked.

"There," Kaine said.

Then Moultrie saw what the reverend meant. A burn mark in the floor jutted out from under the man's side.

"Help me move him, Reverend."

The burns turned out to be just what some sense in the back of the sheriff's mind had suggested. Not a thread of the man's clothing was singed, but there on the wooden floor, as if etched in stone, were the unmistakable strokes of writing.

The sheriff and the preacher stared at the floor and then exchanged a knowing look. The writing was indecipherable, but they had seen its like before. Whatever it meant, Moultrie thought, could not be good.

There were no more mysterious deaths, but Bracton was hardly quiet over the next few days. The feral cats that patrolled the alleys for assorted varmints were nowhere to be seen by Monday afternoon. On Tuesday, the big dog that Tom Hicks, the blacksmith, kept leashed outside his shop, was seen running down Main Street, the frayed remains of the leash flapping behind him. The dog disappeared into the hills and the tied end of the leash bore the plain marks of the canine's teeth. By Friday, people began to notice the absence of any wild birds; the skies were empty and the customary early morning songs had fallen silent. All that would have been strange enough—but then there was the humming.

That the artifact was the source of the sound was undeniable. Sheriff Moultrie had tried to convince himself it was just his own nerves. Deke didn't say anything, but the townsfolk began stopping outside the office and cupping their hands to their ears. The half-buzzing, vaguely-singing sound was loud enough to pass through walls.

On top of it all, the situation with the Whitaker girl had not only lingered, but grown worse. Fear led the parents to call for the doctor from the next county to meet them at the Bracton Sheriff's Office. That was how Moultrie had learned that the girl had continued her strange drawing, using ashes from the family hearth as her eerie canvas. It was also there that he first saw the girl moving her mouth as if to speak. Just as they were about to leave, Selah Whitaker astonished them all—parents, doctor, sheriff, and, after his unexpected appearance, Preacher Kaine—by whispering a single word.

"Divided."

"Wha—what did you say?" her mother asked.

Selah repeated the word, her voice still soft, but no longer a whisper.

The Whitakers seemed unable to decide whether their shock was born of joy or something else. They thanked the flummoxed doctor for coming so far and spirited Selah away. The sheriff could barely hear the child's unexpected refrain: "Divided."

Kaine stayed even after the doctor had gone. The humming of the artifact had grown louder.

"I told you this would happen, Sheriff."

"What's that now?" Deke asked, as much for his own information as to keep Moultrie from acting on the dark look that crossed his face.

"You've stowed a remnant of Babel in that cell. It's speaking again."

"You mean Genesis," the deputy replied. "Can't say as I ever heard no such thing, and I growed up in church."

"Then you know, at least," Kaine continued, "that the people were scattered, and it stands to reason that their tongue was likewise dispersed."

"It's about time we close up, Preacher," Moultrie interrupted.

"There's something sealed in that stone, Sheriff," Kaine said as the lawman ushered him toward the door. "And it was meant to stay that way."

For a couple days after that, everything in town—except for the artifact—seemed quiet. Even Chet managed to stay sober for a time. Then one afternoon Deke returned to the sheriff's office with a stack of papers in his hand. He let himself into one of the empty holding cells without speaking. Moultrie, his curiosity rising, followed him a few minutes later. The sheriff found his deputy seated on the floor, back to the door, spreading the papers in front of him.

"What's all this?"

Deke sucked in a breath through his teeth. "I had a notion . . ." he said, the words trailing off to wherever his mind was.

"Is that right?" Moultrie continued. "S'pose you want to tell me about it?"

"Huh? Oh, right. Yes, well it was when I was over at the Whitaker house. I hope it ain't a breach of protocol. 'Let all things be done decently and in order,' my preacher would always say."

"No, I admire the initiative—so long's you be careful."

"Well, the young girl had taken to drawing again. Used up every scrap of paper in the house, giving her folks quite the scare as you can imagine."

Moultrie nodded for Deke to continue. The sheriff could tell that the man could spin a yarn, but he'd prefer to get to the point.

"So I collected 'em and thought you should have a look."

"And here we are."

"Yep."

"What do *you* make of it all?"

Sheriff and deputy leaned closely over the drawings. They were similar to those first scribblings that drew the crowd that day, yet unlike in a way that Moultrie couldn't quite grasp.

"Well," Deke said, breaking the silence, "to me it looks like some kind of descending spiral; like a funnel almost. Leastways, the way I laid things out."

"I see it, I reckon," Moultrie replied.

"But a funnel that descends . . . to what?"

"That is not a funnel," came a voice from behind the law men.

Moultrie whipped around, startled but ready to fight. The intruder threw up his hands, covering his face and bracing for the inevitable blow.

"Please! The door out front was open. I mean no harm!"

"State your name and your business then, stranger. Foolish thing to sneak up on us like that."

Moultrie eyed his and Deke's gun belts, hung on the other end of the hall, the stranger in between. Giving the newcomer a quick onceover, however, pretty well convinced him the gun belts would not be needed. The man had pale skin, blue eyes, and sandy hair. He wore a black, broadcloth suit of a style Moultrie had never seen before—clean enough that he must have either stepped off the stagecoach only a minute before or spent inordinate time dressing himself. The man was so thin—not to mention drawn in the cheeks—that a stiff wind would be his final and certain undoing.

"I am Doctor Coenraad Hoek of the University of Leyden in the Netherlands," the man said, cautiously lowering his hands. "As I was saying: that is not a funnel. The drawings are of a seal."

"How can you know that?" Deke asked.

"If you will permit me, sirs, I will be most glad to explain."

The next few hours proved intense. Dr. Hoek explained that he had come to Bracton after reports of the earthquake. He was somewhat cagey about his precise area of study at his university; the most the sheriff and Deke could glean was something vaguely related to "antiquities." When the academic learned of the deaths in Bracton, he had developed a sudden and acute interest in the artifact stored in the jail cell. His passion flared hot when the sheriff refused to let him see it.

"This is not acceptable, Sheriff. I am a student of history, well-acquainted with the sciences. We are all men of reason, are we not? Your minister's religious concerns no doubt are sincere, but no less foolish for that."

"The answer is no, Doctor," Moultrie said flatly.

But Hoek was unwilling to accept that answer. He ran through what must have been his full arsenal of rationalisms, most of which Deke seemed to capably parry—though Moultrie himself was less sure. Eventually, however, the stranger's sheer doggedness wore the sheriff down. Perhaps no harm could come of letting him look, and perhaps it was the easiest way to get rid of the man with the funny accent.

Moultrie removed the cylinder from the lockbox, setting it atop a pile of burlap sacks that would have to serve as examination table. Hoek crouched to get a closer look, retrieving a pair of spectacles from the breast pocket of his jacket.

"Most fascinating," Hoek said after a minute's study.

"What's that?" Deke asked skeptically.

"Oh, the symbols—glyphs we call them

in my profession—are almost like . . . well, I shall have to consult my books first."

"You mean hieroglyphics like what I read about that Rosetta Stone?" the sheriff said.

Hoek scoffed, clearly amused by the amateur's attempt to understand. "No, not the same really, Mr. Moultrie. But to explain . . ."

The professor's voice trailed off and his gaze seemed to grow distant as his left hand extended toward the cylinder. The low pulsing to which Moultrie and his deputy had grown almost deaf, grew louder and more shrill the closer Hoek's hand came. The air itself shimmered around the object. Hoek's hand darted the last few inches. As soon as his fingers touched the cylinder, the intense humming popped—or so Deke and the sheriff later called it, having no better word to describe the phenomenon. Hoek's hand flew upward, as if someone had lassoed him. The Dutchman fell back, clutching the hand to his chest, a look of astonished confusion on his face. Sheriff and deputy rushed to his side.

"You all right?" Deke asked. He took one arm and Moultrie the other, helping their visitor to his feet.

"I am unhurt," he replied.

"Well, mostly," Moultrie said, gesturing toward the professor's nose.

Hoek reached a hand to his face, tapping gently at his upper lip, and pulled his fingers away to find them spotted with blood.

"It is nothing," he said. "The dry air of your western territories is so different from Leyden. This is all."

Moultrie and Deke exchanged a doubtful look, but helped Hoek dust himself off.

"I return to my room now, gentlemen."

"And the cylinder? What do you make of it?" the sheriff asked.

"I must consult my books," Hoek replied curtly. "Good day to you both."

"Odd fellow," Deke said after Hoek left.

"You've got that right. But I got a hunch that he knows more than he lets on. That . . . thing in there. I don't know what it is, but it's got to go . . . somewhere."

Deke was waiting for the sheriff at the door when he arrived at the office the next morning.

"Got somethin' to tell ya," the deputy said. "Best get inside first."

"What is it?" Moultrie found himself a little wary of Deke's insistence on such privacy.

"I did somethin' else I reckon I might shouldn't have."

Moultrie sat silently. He was usually one to stand on procedure, but they weren't exactly facing ordinary circumstances.

"Last night," Deke went on, "I went over to the boarding house. Dr. Hoek was engaged in some after-dinner conversation and so . . ."

"And so?" Moultrie raised an eyebrow.

"I let myself into his room."

"You reckoned right. Shouldn't have done that."

"I knowed it." Deke hung his head slightly.

"But you saw something, didn't you?"

Deke looked up. "You ain't gonna fire me or arrest me?"

"Can't afford to lose someone like you in the middle of . . . whatever this is. Tell me what you saw."

Deke then proceeded to summarize the results of his questionable surveillance. Moultrie's hunch was right: Hoek was not what he seemed to be at first glance. He had been traversing the American West for several years, documenting linguistic anomalies and mapping them. His journals were filled with florid descriptions of people speaking in tongues, unexplained discoveries of scripts written in languages long thought to be lost, and of seismic tremors. All of it was taken down in the professor's native tongue and also in English; letters addressed to a "Mr. Smith" at an address in Chicago suggested that the University of Leyden was a believable cover rather than his true employer. All of it added up to this: Hoek's encounter with Bracton was no happenstance. All his efforts had led him there.

"Wish I could say I'd had a quicker hunch," Deke sighed. "But I 'spose this Hoek is more of a snake than we bargained for."

"Normally I'd say let's not jump to conclusions, but—"

An urgent knock came at their door, interrupting the sheriff mid-sentence. No sooner had Deke opened the door than Mrs. Whitaker burst through, carrying a bundle of papers in one arm and towing Selah in the other. The girl freed herself from her mother's grasp and seated herself in a corner, clutching her legs to her chest and rocking gently side to side.

"Ma'am?" the sheriff asked, stealing a sidelong glance at the girl.

"She won't stop, Mr. Moultrie. We've tried everything. Preacher Kaine even came and said a special prayer and laid on hands, but she keeps on."

"Keeps on what, Mrs. Whitaker?" Moultrie replied.

"Here," the woman said, letting out a ragged breath and dumping the papers on the sheriff's desk.

Deke stooped over the collection for a better look and Moultrie joined him. They were similar to the other drawings, at least in terms of the technique, but what they showed was quite different.

"The spirals are there," Deke said, "but the rest . . . you got an idea, Sheriff?"

Moultrie studied the drawings closely, trying his best to block out Mrs. Whitaker's half-frantic efforts to soothe her daughter. Then, like a lightning bolt, it struck him.

"It's Old Lake Carter!"

"What?" Deke asked, cocking his head to one side for a different view of the paper he held up.

"Not from the sky, like a regular map, but from the side, cutting into the earth in a way—a cross-section."

"I see it now, I think. But what's this?"

Deke gestured toward a strange symbol that showed up on each of the drawings, near what must have been the bottom of the lake bed.

"Well that I don't—"

"Mouth."

The sheriff turned on his heel at the word. "What?" he said reflexively.

"Mouth," the voice repeated, a dry croaking sound from the lips of Selah Whitaker.

The rest of that day and the next consisted almost entirely of a train of panicked Bractonians pounding on the sheriff's door. A horse was found dead in its stall, throat torn open, but unstained by any blood. More than one distraught mother reported a young child who seemed to mutter words in his sleep, words in an unknown tongue. The Widow Hargrave—the town's most reliable seamstress and always as serious as a funeral—recounted breathlessly how she had heard the unmistakable sound of her late husband praying, his voice rising from the depths of a nearby well.

Hoek made himself scarce, riding out of town early and returning late. Moultrie and Deke enlisted a band of boys from the town to help track his movements.

All the while, the humming from the cylinder grew louder. It could be heard clearly outside the building; the clerk in the store across the street could hear it faintly but distinctly without even needing to cup a hand to his ear.

Deke got the idea to wrap the thing in a blanket, intending to muffle the sound, and was just about to embark on the experiment when Preacher Kaine arrived.

"Save your breath," Moultrie greeted him. "I know why you're here. I have to do something about . . . all this. Have I read you right?"

The preacher nodded, but held his words.

"Not meaning to sound irksome, Reverend," Deke put in, "but what's a lawman to do about this kind of thing? I hate to even use the word, yet it sure looks like a bit of devilry."

"No," Kaine said. "Not devilry, not directly, in any event. More like judgment or the echoes of a judgment long past."

Moultrie and Deke puzzled over Kaine's words, hoping for some better explanation.

"There is a time for prayer and fasting," Kaine continued, "and there is a time for action. I have done my part and now you must do yours. Bury the item and then we may join all our prayers that we may be allowed to walk away."

Kaine turned and left even before the word "where" had fully formed on Deke's lips.

"Sheriff?"

"I think we both know where."

Deke finished swaddling the cylinder, and the men went to retrieve their horses. Just as they reached the hitching post, Tom Barkley, one of the boyish spies, came running up.

"I seen him, Sheriff!"

"The man I asked y'all to watch?"

"Yessir. He's down at Old Lake Carter and a couple other men with 'im, but I kept my distance like you told me."

"Good work, sonny. Come get your dime when I get back."

Tom trotted away and Moultrie exchanged a knowing glance with his deputy.

"Let's ride," Moultrie said, and the pair mounted up, urging their horses to a steady run by the time they reached the end of Main Street.

They approached the hard pan depression from the south. It took them longer but afforded concealment to their arrival. There was no telling what Hoek might be up to.

"Looks like they're diggin'," Deke said as the two of them peered from behind a tangle of thornbushes. "But what for?"

"No sense waitin' to find out. Let's get down there."

The horses thundered down into the lake bed, but by the time Hoek and his companions looked up, it was too late for them to attempt any ruse.

"Hold it right there, Mr. Hoek," the sheriff called out as they drew up. The other two men Moultrie recognized as hands from the Daniels ranch.

"I mean you no trouble, Mr. Moultrie. In fact, my work is all but at an end."

"Good," Moultrie replied. "Then you'll have plenty of time to explain what you're really doing in my town. I'll hear all about it back at my office."

Hoek ignored the sheriff and the implication. "Your service is most appreciated, gentlemen," he said to the hands. "Your pay may be retrieved from the proprietor of your dining establishment."

Moultrie was content to let them go. Likely they had no real idea who Hoek was or what he was doing. When they moved to leave, the sheriff got his first good look at what the Dutchman seemed to be after. It was half-buried in the soil, but the shape was clear; it was round and very nearly flat, having a slight convex curve to it. It looked black, but in the bright sun, Moultrie could not say for sure. Hoek turned toward the thing, continuing to make no mind of Deke and the sheriff.

"That'll be enough, Mr. Hoek. You won't be doing any more digging today. Sorry to put your little adventure on hold, but—"

"This is no fairytale, Sheriff. Your whole town has seen what the thing does." Here Hoek gestured toward Deke's saddlebag and the humming that seeped through all the wrappings. "Here is the other piece, the part your kind are too uncurious to pursue, or too afraid, but not I."

"You're talkin' nonsense, Mr. Hoek," Deke said. "Now just step over here and—"

"No! Here is the voice that was antecedent to Babel, and I *will* hear its tongue let loose."

Faster than either of the lawmen would have thought possible, Hoek whirled around toward the plate-like object. As the man's shadow passed over it, the Sheriff could see that the thing was as dark as slate and covered with inscriptions. As he turned, Hoek withdrew a hammer from somewhere on his person. The silver of the tool's head flashed brilliantly in the sun as the professor twirled it in a tight arc, bringing it down on the plate—on the seal, Moultrie understood—with terrible force.

The humming ceased, snuffed out like the last embers of a campfire smothered with earth. An instant later, the disc began to sink into the ground, noiselessly. It was only then that the sheriff realized that not only the hum of the cylinder but all sound had died away. He felt a rumbling beneath his feet and then a hot gust knocked him back, dazing him and hurling him to the ground.

Moultrie sat up after a moment, seeing that Deke too had been knocked down. Then he looked back toward the seal. The hammer had broken into several pieces, but Hoek himself was nowhere to be seen. Moultrie started to call out to Deke, but found that no sound would come. He reached over and jabbed his deputy in the shoulder, then tapped on his own throat and tried to mouth "No voice."

Deke made as if to speak, but he too seemed struck dumb. Moultrie gestured toward where Hoek should have been. Deke's eyes grew wide, and he whipped his head right and then left, scanning the area for any sign of their foreign visitor.

Not a trace could be seen of the stranger, but a figure had appeared on the edge of the lake bed. It only took a few moments for the form to draw close enough to reveal the person of Preacher Kaine, leather-bound book in his hand.

The sheriff and Deke rose to meet him, each keeping a wary eye on the shaft that had been revealed beneath the mysterious disc in the ground. Whatever it was felt wrong, forbidden.

Kaine peered past the men toward the shaft and frowned. He pointed toward it and mouthed a word that Moultrie could not make out. Deke tugged on the sheriff's sleeve and pulled him toward the opening.

Kneeling beside it, Moultrie could see no bottom. The pit was no wider than a wagon wheel at the top, but seemed to expand as it went deeper. The outer rim—the same material as the sealing disc—was carved with the intricate spiraling symbols that had become uncomfortably familiar to the three of them.

The air that loomed from the shaft was warm and damp, like a person breathing in the sheriff's face. Moultrie turned away from the mouth of the shaft to see that Kaine had come closer. He held the book open—Moultrie could see that it was the preacher's Bible—and extended it toward the sheriff, pointing to a verse with his index finger.

Moultrie took it and read: "The voice of the Lord shakes the wilderness." He looked up for a moment and then continued reading: "The Lord sits enthroned over the flood."

He looked up and handed the Bible back to Kaine. What he had been meant to learn was unclear. Kaine, however, seemed to have anticipated the confusion and was ready with a scrap of paper and a pencil. He scribbled some words and handed it to the sheriff.

"Guns and fists are no use here. Only the Word."

Before the sheriff could ponder the preacher's meaning, there was movement in the periphery of his sight. Deke's saddlebag had fallen to the ground and the horses shied reflexively away from it. The lawmen approached the sack, and Deke carefully retrieved the contents. Laying the blankets on the ground, the deputy carefully unwrapped the cargo he had only so recently packaged with such caution and uncertainty. The cylinder tumbled out onto the dusty ground, split cleanly down the middle longways.

A tap on the shoulder brought Moultrie's attention back to the present, back to Kaine and the open Bible. The preacher gestured toward another verse, pointed to Moultrie, and made signs that he should read.

The sheriff signed his inability to speak, but the preacher merely shook his head and pointed to the shaft.

He could make no sense of Kaine's thought process, but so many things had not made sense in recent days. He accepted the book, faced the shaft, and began to read where Kaine had pointed, as Deke looked on in bewilderment. Yet no sound came, from Moultrie's mouth or anywhere else. He thought he could feel his vocal cords vibrating, but when he put his hand to his throat he felt nothing. He read on: "Thou shalt not be afraid for the terror by night; nor for the arrow that flieth by day; Nor for the pestilence that walketh in darkness; nor for the destruction that wasteth at noonday."

Just as he reached the end of the passage that Kaine had indicated, something broke in the air, almost like the shock that Hoek had received days before. Then, from behind the sheriff, a sound cut through the silence. He turned to see Selah Whitaker, walking toward them, reciting in a clear, tender voice:

"Our Father which art in heaven, Hallowed be thy name.

Thy kingdom come. Thy will be done in earth, as it is in heaven.

Give us this day our daily bread.

And forgive us our debts, as we forgive our debtors.

And lead us not into temptation, but deliver us from evil: For thine is the kingdom, and the power, and the glory, for ever."

"Amen," Kaine and Deke said in unison.

"Amen," repeated Selah.

Moultrie fell to his knees beside the mouth of the shaft. "Amen," he whispered, overwhelmed at the return of sound.

Another humming had started, though it emanated not from the broken cylinder, but seemingly from all around. Unlike before, the sound was not unsettling, but somehow reassuring, peaceful. Moultrie rose to his feet and backed away from the shaft. A thin layer of white dust, appearing from nowhere the sheriff could identify, had begun to fall into the pit.

"Get back!" Kaine called.

The four of them retreated some yards from the mouth of the shaft as the pale powder continued to rain down. The humming grew warmer and richer, but beneath the ground Moultrie could hear something harsher: the sound of stones falling against one another. He realized that the sound was coming from deep inside the shaft.

The group moved further back. The humming intensified along with the sound of collapsing stones. Then, as if it were the last gasp of a dying beast, the lip of the shaft crumbled, propelling a wisp of the white dust skyward.

For a moment, the silence returned. A breeze caressed the sheriff's cheek and gently tossed the curls of Selah Whitaker's hair. Moultrie took in a deep breath and realized that he could hear himself, something he had always taken for granted. He looked at Deke who clapped him on the back; the smacking sound almost seemed to echo. Then the sound of the wind rustling through the bushes and of birds chirping returned.

"It's over," Kaine said. "The judgment has passed us by."

"Preacher, I still don't—" Moultrie started to say, before he thought better of it. "Let's get Selah back to her parents and then . . ."

"Then I suppose we should have a talk?" Kaine offered.

"Maybe. We'll see."

Deke hoisted Selah up behind him in the saddle and made for the Whitaker's house. Sheriff Moultrie, reins in hand, started the long walk back to Bracton, Preacher Kaine at his side. Perhaps that would have been the best time for a talk, but they walked in silence, satisfied to merely bask in the natural melodies and harmonies of the land that lay around them.

Joseph W. Knowles lives in Virginia with his family, where he writes all kinds of speculative fiction. His stories feature daring heroes, strange worlds, and plenty of action. Find more of his work at The Tidewater Papers on Substack.

Voodoo Man's Curse

By MICHAEL TIERNEY

William Lee's master, a general in the Revolutionary War, has mysteriously died! Lee goes to the last man who saw him before he fell ill, seeking justice for the curse!

Mount Vernon, Virginia
December 15, 1799

The erliest rays of dawn glistened like thunderbolts across the untrodden snowfall covering the trail ahead, so much so that the rider had to slow his horse and shield his eyes, pulling down on the felt bill of his old tricorn hat.

A break ahead in the snow banks and trees revealed a hodgepodge wooden shanty with a porch overhang. A thin finger of gray smoke reached out from the makeshift chimney and stretched for the sky.

The rider pushed the flap of his heavy outer coat back and unbuttoned his waistcoat, slipping a hand to feel the comfort of the hunting knife hanging from his belt. Like his hat, it was a relic he had carried since the Revolutionary War. The blade had not tasted blood since—but that was about to change.

"I ain't seen you ride a horse in a while, old Billy Lee," said the man standing in the shanty's doorway. He held a loaded musket ready in one hand, the muzzle pointed downwards. His other hand suspiciously held something hidden behind his back.

"God knows I hate it," Lee replied.

"Ain't seen you sober since you stopped running dem foxes for youse *Master*. But it's Sunday. Why ain't youse wearing your red sash and sitting in church instead of out riding a mare around in the cold like a man with hot intentions? Been hearing a lot more bells echoing than usual. Is the redcoats coming back?"

"I won't be surprised when they do." Trying to hide his disgust at the way the man had said *Master,* William Lee sighed and urged his horse nearer to one of the porch's roof support beams, then tied the reins to it. "But not on this sad Sunday."

"Most people do that after they get off their horse," taunted the man with the gun. "Who put a bee in your bonnet?"

"I've known you a long time, Elijah," said Lee as he gripped his saddle horn with both hands and painfully swung one leg over his horse's body, then followed it down to the snow-covered ground. The joints in the braces around both knees creaked in complaint as he struggled to free his other boot from the stirrup. "And I've never known you to say a kind word. Laugh if you want, but I'm not taking a chance on having to walk back in this snow."

"As hard as it was for youse to get off that horse," Elijah taunted, "youse should have stayed on. We never was friends. We both know we never liked each other none. I ain't inviting youse into my home."

Elijah raised the gun barrel halfway to level when Lee took a step nearer.

"Last Thursday, the general took a ride to check the farms," said Lee. "Shouldn't have taken him five hours. His hair was covered with snow when he came back, carrying a couple of chickens he said you gave him in thanks for allowing you to keep roosting out here with your brood."

"So? Did he send youse to thank me again? Twern't no need."

"No. I came to ask why you're smiling so big when you ask that? He never was really right after that ride. Caught a chill the next day. Things got bad, fast. Kept wanting to be bled, like he was trying to get something inside him… out."

Elijah could not contain a damning giggle of glee.

"You may live out here alone, but I know you heard the wailing from the big house last night."

"Sounded like somebody died. The *Master*?"

William Lee struggled not to react to how hopefully the question had been asked. He steeled himself not to react, and instead took another half step closer when he replied.

"You smiled again."

"That bothers youse?"

"I've heard about you, how your papa was a Haiti voodoo-man who married a Iroquois medicine woman. The general was always kind to you, but I could tell you hated him. Why?"

"Think youse *Master* is … was … such a great man? Youse and all his other slaves worship him. Youse call me a voodoo man, but youse the ones who had voodoo done to youse heads, mister former valet to the President. Here is truth for youse. Back when he wore the red coat, he burned my village. It wasn't the only one. The Iroquois call youse *Master—Village Fire-Bringer*, it means *the Burner of Villages!* Took those lands and sold dem. That's where youse *Master's* wealth … his *greatness* … come from."

"You hated him."

"Yeah…wouldn't you?" Elijah raised the gun. "Youse wanted to hear me say it? Yeah. Now I said it agin…so git off my porch! Go run like a hound for youse *Master* somewhere else."

Lee took a sudden step forward and knocked the musket out of Elijah's hands. It discharged when it hit the porch boards and startled Lee's horse, but he had tied the reins well. Most of his body might be failing, but he still had powerful hands and arms that were stronger than most.

"You poisoned him with your voodoo!"

"Ha!" Elijah laughed and retreated back inside the shack. "There twern't nothing wrong with dem birds."

Lee followed halfway inside, hesitating with his back still in the door frame as his eyes adjusted to the darkness inside, illuminated by the flickering flames in the fireplace. A chill raised every hair on his body as he finally understood what his wife had meant about being about to smell witchcraft. Looking around, he saw many strange and disturbing things—animal bodies and parts hanging from the ceiling beams, and bizarre things that defied identification sealed inside glass jars lining cluttered shelves. But one thing in particular, seated by the wall, shocked him.

"Why do you have a dead body in here?" Lee demanded.

The voodoo man plucked an effigy of a human figure from where it hung from the ceiling by its own head of dark hair. Elijah then tauntingly revealed another, white-haired effigy that he had been hiding behind his back. Spitting on each in turn, he began chanting in a strange tongue.

"I summon youse spirits to do my vengeance!" Elijah concluded his chant and spit again—this time into the fire.

Lee's heart skipped a beat when the dead body by the wall jolted with life and stood up. His eyelids opened to reveal white eyes with no pupils—they were so rolled back in his head. The corpse then raised both arms and stepped in William's direction.

Lee reached for his knife but was hesitant to draw it as he took a step backwards.

"Go ahead and shoot him with a pistola," the voodoo man taunted and waved the dark-haired effigy. "Shoot him as many times as youse want. Zombies don't feel no thing. Youse can't kilt what's already dead! But he can kilt youse!"

The voodoo man's face then twisted into a vicious smile of evil glee when he waved the white-haired effigy with several long strands wrapped around the neck in a constricting fashion.

"Just like youse *Master* is doing right now! Youse done me a favor by coming here. Now I know the bells meaned what I hoped they meaned. Now youse Master will kill everyone he loves. The person nearest to him dies first—*right now!* Now the world will remember him to be the kind of man he really, really, really be!"

"The Missus," Lee snarled and pulled his knife.

"That's no cobbler's knife," Elijah gasped.

The sight of firelight glinting off the freshly sharpened edge of Lee's long blade surprised the voodoo man, who looked about frantically for something that might counter it.

"Don't need no gun," Lee hissed as he stepped to one side of the zombie and slashed at its neck, giving the blade an extra twist to saw on the spinal column. "You know how many redcoat assassins I kilt with this knife? All of them!"

The zombie's head rolled off its body, but its arms still reached out and grasped blindly at Lee when he pushed it away.

The voodoo man laughed.

"You can't kilt him," Elijah declared with glee, "not even with steel!"

"Maybe not," said Lee, "but steel can kill magic in other ways."

William threw his knife directly at the voodoo man. It thunked like it had struck a hollowed husk when the blade embedded deep into Elijah's chest.

"Too late," Elijah gasped as his eyes rolled back into his head. "Now the world sees your *Master* for who he really be."

The voodoo man fell lifeless to the floor.

Lee struggled fruitlessly to pry the effigies from the voodoo man's gnarled fingers. Finally, he retrieved his knife and cut them free to toss into the fireplace. When they erupted into flames, the aimlessly lurching zombie fell in the same manner as had Elijah, his flesh quickly stiffening with rigor.

As fast as his broken knees would allow, William then pulled burning wood from the fireplace and set the whole shack alight. Opening the doors to the chicken coops, he grabbed a chair and laboriously crawled back onto his horse. With no stable workers to assist him, it took several attempts accompanied by heavenly intonements and more than a few curse words.

The porch roof was already alight by the time he cut the reins and the mare bolted away. Lee grabbed her mane and did nothing to discourage her panicked race home.

"Fly, old Betsy," he whispered into her ear. "Fly."

When Betsy reached the backside of the big house, Lee was falling off as his wife ran out from his cobbler shop.

"It was horrible," gasped Margaret. "I was right. The general...he really *was* touched by voodoo magic!"

"What happened? Is the Missus...?"

"Martha's okay now, but she wasn't." Margaret looked around, anxious to be anywhere else and having any other conversation. As a free woman, she had that choice, but always stayed with William.

"What happened?" Lee urged again.

"The Martha finished ordering the general's coffin. The doctors left right after breakfast. Then Mister Lear and the other aides retired to the study to write the general's kin, leaving poor Martha all alone, when..."

Margaret clutched a shirt sleeve up to her open mouth, as if trying to choke her own words from being spoken.

"...when the general...he just got up and started walking agin, like he was back with the living—but his eyes was blank. When Martha ran to him, he attacked her. Tried to kilt her. So she shot him. Had to. Agin and agin. Shot everything she had loaded, but it didn't do nothing. Then, when he had her cornered, he just falls over and dies agin. But this time it took."

"Sounds horrible."

"It *was!* Martha told the girls to tell Mister Lear that she done the shooting in anger and forbids anyone to talk about it ever agin," Margaret then lowered her voice. "She said it never happened."

"Good," said William.

"Good?" Margaret questioned. "Now she's done locked herself in her room and is burning all the general's letters! She's destroying all the work you did collecting them."

"She's in shock," said Lee. "I saw this in the war. When a body's mind can't deal with something, you just have to shut it, and anything that reminds you about it, completely out. That's what we should do, too. Tell the girls to clean the general's body, then melt wax over the bullet holes and change his gown. Me and a couple of the stable hands will get him back in his bed. No one else will ever know. Like the Missus said ... it never happened."

"Why? Why hide it? Can this undo the freedom you were promised?"

"No." William shook his head. "No point in doing nothing else. The fellow what done this has been dealt with. General George Washington was not flawless, but it's up to us to make sure how people remember him—as a great man."

Michael Tierney's Wild Stars will return later this year as Cirsova Publishing releases both the collected edition of Wild Stars 9: Flight From Reckoning and Wild Stars 10: War of the Gods as a double-featured Kickstarter in the Summer. You can find more of Michael's work at thewildstars.com.

A Necklace of Ghûl Claws

By TAIS TENG

On the eve of a fight to rid the lock of a kraken, Omar meets an exotic ghûl-hunting girl from the Eternal Caravan... Her affections prove more than he bargained for!

Gazelle-eyed Omar ben Hassan was a canal dredger, just like his grandfather and his grandfather's grandfather. In fact, as far back as family records went back, the ben Hassans and their giant beavers had been canal dredgers.

The *Qanat Rayiea*, the Grand Channel to the Mediterranean Sea, started some fifty Sidonese miles from Jorsaleem, at a port city called, with a great lack of imagination, Alexandria. Around the Inland Sea alone, one found no fewer than nine other cities that the great general had named after himself.

Approaching from the east, the first thing you noticed was the entrance to the channel: a gaping hole in the crater wall, flanked by the statues of Hermes and Apollo, both of whom wore the face of Alexander the Great.

That morning, Omar strode along the dock, followed by his beavers. The hairy dredgers were the size of brown bears, and their flat tails could shatter the skull of a full-grown hippopotamus. Not that any hippo would be unwise enough to bother a beaver during his work.

Other children might gaze longingly after the galleons with their silken sails and dream of traveling to the Tin Islands or the endless forests of Iroquois; Omar was indifferent to the whole regatta. He regarded the passing ships with the gaze of a shepherd who, although he could tell each animal from the other, had no romantic thoughts about his flock.

"Yalla, yalla!" he shouted to his beasts, "Faster, faster!" It was of little use. They kept their own pace, and whacking them with his stick was useless. They probably didn't even feel it, and the stick was only intended for scaring off wild dogs, anyway.

Omar knew full well that being late was entirely his own fault. It was quite unwise to dawdle when you could already hear the bells on the piers ringing the seventh hour. The most annoying thing was that his eldest brother would already be waiting for half an hour on the felucca. Gusman's hands were rather loose.

"Shay," a voice sounded from somewhere above his head, "are those real canal beavers?"

A girl jumped down from the quay wall and landed just in front of the first beaver, coming down so hard that her palms slapped the stones.

"I've heard of them, but I didn't know they were so gigantic." She tapped the beaver on the nose, then stroked him under the muzzle.

"Watch out a bit, yes?" Omar said. "My uncle hates people complaining that a beaver bit off a few fingers. Or a hand."

Now Omar didn't like girls much, mainly because they ignored him and only saw him as Gusman's younger brother. Gusman they ogled, then nudged each other and giggled.

"Our beasts of burden are a lot bigger here," she replied. "A ladith can step on a beaver, and he won't even notice. Even if your beaver ends up as flat as a chapati."

"What is a ladith?" asked Omar.

At least this girl talked to him without immediately asking about his brother, which was a completely new experience. It was only then that he realized how incredibly exotic she actually looked: skin like shiny bronze, gray eyes, and then this chain of black claws around her neck. His brother would probably find her unattractive because her locks barely reached her shoulders and she had scratches on her arms. Omar prayed that such was indeed the case.

"A ladith, well, that's an armored turtle the size of a hill. The Hanhari men ride ahead of the caravan on a ladith. They are our soldiers, our caravan guards, though my mother commands them."

"Guards?" he asked. "Of which caravan?"

"The Eternal Caravan of course! We go all the way around the Inland Sea, through the almond groves and the Rusting Dunes. Past the Grand Necropolis where the mausoleums swarm with ghûls." She touched her necklace. "The ghûls, they killed my father and now my mother is hunting them. I do, too, by the way." She nodded. "For he was my father, and the dead are best honored by cruel vengeance."

The Eternal Caravan! That was about as far away as you could get from this horribly boring Channel. It had nothing to do with ruler-straight canals and mud or malfunctioning locks. All the wide land beyond the crater wall formed the territory of the Eternal Caravan. Each day was different from the last, and nothing ever stayed the same.

"You hunt ghûls?"

The girl drew a small horse bow from the case she carried over her shoulder.

"The moon goddess blessed the arrows, and as long as there is moonlight they always hit their target. And my mother, she has a soul silk blindfold and can see just fine on moonless nights."

"So you're a caravan guard, too?"

"It will be official next year. When I turn sixteen."

She's the same age as me. Keep her talking. Ask things about herself.

It was as if a second Omar suddenly appeared in his head, one who gave him orders that he had better follow.

Ask things about herself.

"Your necklace. All those claws? Did you shoot them yourself?"

"Otherwise it doesn't count, does it? And the ghûls have no choice. Like my mother, I stared straight at them until they could count the veins in the whites of my eyes. Now they have to hunt me. Best of all, the

Exarch of Udmarith pays a gold piece for every fresh ghûl skull. He's an alchemist, and ghûl skulls are apparently indispensable for the brewing of certain dark elixirs." She looked at him imploringly. "Is it all right if I ride on his back for a bit?"

Anything you want.

"If Hundu doesn't mind," Omar heard himself say. Which actually sounded better than *anything you want.*

Thank Baal, Hundu was the most benign of the nine beavers, and Omar himself had ridden on his back as a toddler. He had even pulled Hundu's ears and he was still alive.

"Let me give you a foot up. If he smells me, it feels a bit more familiar to him."

"Fine!" She kicked off her sandals and lifted one leg. He bent down, and she put a heel on his clasped hands. One push and she sailed up.

The imprint of her callused heel continued to tingle in his palm, a wonderful, almost sacred feeling.

The rest of the ride across the quay was far too short, and those wretched beavers were now suddenly moving along briskly. Omar saw the felucca's mast, their flag with the beaver's head logo flapping in the breeze. His brother sat on a barrel and lazily raised a hand.

Gusman looked up at Hundu's back and said, "A new face. My name is Gusman. But maybe Omar already told you that?"

Omar felt his brother's charisma envelop the girl. He noticed that his hands clenched into fists and the nails drove into the heels of his thumbs. But what could he do? Some things just happen, and this was one of them.

"No, sorry. We talked about ghûls and whether there is an animal in the whole, wide world that Omar's beavers fear." She slid down Hundu's side and crossed her arms, gave him a nod.

"I am Farisya. A ghûl hunter of the Eternal Caravan. Omar allowed me to ride his beaver for a little while."

"Ah, you're Omar's new girlfriend?"

Omar prayed for the ground to open beneath his feet. Now, of course, she'll shake her head. *No. How did you come up with such an idea? I just ran into him and found your beavers quite interesting. And then she'll look at Gusman and sweep a dangling lock out of her eyes, just like the other girls. Tell me all about your beavers, brave Gusman.*

"That's right," she said, hooking her arm into Omar's.

"Good. It is about time." Gusman nodded. "Find a seat on the bow, Farisya of the Eternal Caravan. At least, I assume you're coming along? It is not too far to the dredging place. I'll watch the beavers."

Omar could hardly believe his ears. Gusman didn't belittle him? Didn't make fun of his little brother?

Suddenly, it became clear to him. *He finds Farisya as interesting as I do, and she chose me over him. For the first time, I am worthy of his respect. No longer the little brother who is so awkwardly hopping from one foot to the other with every girl and can't get a word out.*

Gusman hoisted the sails, and a wind-ghost slid down the mast and filled the canvas. They sailed past junks with sails like opened fans, past cogs with smoking chimneys, past warehouses, each bearing its emblem and guarded by fierce storm birds the size of swans.

All the temptations of Ormazd's Paradisio, the Pomegranates of Eternity, and the rivers of honeydew, all seemed bloodless pleasures compared to the salty breeze in your face, the gurgling of the bow water and your arm around the shoulder of a girl who certainly must be the love of your life.

A curl brushed Omar's cheek with every gust of wind, and the seagulls flew screeching after their barge. Their song seemed infinitely more beautiful to Omar than even the chorus of the yazads, who danced in the crystalline glow of Ormazd's gaze. He knew he would never forget this moment. Blessed is the man who recognizes his happiness, says the poet, and that was exactly how Omar felt: blessed.

"And, of course, almonds from Arrush," Farisya concluded the list of all the wonders the Eternal Caravan carried. "The gardeners promise a mouthful will make a grandmother's breasts full and firm as melons, and let even a ninety-year-old's spear stand tall."

"Is that true?" Gusman asked.

"Who is to say? I don't think any of us three needs such an almond right now."

It was as if Omar saw the city for the first time now that he looked through the eyes of Farisya. Omar's Alexandria was a jumble of floating warehouses, taverns, brothels, and temples clinging to the jetties. Compared to the two-mile-wide entrance to the Channel Tunnel, it all looked rather fragile and improvised.

Farisya's interest made everything new and wonderful, the city no longer a collection of flotsam, but the heaped treasure of some celestial satrap.

The crater wall rose and rose, and then the entrance to the tunnel blotted out the sky. They glided on over oily waters, above which phantom lights bobbed to indicate the safe channel.

"It's still a fair way to go," Gusman said. "The tunnel itself is six miles long, and then we have to be at Lock Forty-six."

"To do what, exactly?" Farisya inquired.

"A kraken has slipped past the nets and is blocking the lock. The perfect place for an ambush. She has already devoured a sloop full of soldiers."

"And then they called Omar and you!" Farisya said. "So exciting to see experts at their job!"

Omar's stomach became a painful knot. A kraken brandished twenty arms, set with barbed suction cups, a beak that could bite through an ironwood bollard, and the harbormaster's soldiers were veterans. Former pirates, they wore their scars and steel-clawed hands as proudly as a general wears his golden laurel wreath.

It's a desperate try, calling us. First the soldiers, and only when she also devours the beavers, it's time to hire an archmagus. One that calls down lightning from the blue sky or rides a tidal wave of ink-black water.

"Our beavers, they fear nothing and no one," declared Gusman. "To them, a kraken is no more than a snack." Only someone who knew Gusman very, very well would detect the tremor in his voice. Omar would have preferred to jump overboard and swim to the shore, despite the Nile crocodiles who, as usual, followed, ever hopeful, in their wake.

When you pray to Ormazd to stretch time—no, to stop it completely!—then it only streams all the faster. Six miles may seem a long distance, but it goes by in the blink of an eye, especially when your wind-ghost blows harder than ever and seems to throw itself gleefully against the billowing sail.

He loves it. When the kraken bites our ship in two and wraps the beavers in its tentacles, he'll be free. With Gusman gone, his geas is broken.

In the distance, a blue star winked on and grew into a circle at an alarming rate. Light fanned out over the ripples, and then the locks lay before them. The water steps descended into a series of oval reservoirs, reaching all the way to the Mediterranean Sea.

The dams were all the work of beavers: logs and twigs, bushes full of juicy blood oranges and lemons. Next to the Channel stretched the willow forest: the self-renewing source of food and building material for the beavers.

"It's the fourth lock from here," Gusman said.

"Shall I string my bow?" Farisya asked.

"Why not? Every little bit helps."

Omar could tell from Gusman's voice that he had no confidence whatsoever. That was understandable: if the kraken could kill the beavers, she wouldn't mind a few oversized toothpicks.

They entered the first lock, and again that strange acceleration of time occurred: as if a quarter of an hour passed in a minute and a minute in a heartbeat. The water receded and they sailed across the second lake.

I must enjoy every moment. I probably don't have that many left anymore. He stroked Farisya's cheek and when she looked up, he kissed her full on the lips. She didn't protest and kissed him back.

"Ayay," she laughed, "are all beaver drivers so forward?" She clicked her tongue. "You're going to ask me to marry you after we defeat the monster?"

"That's not a bad idea at all." All his fear had evaporated into the infinitely blue sky and he felt... Yes, as sure and strong as a Gusman. That was the only correct comparison.

I may not survive this, but at least I have had this. The way she looked at me. As if I were a fearless cobbler's son from a miracle story.

From the dams, the construction beavers watched, creatures not much larger than hyenas. Compared to them, their own beavers were giants, the result of a centuries-long breeding program by the Iroquois who still used them as mounts and warhorses.

Omar knew, of course, that he was absolutely wrong. He and Gusman. Their profession entailed a certain amount of risk, and that certainly was something to be proud of. Bringing a civilian into an emergency situation was reprehensible. The problem was Farisya's enthusiasm. She trusted them completely and believed that Omar and Gusman were heroes. How could he disappoint her? The loss of face was unbearable.

The last lock gate swung slowly open, and they slid onto a lake without any ships. That alone was a bad sign. At least forty ships had been anchored on each previous reservoir, with no intention of continuing until the kraken was removed.

The kraken pulled all ships under. Peeled them open to get to the juicy bits.

Farisya tied on a blindfold of silvery silk, searched the lake.

"There is no one left alive. Not a human soul, but us." She pointed. "There she is. To the right of the lock."

"Can you see her with that blindfold?" Gusman asked.

"Only her soul. She's gorgeous! Magnificent as a forest fire or a tidal wave rushing through a wadi."

"Ah," Gusman said. "Good. Right. We do it like this. We float in her direction. Quiet as mice, disguised as a piece of wreckage."

"Quiet as flotsam," Farisya nodded. She leaned forward. "She saw us and is now heading our way. I bet she doesn't believe we're a piece of wreckage."

The surface of the lake remained a dull mirror, without the slightest ripple. Omar, however, could picture her bulging head crystal clear, speeding through the water, trailing a string of tentacles. Eyes as big as berserker shields and a beak that could bite a felucca in half. The crazy thing was that, according to Gusman, she was just a giant clam, a super mussel that swam around and devoured whole sperm whales.

Gusman hoisted himself onto the bowsprit and gestured to the beavers. Their language was not very complex: a hundred gestures, some grunts, and shrill whistles.

"Enemy," Gusman gestured. "A dam-breaker."

Dam-breaker was the foulest swear word the dredger clan knew, and Omar saw their tails rise, giving an angry drum roll on the planks of the deck.

"Where?" Hundu waved his front left paw.

"In front," Gusman indicated.

A staccato series of splashes, and the beavers had abandoned ship.

"Uh, friends?" said Farisya. "She's not in front anymore." She pointed down to the deck. "She's below us now."

A dozen tentacles rose in eerie silence from the lake and bent over the boat like so many blind serpents. In two of them, beavers had fastened themselves. A third had wrapped itself around Hundu and cracked all his ribs.

Omar had always intended to die like a man, to look death calmly in the eye, preferably with a brave smile on his lips.

So this is what death looks like. Omar felt

that special smile settle on his lips and make his face into a hero's mask.

On starboard, a head broke the surface, shapeless and soft.

"Just a little higher," he heard Farisya whisper. "Show me your beautiful blue eyes."

She put an arrow on her bow and drew the string.

"It isn't night," Omar protested. "Without the moon, your arrows are only arrows. Nothing magic!"

He could have kicked himself in the head. *Don't begrudge her that illusion. Everyone wants to die in their own way.*

"Don't be an idiot. The moon shines as often during the day as at night." She jerked her head, and then Omar saw the moon indeed hovering over the lock, dull as a pebble and no bigger than his thumbnail.

"Mother Ifdalit," sang Farisya, "hear me, mighty goddess. Give me your light and poison my arrows like the spider's bite that killed my father."

Omar saw the light of the moon reach down and tap the arrow on Farisya's bow and make it glow. It was a calm silver glow and somehow brighter than the sunlight itself.

The kraken's head shot all the way up with a bow wave that almost engulfed their boat. Two eyes that seemed far too clever for an animal gazed at Omar, and the look pierced his soul. He had seen cats play with a captive mouse, and in those eyes the same joy swirled, the pleasure of a born tormentor.

"And that is one," Farisya said, and an arrow stood upright in the pupil. The tentacles twisted and jerked under the water. From the saw-toothed beak of a raptor, a scream shrieked that skipped Omar's ears and rang directly in his brain.

"And that's two. Moon venom that frays every flesh and turns muscles into slime."

Omar understood that it was part of the incantation, that Farisya was telling her arrows how monstrously poisonous they truly were.

The pierced eye clouded, like pouring a bag of cement into a carp pool, and burst open.

"She's dead," Farisya said. "Although she hasn't figured it out yet." She shoved her third arrow back into the quiver. "I don't think this one is needed anymore."

The tentacles curled up, spread limply over the water. The kraken had become a mass of shivering flesh, a boneless carcass, and the first seagulls were already descending with happy cries.

Everything had happened too fast to settle firmly into his memory. It seemed to Omar a campfire story told by a stranger long ago. Not something he had actually experienced.

"Thank you," said Farisya. "That was instructive."

"Without you…" Omar began.

"No. Your beavers almost had her. Give them some minutes more and they would have bitten off all of her tentacles. I was just giving her the final push, and if one has a bow it's a shame not to use it." She frowned. "Is it over for today with a cleaned-up lock? I would love to show you around my caravan." She licked her lips. "There is always a lamb turning on a spit."

"Take Omar with you," Gusman said. "I know how badly a canoe rows with a third paddle."

The Eternal Caravan had settled on the Tournament Field, where virgin girls danced with the bulls at Isis's Harvest Festival. They were the counterparts of Mithra's bull wrestlers, who were decidedly virile.

As soon as the drums died down, they threw themselves into each other's arms, and a girl who was still a virgin the next morning clearly hadn't understood anything.

An echo of that atmosphere always hovered over the sands, ghostly sweat, and pools of spilled blood. The bull's horns were equally sharp for both the boys and the girls.

The giant tortoise with its watchtower stood in the center, surrounded by tents of embroidered silk. The wagons formed a makeshift city wall, with hundreds of banners coiling in the breeze like serpents of heaven.

This was a moving village, Omar understood. One that rolled unstoppable during the day and solidified into a massive fortress the moment the sun went down.

A makeshift gate of lacquer panels swung open, and the guard hugged Farisya, kissing her on both cheeks and forehead.

"Light of my life!" he exclaimed. "I smell the joyously spilled blood of a monster. That is a good day's work for a daughter of Yaleena and most certainly pleasing in the eyes of Ormazd and his archangels."

"He here is Hyunne, the only Hanhari man who has stayed with us for more than one trip. He became my mother's third husband and taught me all about hunting stealthy ghosts and sand sharks."

The man seemed a savage to Omar, with his head of hair a windblown bush, and his eyebrows turned up like the tips of a mustache. He was naked except for a bandolier of poison icicles. A glass scimitar was slung over his shoulder, and Omar couldn't make out a scabbard or sling. They had to be fashioned from *marilah,* an alchemical thread so fine that no human eye could discern it.

"Your hunting buddy is my hunting buddy," the man intoned, stepping aside with a wide wave of his arm.

"He's your father?" Omar asked, managing not to raise his eyebrows.

"Women are a scarce commodity in the Eternal Caravan," Farisya said. "That is why every woman must marry three men. Your mother and sperm father will choose your first husband. The second the shamans discover by rolling the petrified vertebrae of a desert hare and the third... Well, I have to choose that one myself."

"I see."

It is not very likely that her mother or a shaman will consider me a suitable candidate. Besides, that didn't fit very well into his daydreams: his own father married four other wives after Omar's mother, as befits a man of distinction. While Uncle Ghalid must have a dozen in his *Hareem*, too many for Omar to remember their names, anyway. And every few years he added another one.

No, third husband of a caravan guard was ridiculous, even if she was as beautiful and lively as Farisya.

The sun and then the moon ducked behind the crater wall and, as Farisya had promised, a lamb was turning on a spit. Several, in fact, and the palm wine flowed quite freely.

A skewer in one hand, a tankard of foaming wine in the other, and Farisya right in front of him with eyes in which the little flames of the campfire danced: like Little Hussein, Omar wanted to cry out to the Lord of Light: "Stop time! Make this moment last forever!"

A woman stepped into the campfire's circle of light, a crossbow over her shoulder, sky-iron studded boots on her feet.

"This is Omar, Mother," Farisya said. "I hunted a kraken with him. His beavers were biting off one tentacle after another until I could fire an arrow into her vile eye!"

The woman smiled.

"Ah, as your namesake Omar Khayyam said:

Shoulder to shoulder,
you with your bow
and me with my sword,
isn't that more exciting
than the hottest kiss?"

Omar couldn't remember that particular stanza, but perhaps caravan drivers read a quite different scroll from the famed poet than canal dredgers?

"We also kissed," Farisya added.

"That is indeed part of it."

"My name is Yaleena, by the way," said Farisya's mother. In the fluttering blaze, Omar could see every wrinkle and black melanoma, every scar. When Omar daydreamed about a bride, he envisioned his uncle's concubines, women barely older than himself. When they came out at all, they strolled in the sifted sunlight from silk umbrellas, under swaying palm fronds and hibiscus pergolas. The wind and the sun had scoured and tanned Yaleena's face, tattooed it with a hundred thousand wondrous vistas and daring deeds.

This is what Farisya's face will look like when she is old, for didn't the poet counsel: "The mother is the mirror of the daughter in her maturity"?

Omar understood then that no price was too great to stay with Farisya, to see her face inscribed day after day with the most beautiful and exciting poems in the wide world. To grow old together. What did it matter that he could only be her third husband? The first two were foreordained, but the third husband a woman chooses herself. A marriage of love.

Farisya rubbed against him, pursed her lips. "Put your chin up?" She untied her ghoul-claw necklace and placed it around his neck. "So, now you're truly a part of my tribe."

It felt like a ritual. *Did she choose me? Am I a caravan driver now? A suitor?* But no, Farisya said nothing more, and perhaps it meant nothing more than when a girl lays three pink shells on the doorstep of a boy she likes and brushes his name with henna on her upper arm. More like *I do find you interesting* than a marriage proposal.

"Right, there you are." A boy knelt next to Farisya and tapped her cheek. "I'm sorry I couldn't come sooner. A terror-bird had the mouth-and-claw disease, and you know how they are. Saying 'It's for your own good' doesn't exactly impress them." He took Omar's wrist and squeezed in greeting. "You must be the guy who hunted the kraken with Farisya. The beaver-keeper."

Farisya got up and put a hand on the newcomer's shoulder.

"This is Faisal. My third husband. The other two are still carousing somewhere in town."

"Welcome here," said Faisal. "Every friend of my wife is my comrade."

A shrieking witch could not have cast a worse curse. "Every friend of my wife is my comrade." *He thinks I'm funny, a little boy. I do not pose any threat to him because Farisya already has three husbands.*

Omar sprinted past the Hanhari men, who huddled humming around a fire of green flames, past the terror-birds and dromedaries, through the open gate. No one stopped him because he was close to invisible and didn't belong here.

The deserted Temple road lay before him, flanked by idols and shrines. The only fires still burning were the ghostly flames above the funeral urns.

As he passed Poseidon on his roaring, shark-toothed seahorse, the darkness moved. A creature that was definitely not human stepped onto the marble flagstones and blocked his way. From his fur wafted the stench of open graves, of cadavers in which maggots thrived. His eyes were black as night, all pupil.

"You wear her stench on your lips," the ghûl said. "Around your neck dangle the severed claws of my sisters. But you are not her."

Omar backed away, reaching for his skipper's knife. It slipped from his suddenly strengthless fingers and clattered against the paving stones, for indeed he was not Farisya.

The creature raised a hand like a hairy paw: claws extended, cat-smooth.

"Don't kill me!" cried Omar. "She doesn't care about me! I am a canal dredger, a humble beaver-keeper!"

The monstrosity lowered its hand and its claws slipped back, no longer scythes of black horn.

"I must have been mistaken. You are indeed not worthy of her. There's no point in killing you." He crouched and pushed off in an impossible frog jump that sent him whizzing straight over a grove of palms.

Four years later, Omar married the girl his aunt had chosen for him. Shanaz was timid and colorless as a night moth, exactly right for a canal dredger who was sure he would never gallop along on a terror-bird with the Eternal Caravan, or put a new talon on his necklace.

Tais Teng is a Dutch writer, illustrator, and sculptor who sold some eighty English stories and three novels. Cirsova published several tales set on the Arabian Nights' shores of the Inland Sea, most recently The Whole Wide World. In a second series, Tais Teng ventures deep into the monster-haunted wastes of Clark Ashton Smith's Zothique.

Tango With Samurai

By RODICA BRETIN

Kayla Blackmoon's whereabouts unknown, her mentor Lorena leads an assault on the headquarters of the Karghan, hoping to find the missing young psychic!

The men were hot on our heels—unseen, unheard, or so they believed. I left them be, for a while. Then I turned and attacked. With my arm outstretched, I felt the vibration of the blade, and before the first drops of blood hit the floor, a head rolled to our feet.

Alix stepped over the body of a second guard, which she dispatched with a blow to the clavicle, sending him into a better world—or not. In how many ways could Alix kill? Several, and each was executed with detached efficiency. If she was trying to impress me, she had done it! Where was Aidan's romantic, shy, sensitive muse? And why were there so many mercenaries armed with Uzis in an abandoned building? By now, we had passed by three patrols, and this was only from the ground to the first floor. Morgan's men were guarding something—or someone. A hostage that was sufficiently important for such massive troop deployment. Could it be her? *It had to be.* Kayla was missing going on forty hours, now. In her place, there was absence, silence, almost as though—but no, she was still alive. Otherwise, I would have felt her passing!

Alix had gone ahead of me and was already at the end of the corridor, where the emergency stairway began. I caught up with her, but not quite as silently. Alix was like a cat when it came to seeing and moving around in the darkness. She probably had other talents that Aidan appreciated.

Alix knew how to be convincing, was one of *them*—that's how she had brought Raven to Kayla's home. Inside the house, Raven had started touching one object, then another, attentive and concentrated. Finally, she looked at me and Alix with an expression that was difficult to decipher. *"Quin wasn't here that night."*

Maybe, but the orders came from him. And in the skull of *Global Vortex*'s security chief lurked the Karghan. Both of them wanted Kayla. Quin would see her dead, while the Karghan had other plans. But where did they keep her? She was in a building that was set to be demolished, Aidan informed us after rummaging through Denton Quin's computer.

We had reached the second floor when, through the darkness, I almost bumped into Alix. We both froze, and then I started listening. First, there was silence, followed by footsteps and breathing. I started counting, but Alix whispered to me: "The more of them that come, the more things are going to get interesting."

"For us or them?"

We were caught in a trap—just as Raven had warned us several hours ago when she had decided to sit this one out, even though Alix had given her a look that could melt a rock.

"Kayla needs all of us together."

"No, she needs only you. Your stupid deaths will help her immensely," Raven had promised before turning her back on us.

And here we were, two teams on an impossible mission, me and Alix, Keeghan and Aidan. They broke down the front door, while we sneaked around through the back, where there were meant to be far fewer problems, or so Keeghan believed.

But he was wrong.

The *problems* came from all sides and, as we retreated, we found ourselves in a room where the darkness rustled like an ant colony. There were twenty or more of them? It was weird that I didn't hear them arming their automatic weapons, only an irritating clanging.

"Chains, machetes, and crowbars," Alix confirmed to me.

I tightened my grip around the handle of my katana, and Alix pulled out her daggers, expertly turning them through the air.

Morgan's samurai-for-hire prudently stepped back. Had the Karghan told them who they were up against? Not likely. But they could see us. Meanwhile, all I could make out were shadows, pressing in closer and closer.

"We had some fun together, Alix."

"That was only the beginning, Lorena."

I felt her smile, arrogant and as cold as a glacier. She made a short gesture, just a turn of the wrist, and a blade sliced through the air, buzzing past heads without touching them. It lodged itself in something—was it a wall or a light switch?

From the ceiling, hundreds of lights spilled their glimmer over the samurai who were now blind, dazed, scratching their cheeks in the rush to pull off their masks and helmet visors. Alix recovered her dagger, then returned to my side and we stood back to back.

That's how the dance began.

A spiral cut through the air with the blade's edge, a howl and the thud of a body collapsing, without stopping the rest of the attackers. The samurai from *Global Vortex* hadn't heard of the Bushido code, nor watched movies with Toshiro Mifune. They all rushed in on us, tripping over each other. I helped them, thinning their ranks. Alix was doing pretty well herself—after all, nothing had been stuck between my ribs yet. But how long could we keep them at bay?

My arms had gone numb, the sweat was weighing down my eyelids, but I didn't slow down, I didn't hesitate, and they kept falling. I was striking, stabbing, and slicing. My heart was beating so quickly it felt like I was hearing a continuous rumble, like a painful vibration through my eardrums.

Morgan's mercenaries appeared to be coming at a slower pace, with decomposed, sequential movements, like astronauts jumping on the Moon. I had plenty of time to pick a target, plan the angle of attack, the force of the blow. I risked taking a glance over my shoulder. Alix was wielding her daggers like a pair of steel knitting needles, weaving a lethal web through which no one could cross. The samurai continued trying and failing, without giving up, even though they were so *slow*. It was only then that I understood that it wasn't them who had slowed down. We were moving with unnatural swiftness, in perfect harmony with one another, in complete dissonance with the rest of the world. Had we just become Berserkers, both of us?

The first, it was believed, were from the ranks of the Vikings, warriors who killed without feeling pain, fear, or hesitation. The only thing that could stop them was death, theirs or their last foe's. Was it a fit of madness, the effect of hallucinogenic mushrooms, or a hypnotic trance in which the subconscious, atavistic inclinations took hold? The chroniclers, historians, and psychologists attempted to explain this *battle frenzy*. Torrents of ink were spilled, where rivers of blood flowed before. A battle of words, that was lost before it began, because the truth was different. The Berserkers had been some of *The Ancients*.

I stabbed empty air and, when I turned, I was face to face with Alix. I looked into her dark green eyes, and then all around. Only the two of us were left standing. I took a few deep breaths until the red mist under my eyelids began to fade, and the rhythm of my heart slowed down. There was still the throbbing rumble between my temples, and now my stomach had rebelled against me, sending acrid waves climbing to my throat. I would have bent over, retching on the dirty floor, over the corpses—but not in front of Aidan's new love. Alix had shaken herself from the madness of the blood with the grace of a cat throwing off ruby drops from her fur, and then she bent down, wiping her daggers' blades on a samurai's sleeve.

My shoulders hurt, and every muscle in my body felt like a too-stretched piano wire threatening to snap. I went ahead and Alix followed me in silence, although the same thought-trains went on in her mind, stopping at the same stations—Kayla, Quin, Russell Morgan. We had another floor left to go, the last. If we didn't find anything there either, we had no idea what to do next.

We hurried up the steps on the spiral staircase, reaching a corridor leading through open doors to identical, vacant rooms, and at the end of it an elevator cabin that, judging by the thick layer of rust on the doors, had been at the bottom of the ocean for a while.

But it was working! There was a screech, and then the light panel came to life. What now, another *welcoming committee*? I didn't have the strength to start it all over again. As if hypnotized, I was watching the number two becoming three when Alix pulled me aside. She was pale and hardly impatient to resume the dance. What were we in for this time, more samurai, ninjas, howling dervishes?

Keeghan and Aidan got out of the elevator. The first held a crossbow in his hand, the other a metal dragonfly.

"Did you bring your flashlight?"

My voice sounded higher by an octave, and, sensing my offense, the insectoid abomination began pulsing. Now it was violet, then yellow, then purple.

"It's still a prototype. It senses threats from the stage of intentions."

Aidan scratched the paranoid dragonfly on its back until it stabilized into a shade of bright green. Could it also purr? I was about to express a few personal thoughts about inventions and prototypes when I stopped, confused—something did not suit the situation at all. The two of them, were so very *clean*. Aidan was just as impeccable as in the moment he had climbed out of a limousine. Keeghan was his usual self, long-haired, bohemian, but without a speck of dust on him. Alix and I looked like we had challenged an excavator to a wrestling contest. And as for them, they hadn't run into a single *problem*?

"We came up with the elevator," Keeghan explained.

This was a joke, right? Typical dark Irish humor. I felt like I was close to exploding, and Aidan's dragonfly started glowing red.

Then a phone rang.

It was on the floor, next to the elevator. I was wondering why I only noticed it now. The device was a classic, black, 60's model. The one in front of us had no wire, but it was ringing shrilly, imperative, and insistent.

I picked up the receiver.

"Lady Argyll, what an unexpected pleasure!"

Actually, Russell was waiting for us. He and his samurai guards had the ambush ready for us to fall into it. But—surprise!—we had come this far. And I was in no mood for a conversation.

"What do you want, Morgan?"

He laughed, in a way that somehow managed to send shivers down my spine.

"The *Black Sun*, what else? In exchange for Kayla."

He knew about the artifact. He had made the first move, and now that he had the upper hand, he could impose his terms. You could never bargain with a Karghan, or stall for time. *Anything for Kayla*, Alix had once said. But did anything also involve the *Black Sun*?

It was a decision I couldn't make alone.

"Keegan?"

He just shrugged. *"I gave it to you, do what you want with it."*

But what could you do with an opaque globe which is heavier than lead, which heats up and vibrates to the touch? An object that was priceless, elusive, and worthless.

Alix was on the same wavelength: *"Give it to him. We have no idea what it's for anyway."*

Or how to use it, but the Karghan had found out. Otherwise, why would he ask for it?

I was wavering, burdened by doubts and fears when Aidan snatched the receiver from me. "We will think about it, Morgan. Don't call us, we'll call you!"

And he hung up leaving Russell Morgan speechless, and me shocked, confused.

"The Karghan is lying. He doesn't have Kayla. He doesn't even know where she is," said Aidan calmly.

Alix exchanged a glance with Keeghan, who looked at me, and then all three of us turned to our infallible scanner.

"Are you sure?" I asked the question in everyone's minds.

Aidan didn't get to answer that. Sharp, untimely sounds broke the marble wall of silence. On the third ring, I took the phone out of my pocket, barely able to restrain the trembling of my fingers. Was it Morgan again?

But it was Raven.

"Do you watch the news, Lorena?"

"I'm a little preoccupied with other things right now."

She was looking at me with an ironic smile from the cockpit of a helicopter. Mine! Just because she had lent me her Land Rover, didn't mean she could use everything I owned.

On the screen, a reporter was now broadcasting live for the six o'clock news. It was morning, already?

"The new *Global Vortex* headquarters, a tower of glass and concrete, thirty stories high, will be built in the place of the warehouse set to be demolished today. The pyrotechnic crews are laying down the last charges, while the police have already set a safety perimeter around the building, the fire trucks are on their way—"

I could hear the sirens of the cars on the speaker, but also from outside.

"Exactly," Raven intervened. "I will be waiting on the roof. Be there in ten minutes!"

We arrived in seven and it took us another two to take off. Raven was at the controls and Keeghan sat in the copilot's seat. In the back, Alix and I buckled our safety belts, while Aidan stuck his face to the porthole, trying to make something out among the dust vortices raised by the rotor.

But we saw the explosion on Channel 8.

First, a wave of fire broke out through the windows and doors on the first floor. The building rocked a single time, and then a gigantic rubble arm rose upwards, stretching towards us, trying to grab us. The helicopter passed through its fingers, and I thought I heard a squeal of helpless rage—or was it the sand in the rotor blades?

Morgan had wanted us there, under the rubble. I could understand him. Karghans killed the same way humans breathed, naturally. And between two breaths they lied, cheated, and stepped over corpses. And they did it all in a very impersonal, uninvolved manner. Their hatred was cerebral, controlled; their vengeance was best served cold, with a slice of lemon and ice. But a Karghan who was bluffing was something new and it could only mean one thing, that Morgan had lost control over Quin.

Which was impossible?

Here is a word that had become devoid of meaning lately. The Karghan was selling us something he never had, Quin had eclipsed himself from the scenery, and Calder's daughter was still missing.

Where are you, Kayla?

Rodica Bretin's Protectors continues in Fall.

Corpse Ala Cart

By TEEL JAMES GLENN

When a dying Elf falls from the sky and onto Jack Silence's dinner table, the Ghostmaker gets served up an intrigue of murder and blackmail amongst fey!

I was just finishing a really good Kobe beef steak when the dying Elf fell out of the sky and smashed into my table sending the plates and food flying.

This corpse ala cart happened while I was out trying to have a normal life, eating an early dinner with my friend La'Shawna Dubois. We were at an outdoor restaurant near Fraunces Tavern in Downtown Manhattan, off of Pearl Street, near the Ferry Terminal, talking about a recent case we'd worked on. I'd had to clear an entire sports arena of ParaFey infestation—those pesky creatures who leaked through the barrier from the Fey Realm to our world and went mad.

My license was as a ParaFey eliminator, a Ghostmaker; it lets me do them in, but Fey spirits are so much more persistent than Mundane, human ghosts. I've often had to hire a banisher or exorcist to get rid of them. More often than not, I hired La'Shawna, in her professional capacity as Madame Vixen, to do the job after I do my bit to get rid of their bodies.

She'd worked overtime on the stadium job, so I was treating her to a lavish meal to thank her and talk about life in general. She was one of my oldest friends.

Right in the middle of her telling a bawdy joke, the six-foot, silk-clad beauty dropped out of nowhere to collapse the table between me and La'Shawna. Beef juice and mashed potatoes splattered all over my new green cloak, ruining it, not to mention my appetite for dessert!

The pointy-eared, dying damsel splayed out on the table still had a few moments of life left in her. When I leaned in to tell her to take it easy, she fixed her golden eyes on me with recognition.

"Ghostmaker," she gasped in breathy whisper, "they killed m—" Then the light went out in her eyes and the Fey beauty was dead. Her golden skin faded to grey like frost on a sunflower as she lost the battle to stay alive. I could almost feel the sudden lessening of the energy all around me, a sort of psychic chill. Then I noticed that her lips were dark and unusually bluish.

Poison, maybe?

La'Shawna, ever stylish in a dayglow green kaftan and with her hair full natural halo, stared with mouth agape at the dead Fey on the table. Without missing a beat she said, "I guess dessert is out—"

"If sack and sugar be a fault, God help the wicked," I quoted. "We'll get you cheesecake to go." By now the other diners had all scattered, the various species, Elf, Gargoyle, Goblin and good old Mundanes, like La'Shawna and I. My guess is they were all afraid of more falling Fey. Frankly, so was I.

"I hope someone has called the cops," I yelled out.

"I got it," the Gargoyle *maître d'* called from where he crouched in a doorway to be sure no Elves would land on him.

Just then, my own calling crystal buzzed. "Boss," my office manager Grondo's voice came through. "Sorry to bother you, but some Fey woman called looking for you. She sounded really desperate..."

"And you told her where I was?"

"Uh, yes, I'm afraid so. She sounded like it was a matter of life and death."

"It was," I said as I studied the dead drop in.

The expired Fey was wearing expensive robes, even for an Elf, had her hair and make-up done expertly yet was wearing cheap canvas deck shoes. "How long ago did she call you?"

"About five minutes, boss."

That means she was only a few minutes carpet trip from here...

There were no visible signs of violence on the body. She looked to be somewhere in her 30s; of course on an elf that meant nothing since they age differently than us humans; she might've been as old as 150 or 200 years. No way to tell without an autopsy, which I wasn't about to do. Heck, I wasn't gonna disturb the body at all and have Morgan O'Flynn from the detective squad yell at me.

She's gonna yell at me anyway for the next thing I'm gonna do.

"Okay, La'Shawna," I said, pointing up to the flying carpet that the Elf had been riding. It was still hovering some thirty feet up in the air. Since the Convergence had caused internal combustion engines in cars to stop working, things like flying carpets, Gryphons, Pegasus, and other flying animals had become the standard. "I need to trace where that carpet came from while things are still fresh."

La'Shawna nodded and went into professional mode as Madam Vixen. She'd been an actress who made money on the side as a fake psychic and tarot reader before the Convergence, when the world of the Fey and our Mundane worlds merged. Since then La'Shawna had, like so many others, latent abilities revealed—in her case, to communicate with and banish spirits.

She also had some limited telepathic ability with the Fey. To that end, she put a hand on the forehead of the dead Elf and assumed a serious expression.

"Okay, Duckie," she said. "But you know the cops are gonna be mighty angry at you, sticking your nose in."

"I know one particular were-cop named O'Flynn who'll be furious," I said, "but I'm really getting tired of this habit of clients dying on me before I get paid."

"This blonde beauty didn't actually hire you, honey child."

"She tried," I said. "So technically I feel obligated. A man's got nothing but his reputation in the end."

"Sort of a John Wayne attitude, Jack."

"If I lose mine honor, I lose myself," I quoted. The Bard really did have sayings for all occasions.

"Well, I don't think it's a good idea, but I'll do what I can." She closed her eyes and concentrated. I couldn't see it, but I knew she was drawing energy from the dead Fey. Like us Mundane humans, the Fey brain was a bunch of electrical impulses and enough of them were left in the dead woman for La'Shawna to tap into them. It would allow me to order the flying carpet that the Elf had commanded as if she were still controlling it.

When it dropped down, I steadied the carpet at my hip height.

"Okay," I said, "Command it to return to wherever it originated."

"What do I tell the cops?"

"That I have no idea what this is about but will clue them in as soon as I do."

"You could lose your license on this, Jack."

"I don't think so," I said as I hopped on the rug. "We have witnesses I had nothing to do with this, and if I don't trace the rug now, her brain activity will be gone."

La'Shawna shook her head and sighed. "Okay, here it goes, good luck."

"Cry havoc! And let slip the dogs of war," I said.

"Drama queen," she snickered then relayed the telepathic command to the carpet.

In a moment it rose and headed off to points unknown. Like it or not, Jack Silence, Ghostmaker, was on a new case.

The flying carpet moved along at about twenty feet up from the ground, weaving in and out of a pattern of other carpets, though the evening rush from the nearby ferries was mostly over, so traffic was light. It seemed to be moving along the shore, cruising past the Staten Island Ferry Terminal, Governors Island Terminal, and a few private piers along the southern tip of Manhattan Island.

In my business, I've had to confront foes as large as ParaTrolls, ParaGargoyles, and even once a Dragon, so I usually carry a shotgun or some other long gun, but heck, I was just having dinner with a friend that night. All I had on me was a holstered Broomhandle Mauser, a Bowie knife, and my hideaway derringer with the silver bullets (werewolves, you know). I felt practically naked.

Still, my ride was intended purely as investigatory, to backtrack the Elf's path. I wanted to have something to tell the police when they inevitably confronted me. I didn't plan to tangle with anyone or thing.

The problem was that since I'd made the papers with a couple of high-profile cases doing some things beside eliminating ParaFey—helping find a missing wife, helping stop a heist from a museum, and recovering a cursed seal that used to belong to Solomon—I'd had a bunch of off-brand jobs come my way.

Here I was following another one, a Fey that, from the looks of her, had been poisoned. She came to me seeking help, though it was doubtful whether or not I could have. Maybe it was leftover guilt for having played so many bad guys back in my stuntman/actor days, but I felt I owed her to find out who had killed her at least.

The carpet took me along the waterfront to near Fulton Street and the South Street Seaport Museum. The flying rug lowered down and deposited me at a rent-a-rug kiosk near the entrance to the pier where the small armada of the museum ships were docked.

There was a restaurant and several shops, with a small number of tourists still enjoying the evening in them. There was also a gun tower where two alert Minotaur guards were 'manning' a machine gun against any Kraken that might pop up in the area—something that was happening with increasing frequency.

At the main gate of the pier, another horn head in uniform was keeping a watchful eye on things. I walked up to him with my best Irish smile.

"Excuse me, sir," I said. "I was wondering if you might be able to help me."

The Minotaur, who stood eye-to-eye with my six-foot-six, squinted at me and gave a little snort. "How can I do that, sir?" He said it with a bored tone but was working to be civil—an achievement with his species, who were more about confrontation than communication usually.

"I wondered if you saw an Elf around here, about a half hour or so ago," I said. "Female, pretty, wearing expensive red silks?"

He snorted again and for a moment I thought he was gonna tell me to take a flying leap, so I added, "I have a letter for her."

"That sounds like Lady Evolla," he said. "She left here a bit ago on a rent-a-rug."

"Darn," I faked, "I wanted to leave it for her at her place."

"Shouldn't be a problem," the horn head said. He cocked his head to the side. "The Lady lives on that yacht over there." The boat he'd indicated was a luxury catamaran at a slip just north of the museum proper. It was at the high end of floating homes, with gold and red pennants flying from the two masts.

"Thanks, pal," I said waving to the beef boy as I walked toward the gleaming boat.

She really is quality Elf material. 'Lady Evolla'!

At the gangway heading down toward the yacht were two Gargoyles sitting and playing a card game. The two were dressed in rent-a-cop uniforms that allowed their folded wings to rest against their backs.

When they saw me they turned their black eyes toward me and clicked their beaks. "What do you want, Mundane?" The tallest of them stood and held up a hand while his partner put a hand on a holstered sidearm.

"I have a message from Lady Evolla," I bluffed.

"Nice try, but she is on the yacht," he said.

"Nope," I said. "Call inside if you doubt me, I just left her at the tip of the island."

Gargoyles have no real expressions, but I'm pretty sure the second guard smirked, making a clicking sound. The one I was talking to looked back at his friend and said, "Call the yacht."

The second guard flicked a crystal set and spoke into it with his back turned to me. He spoke in a low tone that I couldn't hear. After a moment he turned back to us.

"Send him down," he said. "He'll be met."

The first guard opened the gate and let me go down the walkway to the yacht. I could see the name in Elvish on one of her hulls. It translated to "Forever Love."

At the gangplank, I was met by an old Goblin in an expensive yachtman's jacket. Like all his race, he had a bulbous nose, pointed ears, and a leathery-pebbled skin in shades of green, but he had a snaggle tooth sticking out at an angle from his upper lip.

"How you have a message from Evolla?" the little guy said. He had a slight lisp and focused his bulging eyes on me, noting the beef stains on my cloak with distaste.

"From," I acted confused. "No, I told the blue jerk at the gate that I had a message *for* the lady."

He canted his head to the side like a dog hearing a weird sound then smiled. "Oh, yes, of course that makes sense now, since she is here. What is the message?"

Upon my soul, a lie, a wicked lie!

"Oh, just that the order from the salon will be a day or two late. I promised my boss I'd apologize in person since I was gonna be in the neighborhood. Supply chain issue, you know?"

Boy, it's amazing I didn't choke on a piece of the Blarney Stone.

The little Goblin gave a giggle as if he was relieved. "Thank you for your diligence," he said. He reached into the pocket of his jacket and produced a coin and handed it to me. "I will tell her."

"Gee, thanks," I said acting all goofy and turned to head back up the walkway as if I was happy. In fact, I now knew there was indeed something hinky going on at that boat and the little gob was hip deep in it. And to top it off, I was a silver dollar ahead for my trouble—I'd consider it my retainer from the dead Elf.

"How the hell are you always around when dead Fey show up, Silence?" Detective Morgan O'Flynn asked.

"Luck?" I'd flown back on another rent-a-rug to find the police at the restaurant with the defenestrated Fey.

She growled at me in annoyance. When the tall redheaded O'Flynn growled, everyone took it seriously, since she was half-Fey and fully capable of turning into a full-fledged werewolf. Fortunately, she was a good cop and I had been useful to her in the past.

"The only reason I'm not running you in for this," she said, "is because you did the right thing to follow the carpet to get me a name before the essence faded."

"Every subject's duty is the king's, but every subject's soul is his own," I quoted.

"I had a Sasquatch lab tech give a sniff to the corpse," she said. "And your guess was right, this Elf was poisoned, looks like iron filings." Cold iron was fatal to most Fey species, and noses on the big furballs were never wrong.

"You gonna grill the Goblin I met?" I

asked. She fixed me with her green eyes and growled again.

"What I do or do not do is my business, Mister Silence," she said. "I appreciate you helping at this point, but it is an official case now. Stay out of it."

"To hear is to obey," I said with a smile and a bow. She didn't believe a word of it, but she had said what she officially had to say and so had I. We had done this dance before. She knew damn well I wasn't going to let it rest.

After she and her beasts in blue left the restaurant, La'Shawna, hands on her hips, gave me 'the look.' "You're going full scale into this, ain't you?"

"'Once more into the breach' is the term, my dear. I finish what I start—even if I didn't want to start it." I put in a crystal call to my office.

"What's up boss?" Grondo said. "Did the lady reach you?"

"She dropped in, for sure," I said, then proceeded to fill him in on what had happened. By the time I had finished my summary, he knew what I needed.

"I'll have the info you want in no time," the Gnome said. "You coming back here?"

"Nope," I said. "I'm gonna head back to the yacht—it will take time for Morgan to get a search warrant. I have a feeling that Goblin will clean the place up of any evidence before then."

"You are insane, Jack honey," La'Shawna said.

"And that is my good point," I replied.

Grondo may be a living stone Gnome, but he was worth his weight in solid gold because before I reached the yacht he had information for me.

"Seems that the husband of Evolla, the late Lord Marsby-Evolla, had a tragic accident two months ago, boss," Grondo said to me. "He fell off the yacht during a late-night party. Hit his head and drowned. It was ruled an accident."

"Witnesses?"

"Only the crew members," my priceless office manager said. "A Goblin family—Okpo, Gunda, and Zorph Ondoro."

"No one besides the Ondoro family? No party guests saw this?"

"Nope. Just the family, but they all agreed that the old Fey had drunk too much, tripped and fell, hitting his head. He drowned before they could pull him out."

"Old Fey?"

"Yes," Grondo said. "The lady is two hundred years younger than her husband."

"Two hundred?"

"She is only seventy-five years old, a baby for a Fey."

They really do age differently than us Mundanes… like they say, "Fey don't fray."

"She was a Fey commoner when she married the Lord four years ago," Grondo continued, "which was not approved by his family, who thought her a gold digger from what the Fey society pages say. But they seemed happy. In fact, she has been in mourning since then, hasn't been to any of the usual events at all."

"Okay, thanks, Stonepants," I said. "It sure puts things in a new light."

"What are you gonna do, Boss?"

"No idea," I said. "But I'd better do it fast if I want to beat O'Flynn."

I signed off. If I was gonna get a jump on official channels, I had to get aboard that yacht unseen, and approaching via the gangway was out.

I mentally ordered the flying carpet to take me around to the water side of the yacht and approached flying low, just above the surface of the water. I ignored the danger of some Kraken reaching out of the river, hoping that my speed would keep me safe.

I had the carpet hover right at rail level and crawled onto the deck. I stayed low and moved along till I got to an open porthole from which I could hear arguing voices.

"But Papa, I was sure she was sleeping," a female voice was saying. "She's been sleeping a lot lately."

"Well, she wasn't," a gruff voice said. It sounded like the Goblin in the yachting jacket I'd met earlier. "And we have to find her. There was someone from a business with a message for her, and there will be more people wondering why she has not been at any of the parties for this season."

"They think she is in mourning, Papa," another male voice said. "No one has questioned that."

"That will only hold for so long," Papa said. "We were so close—the healer was ready to swear to natural causes. We have to find her."

"She couldn't have gotten far, papa," the male said. "She had no shoes."

"A pair of my shoes are missing," the female voice said. There was the sound of a slap, and the female whimpered. "I didn't realize they were gone till we had to search for her, I'm sorry."

I'd heard enough. These guys were up to their pointed ears in at least keeping the Elf captive if not actively poisoning her. The question was how to get evidence? Or rather, keep them from destroying any.

I had just started to crawl back from the porthole when a shrieking voice from behind me stopped me. "Hold it right there, fella!"

I froze in a deep crouch but risked slowly looking back. One of the Gargoyles from the front gate was standing there with a drawn pistol pointed at me.

"Stand, slowly, and turn around," he said. "Hands where I can seem them, Mundane."

I did as he asked, careful not to excite him. Gargoyles have fast enough reflexes that any thoughts of a John Wayne outdraw of him were pointless. And in any case my license was to eliminate ParaFey—I had no right to shoot normal healthy Fey—or Humans—at least not without good cause. And I was trespassing.

"Hi, beaky," I said. I gave him a full Blarney smile, but he was not buying it.

"Mister Ondoro," the Gargoyle called out. "I caught a prowler."

There was noise inside the yacht, and in a few moments the three members of the Goblin family were on the deck. They were all dressed in expensive clothes, with Papa Ondoro now wearing a gold brocade robe.

The female Goblin was bald like the

males, with the same bulbous nose and pointed ears but along slightly more delicate lines. She wore an expensive silvery dress and heels with a tiara on her head. Next to her was another male, not as old as snaggle tooth, but also dressed like a minor lord.

"Papa," the male said, "I knew this Mundane!"

"What do you mean," Papa Ondoro said. "He was the messenger from the salon."

"No, Papa, I know him from the one sheets—" the younger Goblin said. "This the one that the Mundane's call The Ghostmaker."

The price of fame is beginning to cause me trouble.

"Uh, hi," I said. "I was—"

"What if he heard, Papa?" the female asked.

The elder Ondoro fixed his bulging eyes on me, and his face looked like he had sucked on a lemon. "Yes," he said, looking to the open porthole. "He might. Bring him inside, Gutog," he ordered the Gargoyle.

The beaked guard grunted a response and then barked, "Keep your hands up, Mundane." He got close enough to grab my Mauser from my hip holster then poked me in the back to move me along.

I had no choice but to comply, but unless they literally went off half-cocked, all I had to do was wait until O'Flynn and her guys showed up. Of course, that was providing there was a judge available to give her a search warrant and there was nothing else to distract her. Actually, when I thought about it, I might not have that good a chance of the calvary rescuing me.

That meant it was time to get clever.

"Hey, folks," I said as I was hustled into the cabin of the catamaran. "I know this looks bad, but I was just looking for Lady Evolla to, uh, serve her with some insurance papers about her husband's death."

The elder Ondoro took up a position at the head of a table where a meal was set out. The two younger Goblins flanked him and stood like temple guards while the Gargoyle stayed in the doorway behind me, out of my line of sight.

"What papers?" the old Goblin asked. He folded his arms across his chest and tilted his head up so he literally was looking down his nose at me. "Show them to me."

"I'll need to put my hands down to get to the papers," I said.

"Zorph," the old Goblin said. "Get them."

The younger male walked over to me, stopping just out of arm's length. "Papa, make him promise not to hurt me."

"Of all base passions, fear is most accursed," I quoted. "I'm a teddy bear, junior."

He looked like he didn't believe me, but I guess his fear of disappointing daddy was worse than his terror of me, so he came close.

"Right hand pants pocket, chum," I said. All the while I smiled my most friendly, cuddly smile.

He tentatively reached under my cloak to feel for my pants pocket. That's when I made my move. I grabbed his arm, pulled him to me and spun around so he was facing the Gargoyle at the cabin door.

The winged guard cocked his pistol, but the Goblin was wide enough to hide behind. I pulled my Bowie and menaced his neck. "Hold it, Wyatt Earp," I said. "Put the gun down or you'll be covered in Goblin goo."

"Papa!" my prisoner whined.

Bearlike, they have tied me to the stake, I thought. Aloud I said, "Everybody stay easy."

"What do I do, Mister Ondoro?" the Gargoyle asked.

The elder Goblin made a strangled sound and cursed. "You are an idiot, Zorph," he said. "That you sprang from my loins is my eternal shame."

"I'm sorry, Papa!"

"I should let him shoot you."

"No, Papa, no!"

What a loving family.

"Everyone, just relax," I said. I sidled over to the wall of the stateroom so my back was against it and I could keep both the guard and the Goblin family in my sight. "We're all gonna just have a nice chat. No one needs to be shot at all."

"That remains to be seen," the old Goblin said. "What do you want to talk about?"

"First put the gun on the deck," I ordered the guard. "Then we can talk about ladies and lords, drownings and dreams."

The Gargoyle clicked his beak but didn't move.

"Do it," I said, "or the Ondoro family gets smaller."

"Papa!" Zorph whined.

"He's bluffing," the female Goblin said. "If he kills brother, he will have no hold on us and Gutog can shoot him."

"Good thinking, daughter," Papa said.

What a really loving family!

"But I can cut off junior's ear," I said. "Give every man thy ear, but few thy voice," I quoted.

"No, no!" Zorph yelled. I had a hard time holding onto him as he started to squirm.

"Okay Gutog, put the gun down," I repeated. "Then we can talk." The Gargoyle crouched and set his pistol on the deck then stood.

"We're not going to say anything to you," Papa said.

I pressed the tip of the knife to Junior's neck.

"No, no, stop him, Papa."

"So, Junior," I asked, "what was it? Why were you holding the lady?"

"Don't say anything, Zorph," Papa ordered.

I pressed the knife till there was a little drop of blood.

"Talk!"

"We saw, we saw her," Junior squealed.

It all started to click in for me. "You're saying you saw her kill her husband, didn't you?"

"Yes, yes!" he whimpered. "And then she said no one would believe us, but we know they would."

"So, you blackmailed her to live like lords."

"Zorph, shut up!" Papa yelled.

"Yes, yes," Zorph was crying now, blubbering like a child. "Let me go!"

"What do you want, money?" the female Ondoro asked. The only sound in the cabin was Junior whimpering.

"We all want money," I answered.

"It was Papa's idea," he whined.

"But you wanted more than she would give, didn't you," I said. "You three wanted it all, so you were poisoning her."

"It was Papa's idea, it was Papa's idea!"

"Shut up, Zorph!" the older Goblin hissed.

"You made her sick with the poison and told her you wouldn't give her an antidote until she signed over the papers to this, or put you in her will, didn't you?" I was beginning to feel like I'd have the whole thing wrapped up neatly by the time Morgan showed up and with no violence.

"How much do you want?" Papa asked.

"I've already been paid my fee," I said, thinking about the silver dollar, though now it was clear I had been hired by a murderess to find her own murderers.

"Now everyone sit tight," I said, "And wait for the police." It all seemed settled at that point.

Then things went south.

The Gargoyle guard said, "I can't do more time."

"Then shoot him, Gutog," Papa said, "forget Zorph!"

The Gargoyle didn't waste any time. He dropped to the floor to grab the gun before I could do anything.

He fired from the deck, hitting Junior square in the heart.

I threw my knife directly at Gutog, but the blade hit him handle first—which was, however, just enough to throw his next shot off.

I pulled my Derringer and fired at the guard. It was a lucky one—even if it was a waste of silver—my .22 caliber slug hit the guard right between the eyes. He went down, twitched once, then stopped moving.

I turned quickly to point the gun at the two goblins who had both started to charge me. They froze in place.

"Don't you dare, I've got another bullet in this thing," I snapped. "I only need one someone alive when Morgan gets here."

Then I looked at the two surviving members of the Ondoro family and at least knew what I'd tell her, "Vaulting ambition, which o'er leaps itself and falls on the other."

Teel James Glenn has published dozens of books in multiple genres, and his work has appeared in over two hundred magazines, including Weird Tales, Mystery, Pulp Adventures, Mad, Black Cat Weekly, Cirsova, and Sherlock Holmes Mystery. His first Jack Silence collection "Guns, Goons & Goblins" will be out from Level Best Books in Oct 2026. theurbanswashbuckler.com

Notes

I was sure I'd know what to write when I finally got to this part, or at least have an idea, but here it is, the middle of March, with a ton of projects in various stages of completion [as I write this, there are boxes of Mighty Sons of Hercules all over my living room], and I have no idea what to say.

Thank you to everyone who has supported us over the last 10 years! Readers, editors, artists, authors, advertisers, and even haters. Especially haters—do you have any idea how many of our crappy ideologue "please send stories by and about non-straight, non-white people" competitors we've outlasted?

Seriously, though, it's wild how just sticking around and keeping at something can give you a kind of "elder statesman" status.

But wow, ten years and over 40 issues...

We'd like to thank Mark and Yakov, and Xavier who had to step back due to time constraints, because without them, the magazine would be mess. Their hard work on the copy is a huge reason why we've been able to project a degree of professionalism that is the envy of many of the indies.

We've worked with so many fantastic authors and artists over the years that it would be hard to thank them all here, but we'd like to give particular nods to Anton Oxenuk, Wistmoor Studios, and Collateral Damage Studios for helping us create and maintain the look and vibe of the magazine over the last decade. Also, a tremendous thankyou to our friend Tim Lim, who took time out of his incredibly busy schedule to do our 10th Anniversary Chen cover [which will look familiar to anyone who got the 5th Anniversary variant C cover]. And thanks to ZUN, obviously, who gave us permission.

We hope that you backed Winning Secrets. By now, we ought to be moving into taking orders for Adrian Cole's Dream Lords Legacy [a monumental achievement, which I'm running out of space to fully contextualize, so I won't.]

Later this year, Michael Tierny's Wild Stars will be down the home stretch, where we'll relese volumes 9 and 10 together so that the fact we're no longer serializing them won't delay fans from reading the newest installment.

Even though I'm winding down, 2026 has proven crazy busy, with just one thing after another... 2027 may end up pretty busy, too, at the rates things are going.

Tell you what, if this Anniversary Issue sells as many copies as Winning Secrets, we'll put out a call for 2027 stories...

If not, well, we hope you enjoy the two remaining issues we have lined up for you, they're both fantastic and loaded with fan favorites.

P. Alexander, Ed.

www.ingramcontent.com/pod-product-compliance
Lightning Source LLC
LaVergne TN
LVHW081403110826
845149LV00010B/1653

9781960381675